GATES OF HELL

ANDY DEWITT

ELK LAKE PUBLISHING INC.

PUBLISHING THE POSITIVE
Plymouth, Massachusetts

A Christian Company
ElkLakePublishingInc.com

COPYRIGHT NOTICE

Cover and Interior Design: Derinda Babcock, Deb Haggerty

Editor(s): Peggy Ellis, Cristel Phelps, Deb Haggerty

PUBLISHED BY: Elk Lake Publishing, Inc., 35 Dogwood Drive, Plymouth, MA 02360, 2022

Library Cataloging Data

Names: DeWitt (Andy DeWitt)

Gates of Hell / Andy DeWitt

334 p. 23cm × 15cm (9in × 6 in.)

ISBN-13: 978-1-64949-764-2 (paperback) | 978-1-64949-765-9 (trade hardcover) | 978-1-64949-766-6 (trade paperback) | 978-1-64949-767-3 (e-book)

Key Words: Israel; pagan worship; the god Pan; mystery/suspense/ thriller; police procedural; romance; inventors

Library of Congress Control Number: 2022949251 Fiction

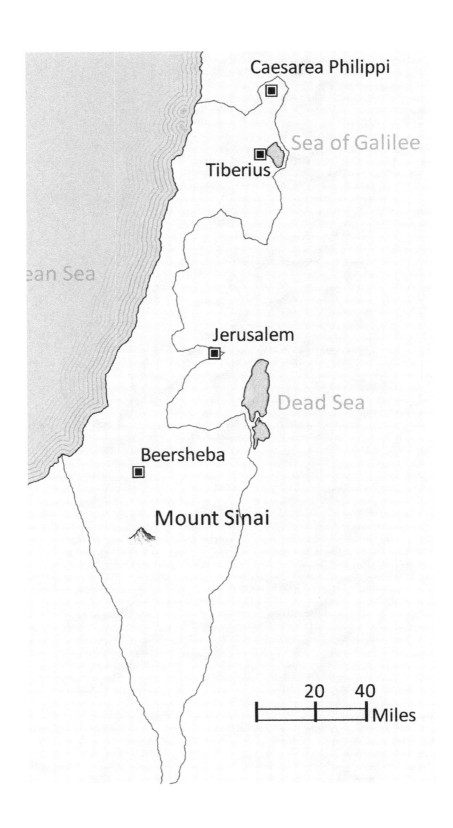

Caesarea Philippi

Sea of Galilee

Tiberius

ean Sea

Jerusalem

Dead Sea

Beersheba

Mount Sinai

20   40
Miles

DEDICATION

For all my kids.

ACKNOWLEDGMENTS

If this had been a one-person project, my wife and kids would have been the only ones to read it. I have plenty of people to thank for all their input and assistance.

Peggy Ellis showed an extreme amount of patience with me. A consummate professional, she read through the manuscript countless times working from every angle. Thank you for your editing expertise.

Erin Healy also displayed expert editorial acumen. Your coaching was critical throughout the writing process. Erin took *The Gates of Hell* far beyond what I could have made it on my own. Are all editors as brilliant as you?

James Rubart gave strategic insight into who I am as a writer. Beyond that, he dove into where I might fit in the publishing world. Seriously, who does that?

Randy Ingermanson is an awesome teacher. Your lessons on writing have been a rudder for me ever since attending your conference and sitting with you for one-on-one instruction.

Deena Nataf, my new Israeli friend. Thank you for taking a fine-toothed comb to the manuscript looking for all things Jewish! As a Jerusalem resident, your specific insight into every city street, character action, and morsel of food was incredible. I'm forever in your debt for your wisdom and experience.

Abigail Johnson and Karna Steel provided valuable input on an early version of *The Gates of Hell*. I appreciate your positive feedback and endless red marks on your copies. I would never have been able to put this book together without you.

Mark Lockwood was indispensable for his expertise on a variety of engineering and technical issues. You know tech!

Peter Lockwood, thanks for being willing to be a model for a villain. Of course, in real life, you are a hero!

Dennis DeWitt, my favorite pilot, generously volunteered his input on everything aeronautically-related. Thanks, bro.

Detective Jon Turbett provided valuable insight into interrogations and police procedures. An amazing professional and friend.

Pastor Dan Allison gave the brief sermon that sparked the idea for this book. Dan, I'll read the Bible differently from now on. Thank you.

Thanks, Mom! It hardly sounds like enough. Your encouragement and inspiration over the years have kept me going in my writing journey.

Dad, you've also been a gifted encourager. Thank you for all the positive feedback over the years.

Words are too frail to convey my overwhelming gratitude for my awesome wife, Anna. You're the reason I've been able to write. You put up with my early mornings, distracted mindset, and missed meetings. A constant sounding board, you listen to all my crazy ideas. I could never have done this without you.

On this rock,

I will build my church, and the

Gates of Hell

shall not prevail against it.

—Matthew 16:18b ESV

CHAPTER 1

Chase Johnson led Abby Radcliffe along the desolate mountainside like a treasure hunter without a map. An unexpected cloud brought scattered raindrops. Then, as they ducked inside a cleft in the rock face, the heavens opened with a downpour.

Abby looked over the vast desert—a flash of realization swept across her face. "This was a special place in Moses's life."

Chase secretly pulled a small velvet box from his pocket.

"God put Moses in a cleft of the rock just like this. Let him see his glory."

Chase dropped to one knee. Abby turned around. Her jaw dropped.

"Will you marry me?"

She stammered, "Yes."

He slipped the ring on her finger then jumped up. "We need pics. Stay here. I'll get Tiffany."

"Wait. The embassy warned us about going off the beaten path in locations like this."

"It's okay, I'll only be a minute." He took off down the path.

Back at the rental car, Chase begged Billy Rawlings and his sister Tiffany to join them.

Tiffany grabbed her Nikon D-10 and turned to Billy. "Coming?"

"I'm good." He leaned against the fender.

Back at the cave, Tiffany captured the event with shots from various angles.

Chase said, "We need a pic with Billy. I'll be right back."

"No." Tiffany stood up straight. "Don't leave us up here alone."

CHAPTER TWO

MT. SINAI

Chase jogged down the wet sandy trail with a spring in his step. When he reached the parking lot where Billy leaned against the tiny rental car's door, he called out, "Come up there with us."

"You left them alone?" At six-foot-five with shoulders of a body builder, Billy towered over Chase.

"They're fine." Chase waved a hand over the empty parking lot. "There's nobody around for miles. A few hundred yards up there will only take couple of minutes."

Billy sprinted up the trail.

Chase followed him aware of the empty jewelry box in his pocket. With his ring on Abby's hand, he couldn't wait to get some final photos commemorating their engagement. They reached the cleft in the rock face.

"My life changed forever right here." The horizon's orange and purple clouds displayed Israel's breathtaking desert. He dropped to a knee. "I waited right here while Abby enjoyed the view. She spoke about how God gave Moses, turned around and—"

"Where are they?" Billy demanded. "Couldn't they stay put for a few minutes? Women!"

Chase sprung to his feet and walked to the cave's end. "Abby?"

Only an echo answered.

Where could they be?

Billy ran further up the trail. "Tiffany?" His deep voice carried across the rocky terrain. In the middle of the trail, he picked up a pink cell phone with a shattered screen.

Chase grabbed the phone. Chills went down his spine. "That's Abby's."

They looked in every direction.

No signs of life.

Chase followed as Billy sprinted further up the trail. After a sharp left turn the path opened into a small gravel cul-de-sac with a dead-end road. Fresh tire tracks coursed between menacing slopes. They stood in silence while in the distance, a diesel engine faded away.

Billy found Tiffany's phone and camera beside the trail.

Chase's world came closing in as darkness engulfed him.

There was no air to breathe.

CHAPTER THREE

Abby slid across the truck's corrugated metal floor resisting the urge to open her eyes. Rough black fabric covered her head while something firm dug into her wrists and secured her hands behind her back. Diesel fumes were almost overwhelming. She tumbled against another body.

"Tiffany?"

No answer.

Abby nudged Tiffany with her knee. "Are you okay?"

Nothing.

She's unconscious.

The truck rumbled along a dirt road into a sharp right turn. About a minute later, it pulled a gradual left. Abby determined to keep a mental record of their trek, noting the curves and time between each. A punishing bump forced her restraints deeper into her wrists. She tried to sit straight but slipped onto her side with the next bump.

Abby kept her focus as they made another right turn. The sound of tires on gravel disappeared as they bumped onto a paved road. The diesel engine's noise increased as they gained speed.

"Tiffany? Are you okay?"

No response.

I need a plan.

Abby bowed her head. "God, I don't understand this. Please get us out of here."

She tried to calm her breathing, inhaling a pungent garlic scent. She steadied herself against a wall as the bumps settled down.

Tiffany pushed against her leg. "What's going on?"

"You're awake, thank God."

"My hands." Tiffany groaned.

"I'll explain. Just take a minute."

"My head is pounding."

"A guy hit you on the head from behind while you were taking pictures."

Tiffany shook her head. "What? Who?"

"I don't know. After he hit you, he put me in a crazy wrestling hold. I couldn't get away."

"What have you done?"

Abby tried to maneuver to look along the fabric's edge. "I ... I didn't do anything."

"He left us."

Abby wished she could make eye contact but said nothing.

"Chase is an idiot."

"I'm sorry. He should have—"

"I practically screamed at him, 'Don't leave us here.' He did anyway."

Abby agreed but didn't want to admit Tiffany was right. She asked, "How badly are you hurt?"

"I hurt all over."

"Nothing broken?"

"How would I know? I can't even see."

Abby scooted away so their legs couldn't touch with the next bump.

"Where are we?"

"I don't know."

"You're just full of information, aren't you?"

Abby sighed. "We're in some type of truck."

They were silent for a minute. Tiffany said, "If your stupid fiancé hadn't left us …"

Tiffany groaned. Another bump forced her to slide against the wall. Restraints sliced into her skin. "Ouch."

"We need to get our hands free."

Tiffany snapped, "You think?"

"I have a Leatherman tool in the side pocket on my cargo pants. Can you get it?"

"They didn't take it from you?"

"I guess not."

"Why do you have a knife?"

"I always carry a knife."

"I guess they wouldn't suspect a knife in your pocket, especially in Israel where carrying one is forbidden."

Abby gritted her teeth. Why can't Tiffany just do what she asked?

Tiffany groaned again. "I can't move."

The truck ambled on as they sat with in uncomfortable silence. After fifteen minutes or so, they could hear cars driving past them causing Abby to say, "We must be in a town."

The truck stopped.

Abby kicked her feet against the metal floor and screamed, "Help. Get us out of here."

She heard footsteps from outside. The door opened. A hand gripped her by the throat. She couldn't breathe.

A deep voice said, "Quiet."

The hand gripped tighter than she could imagine. When he finally let go, Abby collapsed to the floor. Her lungs filled with air once again. Her neck pain persisted. Paralyzed in silence, Abby forced herself to concentrate.

Where are we? What town could this be?

The truck remained still for about a minute before they started moving again. Two left turns later, traffic sounds faded into the distance as the vehicle gained speed.

Abby remained quiet for as long as she could. Finally, she asked, "Are you okay?"

Tiffany coughed a few times. "What were you thinking?"

"I'm sorry."

"I've never been grabbed like that before in my life!"

"I didn't know."

Tiffany swore under her breath. "I thought he'd kill me."

They drove through more winding roads. With the circuitous route, Abby eventually lost track of the turns. "Chase and Billy will find us. Somehow."

"Billy holds grudges." Tiffany said.

"What are you talking about?"

"Chase did this. He's to blame for us being here. Do you think Billy will stay with him? It'll take every bit of self-restraint Billy has not to tear his head off."

After about half an hour, the engine rumbled to a stop. A door squeaked as a strong hand pulled Abby from the truck with her hands still bound together behind her back. She struggled to see along the fabric's edge in the moonlight. They zigzagged down a sandy trail until a blow to the back of her legs forced her down.

A thud announced Tiffany's arrival along with a gust of cool air.

"Why are you doing this?" A profound echo reverberated her words back to her.

A diesel engine rumble with a subtle high-pitched whine faded into the distance.

CHAPTER FOUR

A black telephone sat on a grey Formica workspace within a busy collection of desks at the Beersheba police department. Tired from a long day, Rafi Hadad rotated his shoulders as he rose from his chair, He grimaced when the phone rang.

He answered, "*Shalom.*"

A male voice stammered, "I'm sorry, they put me through to you. You're the fourth person I've spoken with. I'm trying to report an abduction. Did I get the right connection?"

Another American in crisis.

"This is Detective Rafi Hadad. Who's missing?"

"My girlfriend, I ... I mean fiancée. Abby Radcliffe and another girl, Tiffany Rawlings."

Rafi scribbled names down on a notepad. "Your name?"

"Chase Johnson. I'm here with my friend Billy Rawlings."

Hadad turned toward his computer. His fingers rattled quickly on the keyboard. "What happened?"

"We were hiking in the Kadesh Barnea region when they were kidnapped."

"When?"

"Just a few minutes ago."

"Did you see the abduction take place?"

The conversation halted. "Um, no. They were taking pictures together, then they were gone."

Rafi shook his head. "Any chance they're nearby? You haven't found them yet?"

"Their broken cell phones were on the ground. I saw tire tracks." After a frustrated breath, he continued, "Sir, they've been taken."

With his phone cradled under his chin, Rafi brought up Chase's cell number on his computer. A few taps later, he had his location. "Stay put, don't touch anything. I'll be there soon."

Hadad sent Chase's information to his cell phone, then went to the corner office. After a quick rap on the door, he poked his head inside. "Chief Valsburg, we have a possible abduction at Mount Karkom."

Chief Idit Valsburg stared at her laptop screen. Her sharp angular features and straight black hair framed intense eyes which revealed her aggressive nature. She had risen to her position faster than anyone in Israeli Police Department history. With only one week remaining at this post before taking her place as deputy commissioner for the Israeli Police Force, the chief's attention seemed to be elsewhere. Rafi wasn't surprised when she didn't respond. He repeated his statement.

"When?"

"Just now reported. I'll head down there to see if something requires our attention."

"Could be nothing."

He nodded, but said, "With the details the victim's fiancé gave, an abduction sounds real."

"Get the info you need. Work the case from here."

Rafi nodded. He headed to the parking lot where he settled into his silver Skoda Octavia sedan and checked his watch. Just under an hour of travel time. Hadad faced a late night even with less than half an hour on site. Without a wife to come home to, he welcomed extra cases, especially for missing girls.

Several years earlier, someone abducted Laili, his best friend's fiancée. Rafi worked the case through Passover as if his life depended upon it. When days turned to weeks, he re-interviewed everyone involved, doubled back on every lead but came up empty. Ending with a painful apology to his friend and Laili's mother. Rafi kept a copy of her case file on the corner of his desk, a permanent reminder, his inspiration to pursue every missing person like tomorrow doesn't exist.

The smooth desert drive lacked traffic after sundown. The long straight road ended in a parking lot where an average-sized man anxiously paced. A bodybuilder leaned against the fender. His downward facing eyes illuminated by his phone. Rafi parked next to them, and stepped out of his vehicle, extending his hand in greeting. "Good evening. I'm Detective Rafi Hadad. Call me Rafi."

"Chase Johnson, we spoke on the phone." His khakis, red Iowa State T-shirt, and running shoes screamed "American." His flimsy handshake, blotchy face, and general downcast demeanor advertised him as a devastated victim.

He faced the large young man, who challenged Rafi's hand with an equally sturdy handshake. Hair shaved on the sides and gelled on top framed his intimidating stare. A tight teal button-down shirt accentuated his musculature while his honeycomb mesh slip-on loafers completed the look. He could pass as a European until his voice revealed his heritage.

"Billy Rawlings."

Rafi asked, "How are you related to the missing girls?"

"Tiffany's my sister."

"Abby is my girlfriend ... I mean fiancée," Chase clarified.

Rafi grabbed a backpack from the trunk as he made a mental image of the type of footprints each young men had left in the dirt.

Chase said, "We were just getting pictures when it started to rain and ..."

"Details as we walk." Rafi started briskly up the path. Chase fumbled his words as he unfolded the story, including a fair amount of irrelevant minutia. Rafi listened as he surveyed the moist soil with his flashlight. The short, powerful storm had washed away the previous footprints like an eraser on a blackboard. Every imprint like a fingerprint with a time stamp.

Billy followed behind them. "I stayed down yonder at first while they went up. I came up later."

Rafi didn't look up. The footprints had been placed since the downpour. Their story agreed with Billy's report.

When they reached the cave, Chase started a reenactment by getting down on one knee. Rafi shook his head. "Just show me where they disappeared."

Chase dug Abby's phone from his pocket. "We found her phone over here."

Rafi secured her phone in a plastic bag marked with Hebrew lettering. He tucked it into his backpack. "The other one?"

Billy gave him Tiffany's phone. "Found it farther up."

"Did they drop anything else?"

Billy said, "Tiffany's camera, which I put in the car."

"I'll need it." Rafi swept the ground with his flashlight. "Stay behind me."

Rafi walked alone up the trail to where it turned. At the valley's edge, he visually scanned the region before glancing back at the young men obediently giving him space to work. He signaled them to approach. "Did you come up this far before they went missing?"

Chase took a few steps toward him. "No, only after they were gone. Before we didn't get farther than the little cavern back there."

Rafi bent down as he looked a little closer. "Tire tracks." He took pictures, looked along the edge of the parking area where he saw a pair of cigarette butts. He took a few photos, donned a latex glove, and picked up the butts. *Cool and dry. Dropped after the rain.* He stowed the evidence in his backpack. *This is an abduction.*

Chase inched closer. "Can you get DNA off those?"

Without answering, Rafi pulled a tablet from his backpack, aimed the dim yellow light on the footprints, then waved his device back and forth three times in a systematic manner over each print. He did the same for the tire tracks, stood, pressed a few buttons, and waited. Moments later, he announced, "Women's size 7 and 9 shoes, men's size 13 work boots, and tires from a delivery truck."

Chase said, "Wait, what?"

Rafi held his device up.

"Like on CSI TV shows?"

Rafi asked, "You're familiar with analysis of plaster casts of tire tracks in the lab?"

"Sure."

He pointed at the screen. "This takes digital casts. Runs it through an extensive database."

Chase asked, "You already narrowed it down to a delivery truck?"

"I can also tell you detailed brand info and approximate age of each of the shoes, yet we still don't have much."

Chase's eyebrows rose. "Anything to help us find Abby and Tiffany?"

Rafi shrugged, "Shoes are everyday brands, in common sizes. Delivery trucks are used by every mail service and many businesses in town."

Billy stepped back from the screen. Veins in his neck grew. "Are you kidding me? You have to narrow down the truck."

"It's more than we knew five minutes ago." Rafi glanced from one to the other. "Why were you here?"

Chase answered, "Abby wanted to relive Moses's journey."

"Way out here? There are plenty of other places for tourists to visit. Companies who give tours tell stories of what took place at each site. This place is a common hang out for locals. Not the safest."

Chase shrugged. "Abby is a Bible history buff. Her research pointed to this as a likely place where Moses spent some time."

Billy squared off with Rafi. "Tell me the truth. Are they dead?"

Rafi hesitated. "All we know is what we've seen here. Having good friends like you two certainly helps."

Chase said, "Actually, Abby and I just met Billy and Tiffany a couple of days ago at the engineering conference."

Rafi narrowed his gaze.

Billy stepped forward. "You were about to say something else. You know more than you're saying."

"I'm not supposed to tell you this, but if someone is taken without a witness, finding them is quite challenging. With rain this evening, at least we have tire tracks, boot prints, and this." He held up the evidence bags. "We have a start."

Chase asked, "How many times has this happened before?"

Rafi shook his head. "Even one is too many."

Chase said, "How long does it usually take to find them?"

"Abduction is an ongoing problem."

Chase raised his chin an inch. "Doesn't answer my question. How long does it normally take for you to find missing people?"

Rafi looked at Chase without a word then headed back toward the parking lot.

This looks all too much like Laili's disappearance ...

CHAPTER FIVE

MT. SINAI

Chase walked shoulder to shoulder with Rafi down the hillside. Pointing his flashlight at Rafi, he waited for a sign of hope to find Abby while he rattled off detail after detail of her life, desperate to be any help at all.

Rafi didn't respond.

Is he even listening?

When they passed the cave, Billy joined them in silence. With his head hung low, Chase recalled the past twenty-four hours. In the morning, he received international acclaim for his inflatable mattress. His pride and joy, a compilation of years of work which boosted to his already impressive résumé. When Abby said yes, his future opened—life overflowed with possibilities. Then, in a single moment, his entire life collapsed into a nightmare.

In the parking lot, Rafi bagged Tiffany's camera and stowed everything in his trunk. "I have the information I need."

Rafi gave each of them his business card before he slipped behind the wheel. "Email me photos of each girl. I'll post them. Will be in touch if anything comes up."

Chase threw up his hands. "What are we supposed to do now?"

"Stay in town. You might be able to help."

Chase contested. "You can't just leave!"

Rafi placed both hands on the steering wheel. "Guys, I'm going to do everything I can to find them. But staying here any longer will not help me investigate their disappearance." He closed the door and headed down a long straight road.

Billy popped his car trunk where he retrieved a white plastic box and a black device the size of a Pringles can. He pressed a button on the side. Donning wireless earbuds, he directed the machine toward Rafi's vehicle. A hundred yards and growing.

Chase asked, "What are you doing?"

Billy remained focused on the departing sedan. Without a word, he pulled his laptop from his backpack and connected a USB wire it to his device. He tapped on the keyboard for a few minutes, then closed his eyes and groaned like he had taken a blow to his gut.

Chase asked, "What's wrong? Were you able to hear something going on in the car?"

"This isn't right."

"What are you talking about?"

He handed Chase an earbud while he pressed a button. "Listen."

Chase heard Rafi clear his throat as if he had been in the car with him. Rafi spoke in Hebrew. A female voice answered. Chase couldn't understand a word.

Chase's eyes grew wide. "Sounds amazing. How does this thing work?"

Billy held a finger to his lips. He turned his laptop toward Chase. Their conversation had been transcribed through a Hebrew voice recognition program and translated into English. Chase read:

"Did you get the images I sent? I saw footprints and tire tracks."

"It's all vanilla."

"Chief, we have plenty to work with. When I get back, I'll start with a review of all delivery trucks in the area with those tires."

"Already done. Over 10,000 delivery trucks in Israel use those tires. Most are FedEx or other delivery companies. If we extend our search to surrounding countries, there will be three times as many."

"But—"

"If we had a witness who saw the truck out in a desolate area, we would have something. They could tell us about the color or insignia on it. As it is, we have nothing to work with."

"I'll run the cigarette for DNA."

"You know as well as I do those two girls are as good as gone. You're done here."

"However, I think—"

Chase hung his head.

Billy said, "After she hung up, Rafi swore as he pounded the steering wheel."

"I can't believe this."

Billy set the device on the dashboard. "They're done."

Chase turned on his phone flashlight and looked back toward the trail. "Let's go back up there."

They walked up the trail without a word until Chase said, "When I was a sophomore at Iowa State, I worked for a company doing deliveries with an old, converted FedEx truck. We might be able to find something if we look closer."

They walked without a word for a while until Chase broke the silence again. "I missed your presentation at the Engineering Fair, a microphone on steroids?"

"The machine looks at compression of air molecules within sound waves, calculates a corresponding frequency, then reconstructs the conversation."

"Awesome technology. What makes yours so special?"

"Nothing else isolates human voices."

Chase's jaw dropped. "You kidding me? Did you patent it yet?"

Billy didn't reply.

As they arrived at the abduction site, the sloping mountain seemed more prominent than before. They meandered around the periphery of the area where the truck had parked. They scanned one foot at a time with their phone flashlights.

Chase bent over the tire tracks. "No turn-around marks." He imagined sitting in a driver's seat looking over the whole area. "He must have backed in to settle right here. Waiting like a hunter."

He shone his light on the sandy surface by the side door. No sign of a struggle. Inch by inch, he scanned. After some time, on the opposite side, he noticed a few small irregular rainbows glistening in the light.

Billy saw them too. "Motor oil."

Chase playfully asked, "Do folks from Alabama spell the word 'O-O-L' or 'O-L-L?'"

Billy ignored him.

Chase realized this wasn't a time to tease Billy about his accent. "The oil is on the side, not under the engine." He swabbed the oil with his finger, rubbed his fingers together, and tasted it.

"Vegetable oil." He held up his finger looking at Billy.

Billy waved him off.

Why would oil leak from a side of a truck? Who else uses delivery trucks?

Chase remembered the truck he drove in college. He imagined walking around the vehicle like a pilot doing an overall vehicle check. Straight sidewalls, grill, hood, tires, exhaust. Nothing interesting. He imagined vegetable oil dripping from the side. The image in his mind's eye shifted to a county fair back home, standing outside a truck talking through a window, ordering a corn dog. He imagined where oil might build up and drip on the ground below, then looked at the sandy base. Oil.

"It's a food truck."

Billy asked, "Come again?"

"Food trucks are nothing more than converted FedEx trucks. Around here, it might be a falafel truck. They have been getting quite popular in the past few years. An up-and-coming business across the Middle East."

Billy touched the oil with his finger. He rubbed his thumb and finger together. "Olive oil?"

Chase had a glimmer of hope. "We have something to go on." He pulled Rafi's business card from his pocket and dialed.

His familiar voice spoke first in Hebrew, then in English. "You've reached Detective Rafi Hadad's voicemail. Leave a message."

"Rafi, this is Chase Johnson. The vehicle is a falafel truck. That narrows down the possibilities. Call me." He pressed the End Call button, then stood and surveyed the broader area with his flashlight. He looked at Billy. "We're going to find them."

"He won't call back if it's up to his boss lady."

CHAPTER SIX

MT. SINAI

Chase sat shotgun as Billy put his key in the ignition and rolled down his window. A slight breeze did nothing to ease the tension. Billy stared down the long straight road in silence, then threw the key on the dash.

In their silence, three words reverberated in Chase's mind: *You're done here*. Rafi's boss had told him not to pursue the case. He said, "Why are the police shutting us down?"

Billy stared into the distance without speaking.

Darkness absorbed Chase's thoughts as he slumped in his seat. After a few minutes, Chase said, "We can search every business in the area using food trucks. We'll interview the owners. Find out what they're doing, maybe find some type of connection."

Billy grabbed his phone. His fingers moved briskly as they dabbed, swiped, and scrolled.

Chase asked, "What are you doing?"

Billy said, "Contacting the Embassy."

Chase sat up straight, relieved to see Billy joining him in the effort. "You're on their website? Give them a call."

Billy continued swiping the screen. After a few minutes, he held his phone to his ear. "I need to report a kidnapping. Kadesh Barnea, two Americans, Tiffany

Rawlings and Abby—" He looked at Chase, "What's Abby's last name?"

"Radcliffe."

"Abby Radcliffe. We contacted the local police, they looked around, not doing much. Please give me a call." He left his contact information and ended the call.

Chase shook his head. "You had to leave a message?"

"I'll send them an email too." Billy fingers swept over the screen.

Chase's thoughts ricocheted back and forth: the Embassy, Detective Rafi, the tire tracks, Abby. His heart sank when her family popped into his thoughts. He had met them a few months earlier over Christmas break but didn't know them well. They would have no clue his relationship with Abby had progressed to being serious, much less engaged.

I can't call them.

Chase took a deep breath and exhaled. They needed to know what has happened. He checked his watch, The late hour in Israel meant midday back home.

He glanced at Billy. "Hey, you okay?"

Billy shook his head.

"You should call your folks."

His fingers stopped. Billy gazed over the top of his phone. His shoulders slumped.

Chase said, "We need any help we can get from family or friends."

"It's been a long time." Billy stepped out of the car and closed the door.

Chase's eyes stayed on his phone. With the window down he heard Billy say, "Dad?"

He waited a moment, then continued.

"Um, yeah, we're here in Israel. How did you know?"

He shook his head.

"Yeah, you're right. She's always been the better communicator. I'm sorry I didn't tell you we were making the trip over here."

Billy sat on the front fender. The car sank under his weight. "I need to tell you something important."

Billy rubbed his forehead.

"Tiffany has been taken."

His hand fell to his lap.

"No. She didn't find a guy here in Israel. Nothing like—"

He held out his left palm.

"No. Dad. I agree she never was one to conform. Listen, she was taken in a bad way. Abducted. We've contacted the police."

He waited a moment, then continued. "Dad, I said someone abducted her."

Chase leaned closer when the conversation halted. Billy stood like a statue with a phone to his ear.

"No, Dad, she's not off on some project. She was taken." He spoke slowly and clearly. "She was with a couple taking pictures on a mountainside out in the middle of nowhere. The idiot guy left them alone out there. She and the other girl were alone out there. That's when they were taken."

Billy stood up and waited.

"I did already. I called the cops."

His large shoulders drooped.

"Yes, the Embassy too, called and emailed. Listen, Dad, we need help."

"I'm—"

He paced in a circle in front of the car.

"I'm sorry, Dad."

He shook his head. "I know. Can you help us? I was wondering if you could call your friend Mr. Jackson? He's in Congress now, right? Maybe he can put pressure on the Embassy."

"Thank you. Call me if you find out anything."

Chase stared at his phone as Billy returned to the car.

"Must have been tough. How did it go?"

Billy shook his head.

Chase wanted to ask questions. Clearly, this was not the time.

"My turn." Chase dialed his mother and relayed his version of the story. He struggled through her flurry of questions: Why would anyone ... How did they ... Will she be okay?

He had no good answers. With a break in their conversation, he asked, "Mom, is there anyone you know with government connections who can help?"

"Oh, goodness no, dear. I'll call our pastor. He'll put it on the prayer chain. God is the only politician I know."

"Right. Thanks."

After some awkward silence, Chase ended the call, saying he would keep in touch. He gritted his teeth, tapped in Abby's mother's number, then relayed a version of the story with promises to do everything he could to find her daughter. After repeating himself a couple of times, he ended the call with promises to call back soon.

Billy stared at his phone, his thumbs racing.

Chase opened his social media app and saw their engagement notice he had prepared but hadn't posted. Joy had been eaten up by guilt and emptiness.

Billy started the car and headed north on Highway 21. Chase felt every bump in the punishing road.

After a few minutes of silence, Chase said, "Did you see my inflatable mattress at the Engineering Fair?"

When Billy didn't answer, Chase continued. "I was so excited to present it in Tel Aviv. I called it a suicide mattress because I designed the mechanism to be below a jumper. Sensors can detect a falling body. Four powerful fans inflate a nylon-covered nickel-titanium frame, instantly making a giant cushion to break their fall. I called them my cyclone fans as a tip of the hat to my alma mater."

Chase glanced at Billy. "Have you ever seen on YouTube Mark Rober's dartboard which always makes you get a perfect bullseye every time? The computer moves his board to where a dart is headed. I used similar technology, using little jets to position my mattress directly under a falling body."

Billy gripped the steering wheel with white knuckles. "Would you shut up?"

"I was just ..." He turned to Billy and closed his mouth when he saw bulging veins in Billy's temple and his tense jaw.

Heaviness consumed him. They rode on in silence.

Void of any road signs, Chase had no guidance until he saw a dilapidated sign indicating Tlalim—little more than a few buildings in the wilderness. A left turn on Highway 40 carried them farther across miles of dark desert road. By the time they arrived in Beersheba, the presence of streetlights gave no reprieve from their oppressive darkness.

Billy passed through a few intersections then stopped at a red light. A few blocks left waited the hostel where he and Abby stayed in separate rooms for a mere $23 a night. A half-mile north, the four-star Leonardo Negev Hotel awaited Tiffany and Billy.

At the intersection, Chase asked, "Where to?"

Billy glanced to his left, then looked ahead.

Please don't leave me on my own.

Jaw still clenched, Billy drove straight. "We have work to do."

CHAPTER SEVEN

JERUSALEM

In the corner office of a plain steel building in the industrial zone of Israel's capital city, Mr. Manny Lochotzki worked late into the night. Endless spreadsheets indicated his company's sales numbers dwindled while his costs continued to rise. He evaluated employee performance reviews, and his marketing plan. He checked the schematics and performance stats of his revolutionary helio pump. His design had revolutionized the industry ten years earlier. Still their primary source of profit, month after month, sales slowed as his pump neared retirement. Without a fresh innovation, his company would sink.

Lochotzki ran his long fingers through his short-cropped hair. He slumped in the worn chair behind his custom-made desk, built high enough to fit his substantial bony structure. Although he was normally infused with inspiration at his personal retreat, tonight, his numbers showed no future.

For the last ten years, his engineering company, LabStrength, had been nothing short of a rising star in the community. Now he felt his star plummeting like a blazing meteorite. His hope rested in the company's current research project, "Streams in the Desert." *We need definitive results from our research to launch sales of the new pumps.*

Lochotzki stared at a solitary photograph on his wall. A simple picture he had taken as a teenager. Brown, rocky, dusty mountains interrupted by dry riverbeds and deep craters with distinctive beauty. As a young boy, Manny had spent endless hours exploring the Negev. He viewed the scene with mature eyes now. Water lay deep below the surface, geothermal energy waited to be captured and used for his pump. This wasteland could become productive farmland—if only it had water. Now, he would harness underground energy to transport water at a minimal cost to where it was so badly needed. Progress seemed to be two steps forward and three steps back even after years of recruiting and funding talented engineers and geophysicists. His thoughts fractured with a knock on the door. "Shalom, come in."

The door swung open, revealing a smile above a grey goatee. Manny grinned. *There's not another man on the planet who wears a dress shirt with worn jeans.*

"Shalom, good evening, Manny."

His lead engineer's vocal cords must be made of gravel. "Joel, come in. Have a seat. Good to see you. How are you this evening?"

"I'm well. I apologize for such a late visit." He held up three folders.

"Nonsense, come in. I could use some good news for a change."

"Today's news is a blockbuster, sir." Joel took a few steps into the office and handed his boss the top folder.

Joel sat on the edge of the chair. "I spent most of the last few days processing our data. The hydrostatic and lithostatic measurements confirm our findings."

Manny asked, "At Ein Haron or Ein Gedi?"

Joel revealed coffee-stained teeth with his smile. "Both."

Manny rose to his feet. "That is great news. Are they consistent with last month's measurements?"

"Completely."

"What about the final tests going on in Ein Gedi?"

"We should have those results tomorrow. So far, everything looks perfect."

Manny pumped his fist in the air. "Geothermal energy is key. In combination with directional drilling we borrowed from the oil industry, 'Streams in the Desert' will turn almost every desert in the world into prosperous farmland."

"This will change the nature of agriculture all over the world."

Manny stared at a family photo on the wall. His grown children, all standing together, happy, perfect. He opened Joel's file and sorted through their preliminary results. A deep dive into each test and corroborating their results would take time.

Joel pointed to the conclusion on the fourth page. "Here, you can see the readings are consistent."

"Will geothermal energy be sufficient to power our entire irrigation system?"

"Absolutely."

Manny beamed. "And our other project? Tell me about the pumps."

Joel laid a second file on the desk. "Peltier chips convert heat into electricity with more than enough power to run the pumps."

Manny rubbed his hands together. "Our design works!"

We're getting close.

He focused on the folder like an expectant student hoping to find an "A" on a test. When his gaze fell on the numbers, he pumped his fist again. Only one final test remained necessary in a thermally active site before they could start development and sales.

"You will change the nature of agriculture all over the world."

Standing with him in front of his desk, Manny put a hand on Joel's shoulder. "We, my friend. This is a team effort. I couldn't do this without you. Together, we will bring 'Streams in the Desert' to the world."

Joel bowed his head. "Thank you, sir."

Manny smiled at his fellow engineer. Pointing at a file still in his hands he asked, "You have more?"

Joel held up his palm defensively. "We'll cover it tomorrow."

"Nonsense. You have more. I want it all right now."

Joel closed his eyes and held out his final file.

Manny received it with excitement. He read the heading, "Fourth quarter sales"—the same report he had been studying just before Joel entered. He narrowed his gaze. "You've been busy."

Joel said, "Our shareholders might jump ship when they see this."

Manny set the file on the edge of his desk. "All of this goes away when we make our first sale of our new pumps." He pushed the file into his wastebasket.

"We have to deal with questions and accusations from our investors."

"One thing at a time."

Joel took a step forward. He opened his mouth to speak, then stopped.

"Let's review the details in the lab." Manny grabbed his bag and moved toward the door. "First thing tomorrow morning."

Nodding, Joel took a step back.

The conversation closed—but not the crisis.

CHAPTER EIGHT

BEERSHEBA

Chase followed Billy into an elegant hotel room without a word. Two king-size beds filled one side of the room, the other side had a dresser, refrigerator, and desk. On the far wall, a sliding glass door opened to a west-facing balcony.

Chase tossed his bags on a bed. He made two cups of high-quality coffee, set one in front of Billy with cream and sugar. Sipping the other, he sat with his back against the headboard. Billy added cream to the coffee, tossing aside the sugar without a word. He hadn't made eye contact with Chase since they left Mt. Sinai.

Is he going to talk to me at all?

Chase logged into the Wi-Fi and searched for local food trucks. A handful of restaurants had pictures of trucks on their websites. He built a spreadsheet for their basic data. With a little further evaluation, he added their business size, the number of employees, and their number of trucks.

Heaving a deep breath, Chase broke their silence. "I have some information on local businesses using food trucks."

Billy put on his shoes, stood up, and grabbed his laptop. Without a word, he left the room, leaving his phone on the desk.

Chase's mouth dropped open. He jogged to the door, threw a latch to prevent the door from locking him out, and followed Billy down the hallway. In a hushed tone loud enough to be heard but not enough to wake other occupants, he said, "Where are you going?"

Billy walked into the elevator and glared at Chase until the door shut.

Chase returned to the room where he paced from one end to the other until, in frustration, he pulled out his Bible. He gripped the Book in his hands, unable to open it, but stared at the leather cover hoping for something encouraging. His mother's elaborate profound prayers flickered through his mind. He could only mutter, "God help."

His lifeless words fell to the floor. His mind was a vacuum.

Chase picked up Billy's vibrating phone from the desk. A photo of a middle-aged man labeled "Dad" stared back at him.

Chase hesitated. Billy had been gone for who knows how long. No idea when he would return. Chase swiped the screen, brought the phone to his ear. "Hello?"

"Who is this?"

"My name is Chase. I'm working with Billy to find Tiffany and Abby."

"Put Billy on."

"He stepped out for a minute. Mr. Rawlings, have you had any luck with your congressman friend?"

"Have him call me."

The line went dead.

Chase sat comatose.

About fifteen minutes later, Billy's form filled the door frame. He set a stack of papers and his laptop on the desk. Then he turned to Chase with his phone in hand. "You answered my phone? Spoke with my dad?"

"He wasn't very talkative. He asked you to give him a call."

Billy frowned. "Keep your hands off my stuff."

Chase raised his voice. "I'm not the enemy here. Look, we need to work together."

Billy looked as if he wanted to tear him apart. "Without you, they wouldn't be missing. You had to get your precious reenactment for the attention. No one else wanted it. You left them alone. You did this."

Thoroughly steamrolled, Chase bent forward holding his head between his hands. The carpet's fleur-de-lis pattern created the only thread of connection between them.

Billy continued. "Now, you pretend you had nothing to do with their abduction, and you're all excited about finding them—our next adventure. You're ready to go find them. Be the hero."

Chase held his breath,

"Do you care about anyone other than yourself?" Billy turned back to his computer.

The sinister pattern on the carpet blurred as tears covered Chase's eyes. He dared not look at Billy.

He's right. It's my fault they're gone.

Chase sprang to the door like a gazelle fleeing a predator. He walked between palm trees through the downtown district without a destination. His world had been swept out from under him. After a minute, he stopped walking and collapsed onto the sidewalk.

Dim halogen lights illuminated sparse traffic.

The only thing of importance is getting them back.

He imagined going back to Billy's room and getting things right. He ran apology scripts through his head. Nothing could make this right.

He sat alone.

Dreadfully alone.

His mind drifted to the moment when Abby pulled him into the cave to get out of the rain.

Memory of her midwestern professorial tone calmed him. *Historians dispute the location of Mt. Sinai, but I want to see for myself.* She planned Mt. Karkom as a destination. Of all the popular sites to visit, this one didn't make the top twenty list for most groups.

The rumble of a delivery truck stirred Chase back to the present. He looked up as a delivery truck passed him faster than the legal city speed limit. A large window on the driver's side with a dent in the upper left corner. He strained to see more but, with poor illumination, couldn't make out more details.

A food truck?

He didn't take his eyes off the truck. Listening carefully to the rumble, in addition to a typical diesel engine, this truck gave off an intermittent click and high-pitched whine. The sound registered in Chase's mind even as he focused on a smiling cartoon character smoking a cigar and wearing a fedora. The truck turned north and disappeared.

CHAPTER NINE

Beersheba

The delivery truck's image and distinctive sound consumed Chase as he stood on the sidewalk. No doubt, the large window indicated conversion to a mobile kitchen. Chase imagined falafels being cooked and served to happy customers lined up outside, waiting in the sun for their lunch as olive oil spilled down the side dripping on the ground. He pictured a smiling cartoon face with a cigar and fedora. He closed his eyes, searing the image into his memory.

What is it doing out here at this time of night? Could it be them?

Chase noted the street name, Yitzchak I. Rager Boulevard, then hurried back to the hotel room. *If we can track down the truck, we can find Abby and Tiffany.*

Will Billy let me in?

He knocked. Waited.

The knob turned. Door creaked open. He waited for Billy to confront him. Nothing happened. The door remained still, barely open. Chase pressed on the handle and opened it wide enough to slip through. Back at his desk, Billy hunched over his laptop in dim light.

Chase sat on the end of the bed with his hands in his lap. "You're right. Abby and Tiffany being kidnapped is my fault."

Without waiting for a response, Chase continued. "I'm an idiot. I should never have left them." His words hung in the air as he waited for Billy to respond. *I have to tell him about the truck I saw outside.*

Silence. Billy clicked the mouse staring at his screen.

"I'm sorry."

No response.

"I'm stupid."

Nothing.

Wow, how much do I have to genuflect before he talks with me? I'll tell him about the food truck later.

Chase kicked his shoes off and leaned against the headboard. "Fine, we can work in silence."

He answered a series of texts from friends, then slipped into the hallway and called his mother again. As he returned to the room, Billy taped a page to the wall adding to a dozen other pages lined up in rows. Perfectly arranged as if he had used a laser level to align them with care. His top page had the heading "Abductions." Below it, six spreadsheets listed names, ages, locations, and dates. Separate pages reported prostitution abductions from a dozen Mideast countries, some recent, others dated back up to ten years earlier.

A pair of glossy maps separated the two symmetrically spaced columns. The first, a tourist guide to Israel—the same map Abby had used when planning their tour of Israel. Below, a multicolored map of the broader Mideast region. A dozen red ink circles scattered across both maps. Israel had three circles, one around Tel Aviv, the others in desolate regions without large cities. A regional map had nine circles, some around major cities, others in small towns or areas of wilderness. Chase referred to the other list where locations corresponded with abduction sites. He tried to see how the data on those spreadsheets would tell a story but only saw past abductions and prostitution scattered all over the area.

Chase said, "You've been busy." He gestured to a few points on the map with his index finger. "A 200-mile radius from here."

Billy returned to his computer and dug into his keys.

Chase pointed at a spreadsheet. "Women have gone missing each year. How many of them have been found?"

Silence.

Chase's mouth dropped open, "This is bigger than just a pair of girls gone missing."

Billy punished his laptop's keyboard. Within a few seconds, his screen displayed a map representing the Sunni-Shia divide. After saving it, he stopped at a map showing Muslim and Jewish centers. The majority of those countries were red, indicating Islam. Israel stood out as a solitary blue region. Only one Jewish region.

"You think religion has something to do with this?"

Billy's fingers stopped their demanding assault.

Chase walked back toward the door and stopped. "Listen, I'm sorry. I have to tell you what I saw outside."

Billy continued staring at his screen.

"I saw a food truck on the street only a few minutes ago. Why would they be out at this time of night?"

Billy rubbed his face.

Chase continued, "You remember hearing a diesel engine when we were where they disappeared, right?"

"Of course, I remember. I'm not stupid. Where was it tonight?"

Relieved to be back in conversation, Chase said, "Heading north on Yitzchak I. Rager Boulevard. I don't know why they name their streets in paragraphs."

Billy opened a map on his laptop. "What restaurant?"

Chase sat on the bed and opened his laptop. "I saw part of a logo, I think." He closed his eyes. Pictured the smiling cartoon face with a fedora and cigar. *I need to find that image.* He looked at the spreadsheet where he listed restaurants with food trucks. He opened another window and, using the website BatchGeo, mapped out each of their locations.

Billy asked, "You think he's heading where they keep them?

Chase turned his screen towards Billy, pointing out the map's northern portion. "I mapped out a handful of restaurants with trucks in Beersheba."

"Send it to me."

Chase emailed it along with the corresponding data to Billy. One by one, he focused on each with truck service. Albi Kabab claimed to have the best falafels in Israel. Their archaic website showed nothing but a menu, hours, and their location.

He glanced over at Billy's screen. He clicked quickly until a photo of a group of teenagers came up. A boy wore a T-shirt with a cartoon character on it. Chase looked closer. The same cartoon character graced the truck.

"That's it!"

Billy looked up, "What?"

Chase pointed. "Enlarge this image."

Billy zoomed in on a cartoon character with a hat, green sport coat, and brown awkward legs.

Chase said, "I saw something similar on the truck."

"Makes no sense."

"I just saw the face, with the cigar and hat. I don't know about the rest, it somehow felt familiar."

Billy emailed him the link. Chase took a screenshot, and uploaded it to an image searching website, narrowing his search for the Beersheba region. Forty-eight hits appeared. One image took him to a local soccer team's website, another was for a plumber's shop. He continued

40

clicking until he found a restaurant without delivery service.

He turned his screen toward Billy. "This thing is everywhere in this town."

"Looks like you're barking up the wrong tree."

Chase scrolled through images and clicked on a GIF. A video cartoon of a man in a green sport coat and fedora smiled at him. With his hands on his hips, he tipped his hat, and winked. Chase took a screenshot of the body's lower half. Did another search. Web sites for goat care and pricing for goat farming came up. He looked at the whole cartoon image again.

Half goat, half man? What does it mean?

He clicked through one image after the next until he landed on a website for Hakfar High School in Beersheba. The goat-man in a fedora gripped a cigar between his teeth in website's banner.

Why would a school's mascot endorse smoking?

Chase said, "You're right. Wrong tree. I'll keep looking at restaurants."

He saved his search and pressed in on restaurants in northern Beersheba. "What would it take for a restaurant owner to get into sex trafficking? I suppose we could eliminate all smaller 'Mom and Pop' type shops if we're talking about sex trafficking."

Billy shook his head. "Why?"

Chase said, "Kidnapping takes planning and manpower. Smaller shops use every ounce of energy they have just to survive. Countless restaurants go out of business every year. We should focus on larger, more successful restaurants."

"That's not what I mean."

Chase looked at him. "Why what?"

"Why would someone in a restaurant business be into trafficking at all?"

Chase shrugged.

"Makes no sense." Billy stared at the wall with perfectly aligned printed sheets.

Chase shook his head. Young ladies captured and taken who knows where to do who knows what. He imagined a restaurant owner with connections to something bigger, more sinister.

CHAPTER TEN

BEERSHEBA

Chase and Billy continued working, oblivious to the morning sunlight peeking through the blinds. Chase's notes flowed across the floor and over his disheveled bedspread. In contrast, Billy's workspace remained tidy. Only empty coffee cups revealed he had worked through the night.

Chase took a final swig of coffee and grimaced at the cold, bitter grit of coffee grounds. Glancing at his watch, he asked, "Do they serve morning coffee in the lobby?"

Billy nodded.

Chase checked social media while he waited for the elevator. His mother had posted a plea for help. Unending emojis and comments gave nothing helpful. Disappointed yet not surprised, he headed to the lobby where fresh, high-quality Mideastern coffee beckoned him. He dosed two cups with cream and gingerly carried them back to the elevator.

Pressing the fourth-floor button, he put himself in Billy's shoes. His sister was missing. The only one here working with him is responsible for their abduction.

I'll apologize again.

His knuckles rapped on the door. After a moment, it creaked open. A stench of male bodies working through the night without ventilation hit him as he stepped through the doorway. Billy had his phone pressed to his ear.

Chase opened the blinds, illuminating the room with sun. He placed a coffee cup on the desk and returned to his post on the bed. He eyed his Bible lying on the floor and longed for hope or inspiration.

Billy stared at the wall. The person on the other end of his phone must have been doing a fair amount of talking. Eventually, he said, "Keep me posted. I'll call again soon, Dad."

Catching Billy's eye, Chase pointed to the coffee. "Cream, no sugar."

"I'll get you a key."

Chase felt a glimmer of hope. We're a team. As Billy turned away, Chase realized Billy had not invited him in. Instead, he created an arm's length of separation. With his face parallel to the floor, Chase said, "Listen. I'm sorry, I can't imagine what it takes for you to put up with me."

"Okay. We have work to do."

Chase proceeded as best he could. "Did your dad have any luck with the congressman?"

"No."

"I heard about an abduction in Tennessee. People posted details which went viral. Hundreds of thousands of people joined the search. They found the girl in one day. My mom lives on social media. She posted a plea last night. Who knows? Somebody might know something. Let's get some people ..."

"I saw it. Reposted. A dozen friends who are social media gurus reposted it too." Billy pointed to another column of pages on the wall. "These people will post too."

Chase looked at the accumulation of Billy's work. Through the night, he had continued printing and posting. Page after page of social media posts. Pages had metastasized to cover half the room.

"Impressive." Neatly nestled between sex trafficking reports and information on food trucks, sat a printout of the goat-man.

"We know a fair amount about the rate of abductions." Billy pointed at other columns. "We have police reports, religious cults, restaurants, food trucks, and sex trafficking."

"Where do we go from here?"

"Keep looking."

"There has to be photos of the food truck somewhere. If we were back in Iowa, we'd be looking at outdoor celebrations like 'Taste of Des Moines' or the Iowa State Fair."

Chase used a variety of search engines and combed through activities community events. One photo after the next flowed across his screen. At an outdoor award ceremony, he saw a collection of about a hundred people in a park with rolling grassy knolls, beautiful walking paths, and scattered bicycles.

How could such a beautiful park exist in this desert?

He double-checked the location, Beersheba River Park. More photos revealed about a hundred people gathered in front of a makeshift platform where a man with a microphone announced winners of the Negev Award for their Community Contributions. At back of the crowd, Chase noted a partially visible silver truck under a large shade tree.

His eyes widened. He enlarged the photo but didn't see any markings. He searched the event site for more pictures at Beersheba River Park. As he enlarged a photo, his screen filled with a shiny truck with a dent in the upper left corner, a goat-man on the back, and the restaurant's name: Albi Kabab.

"Bingo! I found a picture of the truck." Chase turned his laptop toward Billy.

"Are you sure?"

"Absolutely! Same truck I saw last night with an unmistakable dent in the corner. I know I didn't mention a dent earlier, but it was there." He pointed at the screen. "The truck which took Abby and Tiffany."

"Okay. We have a place to start." Billy plugged the restaurant into this laptop and scanned the limited website. "How long have they been in business? How many employees do they have? What connections do they have with criminal organizations?"

Chase asked, "How do you get such information?"

"No idea."

"We could visit them in person."

Billy looked at his watch. "Soon."

Chase pointed at his screen. "Looking at a business online is like getting a view from 30,000 feet."

Billy picked up Tiffany's blue and white designer suitcase. "What if we could truly look at the city from above?"

Chase furrowed his brow, "Huh?"

"Let me introduce you to *Şeker Bayrami*."

Billy removed a pair of large curved black panels from Tiffany's suitcase. Taking his time, he delicately assembled a model airplane with a series of snaps.

Chase's eyebrows rose. "I'm intrigued."

Billy picked it up at the center of the fuselage with one hand like a proud uncle. "May I present to you Tiffany's pride and joy."

Chase gazed at the machine. A quad-deck wing provided maximum lift, a boxy appearance only a mother could love. "Is it a glider?"

"Drone."

"There's no prop or jet engine. What provides thrust?"

"Ion propulsion." Billy pointed at fine wires under the wings. "No moving parts."

"I saw a prototype where ionized nitrogen forces airflow across the wing. They had problems with low propulsion."

"Tiff tripled the ionic wind with palladium-titanium alloy." He pointed at the top wing. "The upper surfaces are a new light-weight solar panel."

"Solar-powered ionic wind?"

"Fully charged, ready to fly. She built it for the specifications of the contest in Tel Aviv. Her ticket to a promotion."

Chase raised his eyebrows. "Promotion?"

"Three years as an associate, then she'll move to a bigger firm. Within ten years, she'll be a CEO."

Chase couldn't remember the last time he planned more than a week ahead of time.

Billy pointed to a series of tiny circles on the hull's underbelly. "This is my personal addition, a camera, infrared thermal sensor, and night vision."

"A solar-powered drone can't fly at night."

"Theoretically she could fly forever with a fully charged battery and enough altitude at sunset."

He tapped his phone. "You control it with this. All the controls a pilot needed at his fingertips. Program a course. She'll fly it."

Chase held the phone, reminiscent of a flight simulator game. He pointed to the name artfully embossed on the hull. "What's Şeker Bayrami?"

Billy gently disassembled the wings. "Tiffany spent a semester studying abroad and did a lot of traveling. She fell in love with Turkey. After thirty days of fasting during Ramadan, they have a festival called Şeker Bayrami."

"Never heard of it."

Billy continued, "Like Mardi Gras to the Lenten season. Literal meaning is 'Sugar Holiday.' Ever since her visit, she's cooked their traditional sweet desserts and has celebrated it the way most people celebrate Christmas."

Chase forced a nervous smile. He looked at his Bible on the floor then considered how far apart he and his new friends must be on a theological basis.

"This drone is her Şeker Bayrami." Billy zipped up the suitcase. "Four patents are pending on this model alone. Two manufacturers in Tel Aviv approached her to purchase the rights to her ionic wind generator."

Chase sat down on the bed. "She's going to sell her patent?"

"She'll leverage it to forward her career." Billy shrugged, "Being a CEO is more important to her than financial gain."

Chase once again felt the burden of her disappearance. He turned to the wall's pages, volumes of information in one night, yet still, they had no idea where to look. "What do we do now?"

"If the drone gets high enough, she can scan the whole city at once. We can program her to look for delivery trucks. Even look for your goat-man logo."

Chase considered a playful joke, "The wrong tree?" He held his tongue as he opened the balcony door. "Let's do it."

"Not here. Illegal to fly a drone within city limits."

"So, we head into the desert. Will anyone be able to see it?"

"Doubtful. She's practically invisible and virtually silent, as stealth as it gets."

CHAPTER ELEVEN

Chase followed Billy out the elevator and through the hotel lobby. As they reached his rental car, Billy placed the suitcase in the trunk like a sleeping child he didn't want to wake. A handful of jokes ran through Chase's mind about how Billy took special care of Tiffany's luggage. Certain his jocularity would backfire, he refrained from stretching the limits of their tenuous relationship. He climbed into the passenger side with a simple hope of working as a team.

Chase asked, "If Abby and Tiffany were in the food truck, how do we find it?"

"Let's head north."

The Kia Picanto's anemic engine sputtered to life. They lurched forward. Within a few turns, they were heading north on Highway 406. Wind noise in the tiny car punished them. After a few miles, the road merged with Highway 40 heading into the Duda'im Forest. Israel's definition of a forest in Israel amused Chase. In a country the size of a postage stamp, every slice of ground has a story. This forest was simply rows of pine and eucalyptus trees.

Billy exited on an unmarked junction and continued past massive power lines paralleling the highway. Trees would provide the cover they needed to prevent visibility from road traffic.

Chase said, "Will the drone be able to navigate through the branches?"

Billy turned into a shallow depression and parked. No nearby roadside cameras. He gently snapped Şeker together.

Chase asked, "Have you flown her before?"

"I've flown with Tiffany several times. But never launched her baby without her. This is what she would do if our roles were reversed."

Billy held the assembled drone, wiped the black solar panels with a clean flannel rag one final time. The ion propulsion system created a subtle purple glow under the wings. On the app he ran a complete avionics system check. He checked the westerly breeze and tapped his phone. The drone pulled his arm forward. A soft hissing sound revealed her readiness to sail into the heavens. Billy adjusted his stance. Using a fluid motion reminiscent of throwing a dart at a dartboard, he delicately launched Tiffany's drone into the desert air. Silently, she drifted forward. Rising through the sparse canopy of trees. She swerved left, then right, avoiding branches.

Billy looked at his phone. "She'll fly over Beersheba in a grid pattern and stream a video feed."

Chase looked over Billy's shoulder at an impressive assortment of monitors on the small screen. Billy dabbed and swiped left. A map came up with his pre-programmed course. A second later, a blue dot appeared in line with the prescribed flight plan.

Chase asked, "Have you programmed it to look for any specific images?"

"Not yet." Billy climbed back into the car and opened his laptop. He slid his finger along his mouse pad. The drone's video feed streamed in. He clicked. The screen changed from a video to a dark screen with lines of code. He scrolled through hundreds of lines before tapping furiously on the keyboard.

Chase said, "If I were doing this, I'd piggyback on a common facial recognition software including pics of the girls as well as a few variations of our goat-man."

Billy rolled his eyes.

While Billy absorbed himself in lines of code, Chase removed his backpack from the car and walked a few yards where he set it down and flipped the power switch. Tiny green lights flashed in a series around the base. Fully charged. Sensors working. Latches intact. Dozens of sensors analyzed its surroundings and sent thousands of data points to an internal computer. He picked up a large branch.

He turned to Billy. "Watch this."

Chase tossed the stick high up into the air. Suddenly, turbofans inside the backpack screamed like a jet engine as they forced an incredible amount of air into the growing nylon mattress. Chase felt a gust of wind rush past him as massive amounts of air poured in. Within a second, a full-sized structure supported by a nickel titanium frame stood in all its glory as the branch gently settled. A perfectly safe landing.

"Voilà!"

"What's wrong with you?" Billy suddenly stood next to Chase. "These things are not toys."

Chase carefully folded the mattress then looked up. The drone rose skyward. To his right, a red-tailed hawk caught a thermal updraft and ascended into the heavens.

Not a bad way to fly.

"You should program her to use thermal imagery sensors to seek out updrafts so she can gain altitude like an eagle."

"She doesn't need your help." He stormed back to the driver's seat and continued coding.

Chase slumped onto the fender. He found Rafi's number and pressed "Dial."

CHAPTER TWELVE

Rafi's cell phone rang as he arrived at his desk. He tossed his jacket over his chair and answered the phone in one fluid movement. "Hello?"

"Do you have DNA results yet?"

"Good morning, Chase. How are you holding up?"

"Fine. Good morning. The test?"

"I sent it to the lab last night. Our team will start processing it this morning when they arrive."

"How long?"

"Typically, DNA tests take two to four days." Rafi logged into his computer. "You're a resourceful guy. I'm sure you did a quick search and knew this already. You're calling to see if I have anything else."

"Guilty as charged. Do you?"

"Listen, we're on this, but we don't have anything yet."

"You need to check your email."

Rafi entered his password. His inbox held a dozen messages from Chase. "What's all this?" He scrolled down. Clicked his first message.

"I passed along a handful of things we uncovered last night."

Rafi clicked through the first few messages digesting information on falafel trucks, restaurants, and abductions. "You've been busy."

He continued the email before turning to Chase's mother's social media posts. Then a dozen replies. People gave creative expressions of alarm, but nothing helpful.

Rafi cautioned, "Don't put your faith in social media. I know there are some anecdotal stories of a post leading to a missing person being found. Those are few and far between. The majority of crimes are solved with eyewitnesses, evidence, and confessions, not social blather."

"We called the Embassy. Have they contacted you yet?"

Rafi continued clicking through email. "Nothing yet." He checked the time. "It's understandable since nobody at the Embassy has even sat down at their desk yet this morning. Listen, I have a friend over there. I'll get in touch with him. See what he knows."

"Thanks." Chase hesitated. "I just have one more question."

Rafi sighed. "Go ahead."

"Why are there images of a half-goat half-man all over town?"

Rafi opened his final email with an image of the goat-man. He sighed, "A weird high school mascot is nothing criminal." Leaning back in his chair he said, "Please understand, we are on this. I'll call you if we have anything." He hung up with a sigh.

This guy will be a thorn in my side until this is finished. He sent a quick email to the lab asking them to expedite his DNA test. *Hopefully, it can come back today.*

He composed a new message:

Avi,

I'm looking into a report of two missing US citizens, young ladies in their mid-twenties: Abigail Radcliffe and

Tiffany Rawlings. The fiancé and brother are in town. Pressing into it. If you hear of anything, please let me know.

Thanks,
Rafi

He logged Chase's phone call and his email to Avi. Then turned to the stack of paperwork begging for his attention. He usually worked ten cases at any given time, each one represented by a single folder with a description of a crime, a summary of evidence, and next steps to take. Some cases had boxes of evidence in storage, an endless list of witnesses to interview, or depositions to take. He made it his personal goal to make a substantial step of progress in every case before the Chief arrived and his day formally began.

Behind him, a rhythmic click of two-inch heels announced Chief Valsburg's presence. He quickly stowed the file on the American girls at the bottom of his stack and busied himself with another folder.

CHAPTER THIRTEEN

Abby sat on the dirt floor as the truck rumbled away. "Tiffany, are you awake?"

No answer.

With her hands tied behind her back, Abby rose and felt her way along cool limestone walls. She bumped into Tiffany and slumped down next to her. Quietly she prayed, "God, please get us out of here. When things look hopeless, you are our hope. Father God, please provide a way out. Keep us safe ..."

"He isn't here. Just the two of us."

Shocked, Abby sputtered, "I'm sorry. I was just ..."

"Where's your knife."

"My side pocket. My Dad took me hunting growing up. He taught me to never leave the house without a knife."

"I don't need your backstory. Just let me get it."

Tiffany worked her way into Abby's pocket for a few seconds then pulled away.

Abby held her hands out. "I'll cut mine, then free you." A few moments later, Tiffany grabbed her hands. Abby felt a back-and-forth sawing motion until something snapped. With her hands free, Abby made quick work of the fabric over her head. Rubbing her wrists she said, "What do they want from us? Ransom?"

"My parents don't have money. They aren't anything special."

"Some kidnappings are for political reasons."

"My family doesn't have any of those type of connections. Does yours?"

Tiffany stared at the wall, motionless.

Abby looked around the room. Untouched by a tool, these walls made a ten-foot enclosure. On the far end, a cinderblock wall held a heavy steel door with industrial hinges. Free of furnishings, their empty space had nothing but rocks and a partially sandy floor.

Abby collapsed to the floor. After a few moments, she closed her eyes.

We're just a couple of engineers. Why would they do this to us? What will happen when he returns?

The wind rustling through brush outside provided the only sounds. Abby had no words. Apparently, her new roommate had no interest in speaking.

Eventually, desperate for some type of connection, Abby turned toward Tiffany, who sat in a cross-legged meditation pose with each foot on the opposite thigh breathing slowly. She whispered, "Turn your wounds into wisdom."

Abby said, "What?"

Tiffany finally pulled her legs out of the meditative position and flipped her long white hair behind her shoulders.

My goodness, how can I relate to her?

Abby asked, "Do you think Billy is working with Chase to find us?"

Tiffany let out a subtle huff.

Abby said, "They're smart and resourceful. They'll contact the police. Whatever it takes, they'll find us."

"I'll bet Billy won't even look at Chase after what he did."

"What do you mean?"

"Billy isn't what he seems."

"What?"

Tiffney spoke slowly. "He wouldn't do well with this kind of thing. Mother's death was hard on us kids, especially Billy."

"I'm sorry."

"Dad didn't handle her death well. He found solace in a bottle. Billy and I stuck together, we were both devastated, but we relied on each other."

Abby asked, "How old were you?"

"Fourteen. He was sixteen."

"I suppose you two were very close."

"Inseparable. He helped me with my homework, took me to gymnastics practice. He guided me through school."

"Like a surrogate dad." Abby searched her face for emotion yet found only pain and loss. "What about your real dad, is he still in the picture?"

Tiffany shook her head. "Not really. We chat sometimes. He follows me on social media."

"How about Billy?"

"Billy and Dad?" Tiffany scoffed. "Oil and water. They haven't spoken since Christmas."

"Did you two go to the same college?"

"Of course. He attended Auburn, so I went there too. He dated a girl for a couple of years. He dropped out of school when she dumped him. Had a breakdown. I convinced him to take a semester off before he finished his degree. He transferred to Clemson to get away from her, graduated Summa Cum Laude."

Abby's eyes grew wide. "Do you think he can find us?"

"He's smart and methodical." She looked at the walls and the no-nonsense door. "If anything gets us out of here, it will be technology."

CHAPTER FOURTEEN

Manny clicked through the day's news on his computer, avoiding his email. After perusing a few news venues, he clicked on a local newspaper with an article about LabStrength's financial woes, including a new low for the stock price. The biased piece, though somewhat accurate, used unnamed sources and few details. Fortunately, the small online journal had a low readership. *As long as this doesn't gain traction with more important papers, we can weather the storm.* Thankfully social media had been quiet. After delaying as long as he could, he clicked on his email only to be bombarded with messages from board members. The board chairman demanded an immediate meeting. Manny's shoulders slumped as his heart sank.

When he'd made his initial public stock offering a year earlier, he had traded anonymity and independence for much-needed capital. The cash infusion fueled their first several rounds of research. The tradeoff sucked the life from him. A board comprised of investors and bean counters, who only cared about current sales numbers, gave marketing advice. They didn't take time to read his scientific reports or even understand the arduous processes he undertook to make such landmark progress.

Yet, he remained obligated to report every business decision and financial data point to these bean counters.

The first email, copied to every board member, demanded a meeting. A few lines later, the board chairman had scheduled an emergency meeting this morning.

Can't this wait until after Passover?

He verified the meeting time. Checked his watch. Ten minutes.

A rap on his door surprised him. "What?"

The door cracked open. Joel had a look of joyful anticipation. "Good morning, sir. You wanted to see the results we talked about last night?"

"Right." He recalibrated his emotions. "We have a change of plans. Will have to wait until after a meeting with the board."

"You scheduled a meeting for this morning?"

"Not exactly. Bring your laptop. Time to play politics."

He marched down the hall ramrod straight. The ten-by-twenty-foot white room served as the company's welcome center, brainstorming region, break area, and board room. Joel opened his laptop while Manny grabbed a coffee pot.

The door swung open. "Mr. Tulenfeld, welcome. Good to see you."

A short, muscular man built like a deep breath entered without a word.

"How's your family? Can I get you a cup of coffee?"

"No." He unbuttoned his jacket as he took a seat.

Behind him, two well-dressed men and a tall, elegant woman filed in and took seats at the table. Each of them had built their businesses as stern, demanding leaders. Manny made eye contact one at a time, still he couldn't read their poker faces.

Mr. Tulenfeld leaned forward on his elbows over the table. "The others won't be able to make it. This is everyone."

Manny took a seat at the head of the table. "Thanks for coming on such short notice."

"We know you don't want us here, but we each have plenty of skin in the game. If we dump our shares now, we can get out before we lose everything."

"The article you read referred to some challenges we've had recently."

"Challenges? You're bankrupt."

"I don't know the journalist's source, but much of it is untrue. I think you'll change your mind when you see what's going on behind the scenes. We are on the brink of a new development which could dwarf everything we've done before." He motioned to Joel, who turned on the projector. "Our geothermally powered pumps, in combination with directional drilling developed by the oil industry, will allow us to create large-scale irrigation systems without an external power source."

Mr. Tulenfeld interjected, "You've told us about 'Streams in the Desert' before. All hype. You haven't generated a single shekel."

Manny nodded. "What the newspaper didn't tell you is our supply pump with an endo-skeletal-matrix quadruples a water supply using geothermal power."

Joel walked them through some details of their recent trials, sharing a simpler version of what they had reviewed the previous night.

Mr. Tulenfeld shook his head. "When things are too good to be true, they usually are. Show me."

Manny brought out a small black tank about the size of a coffee cup. He filled it with water and held it in front of Mr. Tulenfeld. "Hold this."

He took it with an open palm.

"Press your hands on the sides."

Tulenfeld obeyed.

"The bi-metal internal lattice works like a scissor jack, absorbing energy from your hands."

The object in his hands grew to the size of a soccer ball.

Manny smiled. "Now, we have a vacuum inside. Imagine large tanks with daytime expansion, contracting at night. This plus geothermal electricity powers our pumps."

Mr. Tulenfeld set it down. "You have my attention. Can I see it in action?"

"Absolutely," Manny interjected. "Follow me." He led them down the hall through the double doors to their lab.

Pristine countertops lined with computers and lab notebooks separated the large windowless room. Alone in the room's center, Manny hunched over a black industrial tank, his baby. The size of a barbeque grill, sensors, clear tubing, and wires covered every surface of the device. He ran his hand over it, familiar with every joint and copper coil deep within the machine's bowels.

Life giving.

Hope.

Board members stood awkwardly among wires on the floor. A dozen tubes headed across the sparkling clean grey floor to the far section of the room, where an industrial boiler, cooler, and large compressor rumbled. A large screen TV showed LabStrength's blue flask logo.

Joel brought up a spreadsheet. "Numbers tell results, but there is always more to the story."

Manny said, "Reset the system to replicate those numbers you showed me last night."

A low rumble emanated from the machinery as Joel evaluated every pipe fitting and joint with the diligence of a government inspector. With all settings perfect, he clicked away on the computer as the wall screen provided live data.

Manny stood ramrod straight silently hoping his audience would understand the significance of his findings. "This expanding tank has snap action bimetal switches trip at a set temperature and pumps the three-dimensional matrix—"

"Enough." Mr. Tulenfeld said. "Simplify it for us."

Manny pointed at the numbers on the screen. "This is a world changer. Every ounce of electricity the pump uses to move water is extracted from an existing underground temperature gradient."

Mr. Tulenfeld squinted. "Water leaves the pump at room temperature?"

"Actually cooler. The colder it leaves, the more energy we harvest. At this rate, we'll be selling electricity."

Joel ran his cursor across a spreadsheet. "The numbers were replicable. Consistent with success."

Manny ran a hand over his pump, wondering if they needed more data or if he should return to re-phrase the big picture. He concluded, "We are on the cusp of reinventing agriculture in desert environments."

Board members turned toward one another. Manny took comfort in the labyrinth of wires as gentle rolling of industrial machinery hummed in the background.

Mr. Tulenfeld took a step forward. "Don't waste my time. We need to know if it will bring in enough capital to turn a profit?"

"Absolutely. Arid lands across the planet will be clamoring for our technology. The only thing left is to test it in a thermally active site."

Some board members shifted their weight. Their poker faces replaced with grim concern.

"You need more tests?" Mr. Tulenfeld ran his open palm across his face. "I thought you were finished."

"We almost are. As long as our tests are replicated in a thermally active site, we will be able to implement these pumps anywhere."

Mr. Tulenfeld huddled with the other businessmen. A minute later, he turned back to Manny. "You have one month. If you don't have purchase orders in hand, we are out."

CHAPTER FIFTEEN

Manny shook hands with each of his guests as he walked them to the front door. After confident promises of success, he returned to the lab and collapsed into a chair.

Joel sequentially turned off all machines and sat next to his boss as the lumbering sound of machinery slowly settled down.

Manny said, "Where can we do our final tests?"

"I'll call the division chairman at the Israeli Department of Agriculture. If we show them these results and they understand what they are looking at, they will certainly give us access to a site with hot springs and another grant."

"No. We need private land."

Joel's raspy voice halted. "We don't have access to any private land meeting our criteria."

Manny nodded.

Joel ran a hand across his smooth head. "I don't understand."

"If we try to get further access to government land, we will have to show our data to someone in the Ministry of Agriculture and Rural Development, which would be suicide before obtaining patents. We risk them stealing our rights to the technology and end up with nothing."

Joel suggested, "We could have them sign a confidentiality waiver."

He shook his head. "Waivers are fine for a private individual or business, however I would never trust a government official with a waiver. They don't need to hire lawyers to sue us. They simply change the law. Take what they want."

"Maybe they will extend us one more grant? We could use the money to rent land."

"When they gave us their last grant, they warned me it would be their final one." He tilted his head to the place where the board had huddled before rendering their verdict. "Those guys aren't going to fund anything. We're on our own."

Joel tapped a few keys on his computer. A map of Israel appeared on the large screen. He zoomed in to the Sea of Galilee, then further to a smaller section on the western shore. "Have you made any progress at Tiberias?"

"I've reached out to a man named Alon Elkayim. He owns extensive tracks of land along the Dead Sea and the Sea of Galilee, including Tiberias. I've contacted him numerous times. Set up meetings."

"How have your discussions gone?"

"He answers email just fine, but he rescheduled our last three meetings."

"He's a busy man—opened a new hotel last month, didn't he?"

Manny nodded, "Two of them. He hobnobs with uber-wealthy people in his high-end businesses. Tough to get his attention, especially for something like our type of research."

Joel said, "If you entice him with riches, you'll be speaking his language."

"I've tried. No doubt riches will follow this breakthrough, yet it's hard to show him any money before we have it."

"There may be another way to get an audience with him."

"What do you mean?"

"His nephew, Moshe Elkayim, is a student in the United States at the University of Arkansas. My son also attends there. They're classmates."

"What's your point?"

"Moshe's field is geothermal research at hot springs in Arkansas. He coauthored a paper very similar to our project. As a fellow scientist, it wouldn't be hard to convince him of the validity of our research."

"Can he get us an audience with his uncle?"

"Possibly."

"We'll need to connect with him right away."

"I already did," Joel said. "He's old friends with your daughter Miriam. They're having lunch at the Zahav Bistro today, noon."

"We'll join them." Manny tapped his phone. An image of his daughter with long black hair and a dazzling smile filled the screen. He remembered when he took the photo at the ribbon-cutting ceremony when they opened their restaurant. She remained blissfully unaware of how he had leveraged his business to obtain the loan for her enterprise. He pressed the button to dial.

"Father?" his daughter responded.

In the background, he could hear a bustling commercial kitchen. He tried to put a smile on his voice. "Good morning, dear. How's Zahav Bistro today?"

"Busy."

"I hear you're having lunch with a friend."

"Yes," Miriam answered. "Moshe is an old friend. How did you—"

"I don't mean to intrude, but I think we may have a lot in common. Would it be okay if I swung by to meet him?"

"You won't embarrass me in front of my friend, will you?"

He laughed. "No, I'd just like fifteen minutes to chat with him about nerdy engineering stuff."

"No problem. I'll text him."

"Thanks, see you at noon."

Joel stood up. "I'll get a confidentiality waiver written up."

CHAPTER SIXTEEN

Chase sat on the car's fender checking social media on his phone waiting for Billy who continued writing code for the drone.

Billy closed his computer. "She's scanning the Beersheba region for anyone with facial features similar to Tiffany or Abby."

Chase opened the passenger door. "How about the goat-man image? Did you add it?"

Billy stowed his laptop and Tiffany's suitcase in the trunk. "Let's check out those restaurants from our list unless you need more playtime?"

Chase closed his eyes. *What will it take to work with this guy?*

Billy slipped into the driver's seat and headed south onto the highway. Beersheba was in full swing, bustling with activity. Powerlines covered single-story cinderblock buildings like overgrown ivy. Men and women dressed in traditional Arabic and Jewish garb crowded the sidewalks next to ancient streets on their way to work. A group of backpack-laden children hustled to school, with one straggler ten yards behind.

Chase read from his laptop as they drove. "Beersheba is home to 200,000 people. Just a couple of miles away, the ancient city of Tel Beersheba boasts thousands of years of history starting with Abraham and Abimelech settling their differences over a well of water."

The article sounded exactly like Abby. He could see her brilliant smile and sense her boundless energy. The memory of her infectious laugh made his heart ache.

We will find her. We have to.

Chase looked at his phone. "We should check out Albi Kabab and Ben Yehuda. They are both on the north end of town."

"Ben Yehuda."

Chase plugged the address into his phone. "Turn right. Just a few blocks down."

They approached a bustling restaurant. A line of people waited at a counter for their morning coffee to go. The breakfast crowd of businessmen and women filled the long narrow restaurant. Meeting for social meals or business meetings before office hours began. As Chase entered the front door a hostess greeted him. He held up a photo of Tiffany. "Have you seen this girl?"

Billy rolled his eyes. Held up two fingers. "Breakfast, please."

The waitress grabbed two menus and sped toward a table in the back. Waitresses bustled from table to table, taking orders and delivering breakfast plates. Only a few tables were open. Behind a metal door with a small window, a crew filled the busy kitchen.

As the waitress stopped at an empty table, Chase said, "I'm looking for my friends. They were taken last night. Can you help me?" He switched the photo to an image of Abby. Held it in front of her until she acknowledged him.

She shook her head, "I'm sorry." She looked closely. "I haven't seen her or the one with white hair." She moved on to her next customer, taking their order in Hebrew.

Chase took a seat. Something at the entrance caught his eye. He walked back to the front. Standing among the line of pre-caffeinated patrons, a bulletin board displayed fliers from local businesses advertising their services and products. He recognized most businesses from their research the previous night. Still, the menus for Zahav Bistro, and 'Ez Falafel restaurants were new. He looked closer. Both establishments had Jerusalem. *Why are those restaurants advertising here?*

In the bulletin board's upper right corner, a six-by-nine-inch image caught his eye. A cartoon of a goat-man smoking a cigar stared back at him. Chase quickly took a photograph of the entire bulletin board. From behind, he heard a male voice say, "Sir, if you're not going to order anything, I'm going to have to ask you to leave."

Chase turned toward the voice. A muscular, masculine figure in his thirties. Chase said, "I'm sitting with my friend in the back." He pointed to Billy. "His sister and my fiancée are missing. I'd appreciate any help you can give us in finding them." He showed him a photo of Tiffany holding a flower.

"Oh, I'm so sorry. Let me take a closer look. My name is Yosef, by the way." He held out a calloused hand which Chase shook. "I'm sure I'd remember white hair on one so young."

Chase looked around the restaurant. Almost every head covered with something, a yarmulke or some type of hat. Those without coverings bore dark black or brown hair. There wasn't a blonde head in sight.

Yosef led the way toward Billy's table. "Tell me about your friends."

Chase pointed to Tiffany's picture, "My friend's sister." He showed Abby's picture, "My fiancée."

"Congratulations. Do you have a date for your wedding?"

"Not yet. But I'm sure she'll have it all planned out in a heartbeat."

"I'm so sorry. I hope you don't mind me asking, why not go to the police?"

"We have, sadly they haven't been very accommodating. We're just trying to do whatever we can."

As they arrived at the table, Chase said, "This is my friend Billy. Tiffany's brother." Billy shook Yosef's hand.

Yosef waved to the waitress as he said, "How about some coffee on the house?" The waitress glared at Chase. Yosef said, "Appears you've already met my sister, Rebekah."

Chase took his seat. "Yes, thank you very much."

Rebekah stood before them impatiently while Yosef slipped away.

Billy simply said, "*Nes.*"

Chase held up two fingers. "*Boker Tov, café barad. Toda.*"

She smirked at his rudimentary Hebrew. "You want two cups?"

"No, um ..." Chase looked at his hand, then dropped his chin. "I'm just used to ordering a cup for Abby."

"One?"

If she had been here, she would have ordered perfectly and made us look amazing.

He felt his face flush.

Where could she be?

Billy stared at Chase with narrowed eyes. "Learn some discretion. If you stumble around like an American detective, you'll get us kicked out of here. We won't learn anything."

"Sorry, I was just trying to ..."

Billy interrupted. "Listen, they have offered us a gift, a simple cup of coffee, which we must honor. We are obligated to take our time. Avoid any sense of rushing or hurrying."

Chase nodded.

"Show appreciation, respect."

Chase took a deep breath. "I meant to … you're right. I'm sorry."

Billy scanned the room.

Chase asked, "Where did you learn Hebrew?"

"I picked up a few words here and there."

"My parents took me on a trip to Israel when I was a kid. I've dabbled in it ever since. Took a couple of Hebrew classes in college just for fun." Chase asked, "You ordered nes. One of your favorites?"

"Easiest thing to say."

Chase said, "You'll love it. Nes is a type of freeze-dried coffee which completely dissolves in hot water. The Hebrew word Nes means miracle. Original instant coffee here was Nestle brand. Taste's quite good. The name stuck."

Billy looked at him with a tired gaze.

"We need a nes, a miracle, to find any clue leading us to the girls." Chase showed him his photo of the billboard. "Our little goat-man made another appearance."

A few minutes later, the waitress returned with hot steaming cup for Billy and a chilled glass overflowing with a brown frozen drink for Chase. As she served the next table, he took a sip. "It's like a coffee slushy with milk and sugar."

"You ordered a barad," Billy said. "Means hail."

Chase's eyebrows rose. "You do know Hebrew."

Billy ignored him.

Chase joined his gaze toward a window. "A word like 'Hail' is a bit ironic in a country where it hails once in a blue moon."

Fully caffeinated, Billy left a healthy tip and rose. Chase found Yosef behind the register and gave him two pictures of the girls with his contact information on the back. "Thank you for the coffee. If you see either of these girls or hear of anyone who does, please give me a call."

Yosef took them. "Of course, I wish you the best of luck."

As they passed by the bulletin board, Chase made eye contact with Rebekah. "Thank you for your help."

She replied, "Did you enjoy your coffee slushy?"

Embarrassed his faux pas had been overheard, Chase changed the subject and pointed to the bulletin board's goat-man picture. "What can you tell me about this?"

She answered, "Pantheon?"

Chase raised his eyebrows. "Right, Pantheon. Tell me about it."

She stepped back. "Our high school mascot. He brings us luck."

Abby loved symbolism. What would she say about it?

"Looks spiritual, like some type of pagan symbol. I've never seen anything like it in Jewish or Christian literature."

Rebekah took a step back, her face flushed, even her ears turned red. She turned around and slipped into the sea of customers once again. Chase followed Billy outside and said, "There's more to the goat-man image than simply a high school mascot."

Billy shook his head.

Chase continued, "You should have seen her face when I asked for more information. Looked like she swallowed a fly."

CHAPTER SEVENTEEN

Abby sat with her back against the rock wall, hugging her legs to protect from the chill. A minimal light snuck below the door. She swiped her thumb over her solitaire diamond ring. "I can't believe he asked me to marry him."

Tiffany lay on her back in silence

"I didn't even know he bought a ring.

"Yesterday, in Tel-Aviv."

"What?" Abby's voice rose.

"He watched some YouTube videos on how to propose and wanted a meaningful place with a sunset."

"How did you know this?"

"He showed me your ring after the award ceremony. Asked for advice on a proposal. He said he wanted a woman's perspective."

"What was he thinking? We never talked about marriage."

"How did you guys meet?"

"We took a robotics engineering class together at Iowa State—worked together on team projects." Abby managed a mild grin. "Over the next two years, he drained his meager bank account with dinner dates and flowers."

An awkward silence hung in the air.

Abby asked, "Are you dating anyone."

"Just my work."

Abby stood up and inspected the door. She ran her hand across the sturdy lock. With a glimmer of hope she reached into her pocket and retrieved a black device a little larger than a thick fountain pen, though four times the mass. She said, "I have an idea."

Tiffany's eyes remained closed. "What?"

"Did you see my presentation?"

"I saw your video. People were talking about a powerful laser."

"My incendiary laser didn't win any competitions. However, we might find a way for this to help us."

"Can it destroy a lock?"

Abby shook her head. "Only works on organic material."

"The locking mechanism? Hinges?"

"Sorry, it would just reflect back at us."

"What about those rocks the hinges are secured in?"

Abby gritted her teeth. "Nothing flammable there."

"So, it's not a Star Wars-type of blaster?"

"Not quite, but it does ignite anything flammable." She felt the buttons on the side. "It has two phases. First, you aim at a target with a low-intensity laser. Sensors analyze the target and calculate proper wavelengths needed to light each material on fire."

Tiffany pretended to fire it at a target. "Then, boom!"

"More like whoosh."

"Instantly?"

"Not really. Just causes a flame at point of contact."

"Fully charged?" Tiffany asked.

"Yes. We never used it at the Tel Aviv convention. I planned to demonstrate how it works, but the safety committee deemed it a fire hazard. The judges decided to defer a live display and relied on our video presentation."

"On your video, the pile of wood went up like a flash."

"Looks can be deceiving."

Tiffany handed it back. "What do you mean?"

"We soaked a log in gasoline before making the video."

"You cheated?"

"When we filmed it, we didn't know they would use our video at the conference. We lit it on fire, using just the laser. Amazing. Gas on the video makes it look a thousand times better."

Tiffany leaned back. "I'll bet it did. So, when they decided to use your video, you didn't protest?"

Abby shrugged.

"Without gas, does it still work?"

Abby nodded. "It's not as impressive, but it will light things on fire, even clothing." She took her position as a lookout, aimed. Ready.

"The next road is always ahead." Tiffany sat up, brought her feet over her thighs, and closed her eyes.

Abby held the laser steady staring at the door. She knew she should pray. Silently, she found whatever words she could. *God help, let this thing ignite whatever comes through the door. Please get us out of here.*

She continued praying, yet her words seemed to fall to the ground without effect. She sat quietly for a long time, her laser swaying in her hand. Eventually, she pulled out her knife and exposed the blade. She swayed with her laser in one hand and a knife in the other feeling power in hope of using these tools for their rescue.

Anyone who had the skills to incapacitate the two of them and lock them up wouldn't be threatened by a two-and-a-half-inch piece of sharpened steel.

What if they were on fire?

She could only hope.

Tiffany remained motionless in her meditative pose.

A hint of light began to show the door's outline. Abby broke the silence. "Obviously, they don't know about the knife or laser, or they would have taken them away. Who do they think we are?"

Tiffany emerged from her position. "We are just a couple of girls to them."

Abby knew the implications of men capturing girls. She didn't want to talk about what could happen to them if they were involved in trafficking.

Tiffany pressed her ear against the door, playing the role of a sentry. After a few moments, she said, "It's quiet out there."

Abby ran her hand along the walls. "This area is desolate. Nobody is around for miles."

"What will happen when this door opens?"

CHAPTER EIGHTEEN

Billy drove down Shazar Boulevard as scooters and sedans wove past him like water rushing around rocks. Chase announced, "Albi Kabab is only a few blocks. This is one of two restaurants with truck service on the north end."

He turned north on Yitzchak I. Rager Boulevard, continuing until he saw a wilted awning announcing Albi Kabab, the Arabic and Hebrew lettering presumably repeated the message. Billy pulled to the side of the busy street and parked. He circled a blue and white Vesper scooter near the entrance then approached the glass door with Chase on his heels. "Let's say hi."

Seeing lights on and two workers mulling about inside, he assumed they would be open. He pulled the handle. Locked.

Billy stepped back. The door swung open, and a man Chase's size in a black shirt emblazoned with Albi Kabab in pink lettering burst through the door and stood in front of them. The man had short brown hair and a scar on the left side of his forehead extending over the bridge of his nose.

"Excuse me," Chase called out. "Are you open for breakfast?"

He looked Chase in the eye and said a few words in Hebrew.

"Do you speak English?"

He pointed at his watch. "*Sagur.*"

Billy gave him a thumbs up. "Toda."

He slipped between Billy and Chase with the agility of a soccer player, mounted his scooter and drove off.

Chase looked at Billy. "What did he say?"

Billy opened the driver's side door while Chase stayed at the window with his hands cupped over his eyes looking through the glass.

"Let's go," Billy demanded, halfway inside the vehicle.

Chase held photos of the girls to the glass. "Have you seen these girls?"

A heavyset bearded man with a white tank top came crashing onto the sidewalk with a flurry of words and gestures.

Chase stepped back. "I'm sorry, I ..."

Billy grabbed him by his arm, spun him a hundred eighty degrees and shoved him onto the passenger side door. He looked back. "*Slicha.*"

"Apparently, not everyone is in a chatty mode today."

Billy ran back to the driver's side. "Get in."

He slipped the vehicle in gear. Slammed the pedal to the floor. The car lurched in between sedans in the direction the scooter had gone.

"Get eyes on the guy on that blue and white scooter."

"Wait, what?" Chase grabbed the dashboard as Billy aggressively entered traffic. "Why?"

"The two of them were in the middle of a fight when you interrupted." Billy sliced between a pair of sedans.

"So?" Chase saw the blue scooter turn two blocks ahead. "He turned right."

Billy accelerated, pushing the anemic engine's limits. "Boss was mad. The young guy was embarrassed like he had done something wrong."

Chase shrugged. "How do you know?"

"His face was red, jugular bulging." He turned to follow the scooter. "Could have been out late last night with the truck."

Chase saw the scooter, a little closer now. "Over there." They followed him, catching up quickly. He turned again. "You'll get a speeding ticket."

Billy leaned into the turn. They had pulled within a half block from their target as he turned into a utility garage with a large open door. Billy slowed to appropriate city speed then stopped a few yards past the building.

"Let's go in."

Billy rolled down his window. "No. Just keep an eye on him."

Chase turned around as best he could to watch him from the confines of their vehicle. The man parked his scooter and disappeared around a building. A few minutes later, a silver food truck pulled out the way he'd come in. "Albi Kabab" had been painted across the side. Though daytime lighting gave the goat-man a different look, the dent in the corner, the high-pitched whine, and the intermittent click were unmistakable.

"Bingo."

The truck turned opposite the direction they were facing and threaded through a series of small sedans. Billy squeezed into southbound traffic, nearly kissing a bumper on a small flatbed truck. He followed traffic flow swinging into the left lane.

Chase looked over his shoulder as the truck grew smaller. "Turn around!"

Billy struggled through the sea of vehicles. With a U-turn out of the question he turned right, going around the block. They lost visual contact. Another hard-right turn. Chase grasped the dashboard again as he watched one near miss after another. Billy worked his way back to the street with another turn and swore under his breath. As they approached the busy street, Chase saw the truck two blocks away. As Billy dove into the line of traffic, a construction truck pulled in front of them and stopped.

Chase yelled, "No!"

Billy came to a stop inches away from the truck's bumper. He put the transmission in reverse. A slow-moving sedan blocked him in. "Where did he go?"

Chase looked to where he had last seen the food truck. "No idea."

Billy slammed his palm against the steering wheel. He pulled forward when the construction truck finally moved on. "How well did you see it?"

"Clear as day."

"The logo?"

"Same truck. I guarantee it. Sounded the same as last night."

"Just a diesel."

Chase shook his head. "I drove those things, you know. Each truck has a character of its own. I'm no diesel mechanic, but I spent enough time behind the sheet metal and rivets to recognize a few extra nuances. This one had a rattle and a whine." He flicked his fingers like a musician imagining a melody. "It was him."

"Let's find him."

CHAPTER NINETEEN

Rafi closed an embezzlement case file. His first of his completed tasks for the day. He opened the second file in his stack, a series of breaking and entering robberies in the University District. He pulled up a map. Scrolled out to a larger city grid looking for a pattern. His phone vibrated—his friend at the State Department.

AVI: Just sent you an email.

He picked up a framed photo of the two of them on his desk. A standard pose, a routine picture, yet it meant so much more to him. Rafi and Avi bonded when they enlisted in the army and enrolled in the Military Police training program. Every young man in Israeli serves in the military for three years, young women for two.

When Avi proposed to Laili, Rafi agreed to be his *shomer*—best man. However, after Laili had been taken, the two men grieved together for months. Deeply moved by the pain in his friend's heart, Rafi silently vowed to refuse to entertain the idea of marriage until Avi had found a soulmate once again.

Rafi,
Good to hear from you. Regarding your missing person's case, our office had contact from an American last night.

The individuals have been missing less than twelve hours. From our end, there is little evidence of foul play, but we are attending to the matter. We need to catch up soon, troublemaker.

Avi

Rafi read the message a second time. Throughout their long friendship, Avi had plenty of unique names for Rafi but would never refer to him as "Troublemaker." The two of them had used this code word for a diplomat they knew to be guilty of corruption at high levels. For Rafi, this message rang loud and clear. He needed to tread lightly from a political standpoint.

Rafi closed Avi's email. No other messages in his folder except Chase's multiple messages and junk email. He sat back in his chair when his phone vibrated.

AVI: Daniel 8:5

Though they had been friends for years, neither of them had been remotely devout in their Jewish faith. Rafi quickly searched the reference.

> A male goat came from the west across the face of the whole earth, without touching the ground.

Rafi hadn't read the obscure passage since he was a boy in a Bible class in school. He remembered someone making a joke about a goat who flew across the world. This text didn't make sense to him then and certainly didn't mean anything now, especially about a missing person case.

He dialed Avi. The line went to voice mail. A moment later, another text appeared.

AVI: Follow the money.

Rafi studied his phone. Avi couldn't talk. Something odd had to be going on. Rafi knew all his phone conversations were recorded, both landlines and cellular. Emails and texts were available to anyone higher up in the chain of command.

Rafi sat back in his chair with his hands interlaced over his head. He felt distant and longed to talk with his friend. He glanced at Chief Valsburg's office. She had ordered him to set aside the missing person's case. She might as well have told him to file it away.

Rafi prepared to respond to Avi's email when he remembered Chase's copious messages.

There's a guy who could use a little project.

He started typing an email. His fingers froze. If there were corruption at the higher levels, an email would be immediately flagged. A text would be less noticeable.

RAFI: Daniel 8:5 Follow the Money

Chief Valsburg's door swung open. She stood in her doorway looking around the busy room. Rafi stowed his phone. Refocused on the city grid.

CHAPTER TWENTY

BEERSHEBA

Billy completed a grid pattern of the north end of town in search of the food truck. Unsuccessful, he turned back to Albi Kabab. He parked the tired little car a half-block away, with the restaurant in sight, and stared at bustling pedestrian activity. A little less congested than earlier while plenty of foot traffic flowed by.

Chase's phone buzzed.

RAFI: Daniel 8:5. Follow the money

What the heck?

He quickly dialed Rafi. A voice message, first in Hebrew then English. "You've reached Detective Rafi Hadad. Please leave a message."

Chase said, "Rafi, we saw the guy driving the food truck. Albi Kabab. I know it's him. About five foot ten with dark hair. About twenty to thirty years old. Athletic. Maybe a soccer player. Oh, I have your message. Don't understand it. Call me."

Billy turned toward him. "You described every young man in this country."

Chase shook his head. "I sounded like a blundering idiot."

"Yep."

"I didn't even mention the scar on his forehead."

"Maybe think before you talk."

"Why didn't he answer? He just texted me. He probably still had his phone in his hand."

"Show me the text."

Chase handed over the phone. Billy shook his head. "What does it mean?"

"I have no idea. I sent Rafi a bunch of emails. This is how he responds."

"What did you send him?"

"A bunch of things we found last night."

Billy closed his eyes. "I suppose it wouldn't hurt."

"I'll follow any rabbit trail at this point."

Billy pressed his phone a few times. "Nothing from the Embassy."

Chase checked his email. Without Wi-Fi, his messages downloaded slowly. He scanned through them. "Not on my end either."

He checked the social media posts. Countless friends had reposted his plea for help—the comments were expanding. People all over the US expressed concern and posted various expressions of surprise along with toxic levels of emojis. His message proliferated but not enough to be called viral. A few friends mentioned they would contact their congressmen. Sadly, nothing helpful came from Israel. Not a hint of helpful information to point to Abby's location.

He looked up at the Albi Kabab doorway.

They are at the center of this. If I were an unhappy customer, I'd go online and—

With adrenaline surging through his veins, his thumbs pounded his phone. He threw together a brief but scathing post about the restaurant. Pressed "send" then slammed his phone on the dashboard.

Billy scanned in silence. Chase said, "Let's head back to the hotel. We can log into Wi-Fi. Figure out what Rafi's text means."

Billy's phone buzzed. He sighed and looked at Chase. "Really?"

"Huh?"

"Somehow, you think throwing around accusations at a tiny restaurant in this obscure town will help?"

Chase pointed at his phone. "This is the biggest voice we have."

"My god, you're an idiot."

"We have to get the word out."

"Just stop. We don't know anything yet. We saw a guy, heard a truck—it may have been nothing."

"Same truck!"

Billy shook his head. His phone rang. A deep voice said, "Any news, son?"

Billy closed his eyes. "We're tracking down everything we can think of."

"Tell me details."

"We saw a guy in a food truck this morning. He might be connected with the truck involved in taking them."

"Albi Kabab? Apparently, I should never eat there."

"How did you ..." He glanced at Chase. "Yeah, news travels quickly."

"Tell your friend to cool his jets. He's doing the opposite of helping. Some posts help find what you are looking for, while other types of posts do nothing but cause distraction. There's an art to posting well."

The veins in Billy's neck bulged. Wrinkles in his forehead sprang from nowhere. "You're on speaker." He glared at Chase. "He heard you."

"Good."

"Our best hope right now is for you to find him when he returns." Mr. Rawlings's tone softened. "Billy, tell me about your project."

Billy took his phone off speaker. "Thanks for asking. I call it my microphone on steroids. First, it takes a distance measurement to the target site ..."

Chase pulled up the Albi Kabab post. Nobody had commented on it yet. *Is it really offensive?* He reread then deleted it. He glanced at Billy, fully engaged in conversation with his father. Unable to be included in the discussion, he pulled up Rafi's text again. He longed for Wi-Fi to figure out what he meant.

After a few minutes, Billy said, "Thanks, Dad. I appreciate your help." He hung up and continued to face the restaurant's front door.

Chase asked, "Anything interesting from the drone?"

Billy opened the app. "Fully charged. Flying smoothly at a thousand feet." He swiped to find the photos but found a blank screen. "Images are big, it will take a minute."

A message appeared on Billy's phone. "I'm proud of you, Son."

Billy's shoulders relaxed. Lines on his forehead smoothed as his neck veins melted away.

Chase guessed this might have been the first meaningful conversation Billy had with his dad in years.

Chase said, "Let's go to the hotel."

"We need to wait here."

"We lost him. Now we have another lead."

"I'm staying."

"We need to look into this. We can't just sit here."

"Go."

Chase shook his head. "You're getting rid of me? I thought we were working this together."

Billy gave him a blank stare as a red and yellow scooter passed them. He looked back toward the Albi Kabab doorway.

Chase plugged the address into his map. A half-mile, no problem. "Send me the drone images. I'll text you when I have something." He joined the flow of pedestrians.

CHAPTER TWENTY-ONE

JERUSALEM

Manny Lochotzki maneuvered his black Lexus smoothly through congested traffic in downtown Jerusalem. After a couple of near-miss encounters, he turned from Betsal'el Street onto Mordehai A'liash Street. He found relief in a parking garage for Bank Leumi and turned to Joel. "This is as close as we can get. Parking this time of day is ridiculous."

Joel agreed, "Especially the day before Passover."

Inside the Zahav Bistro, Manny peered over a sea of heads scanning for Moshe Elkayim. He found himself face to face with an olive-skinned woman in her mid-thirties, tall enough to meet his gaze.

She greeted him with a hug. "Abba."

"Miriam," Manny returned her embrace. "Any sign of our guest?"

"You should probably sit down. When Moshe comes, I'll introduce you." Her tone turned serious. "Before you leave, I have a question for you."

A minute later, a young man entered. Miriam burst through the crowd. "Moshe!"

"Miriam!"

Almost a foot taller than Moshe, she gave him an awkward side hug pressing the side of his face into her rib cage under her arm. "It's so good to see you. Has the American lifestyle completely corrupted you yet?"

"Absolutely. A perfect reason to come home for Passover."

"Thanks for agreeing to have my dad join us."

Moshe pulled away. "Sure. I'd love to meet him. I've known about his company for years, but I thought they just sold water filtration systems."

"Let me introduce you." Miriam turned toward her father.

Manny began to rise from his chair. Already eye to eye in a seated position, Moshe's face fell as he watched him elevate. He took a step back. His mouth dropped open. Manny continued to gain altitude until he reached his full stature. Moshe stepped backward and collided with a passerby.

Miriam grabbed him by the arm. "Moshe, I'd like you to meet my father."

Manny reached out for a handshake. Moshe reciprocated, his small hand completely enveloped within Manny's grip. Moshe greeted Joel, then looked to Miriam for help.

Miriam laughed out loud. "Let's get you two on a level playing field. Follow me." She escorted the three men to a quiet private table in the back of the restaurant instructing them to take a seat.

Manny did his best to put Moshe at ease. "Miriam has told me quite a bit about you."

"She's a good friend. Is LabStrength interested in geologic research?"

Manny nodded. "The water filtration systems started our business."

Joel said, "He's done very well. He's helped fund housing projects outside Jerusalem and a high school in the South."

Manny shrugged. "We've had some early successes. Now our primary research is on using natural resources to power irrigation pumps."

"Geothermal energy?"

"It's quite similar to your work in hot springs."

"I didn't know I had groupies in Jerusalem," Moshe laughed. "The Arkansas hot springs are fascinating geologically. We analyzed the source hydrostatic pressures with some ingenious methods. We took the direct low-pressure head measurements, and high-pressure head indirect measurement—"

Manny interrupted, "And the hydrostatic and lithostatic measurements were consistent."

"Right."

"Even when the static water column was salinity controlled?"

"Exactly."

Manny leaned forward. "I think I can convince you to come work with LabStrength. You can help create world changing technology."

"What are you talking about?"

Manny slid a small stack of papers across the table and placed a pen on it. "To go any further with this conversation, I'll need you to sign a confidentiality agreement."

"My uncle will offer a handsome salary."

"A healthy salary working at a hotel."

Moshe shrugged.

"Change the world and get paid for it. Stock options come in as a bonus when our company takes off."

Moshe flipped through the pages. Scrawled his name on the bottom line. "Impress me."

Manny laid out a series of spreadsheets on the table. "Geothermal powered pumps with directional drilling will create large-scale energy independent irrigation systems."

Moshe's eyes darted back and forth as he took in the raw data.

"Imagine if every acre of the desert could be transformed into farmland. This technology works." Manny pointed to a data point on the second page. "Every desert in the world has water underneath. When the initial investment is minimal, every desert can bear fruit."

Moshe shook his head. "They've been talking about this for years. Too expensive. Not sustainable."

Joel produced more blueprints. "We will hold the patents. Affordable. Sustainable."

"Where have you conducted your research?"

"We've worked at natural springs on government-controlled land. They give us access for a few days here and there when the sites are shut down for maintenance. Slow going."

"Have you conducted your studies in areas with hot springs?"

"You understand this better than most."

Moshe shrugged. "You don't want to cook the crops before they have a chance to grow."

"What do you mean?"

"In Hot Springs, Arkansas, one of my crazy friends holds a unique 'reverse wishing-well' competition every year. He gets people to reach into a steaming pool and retrieve a coin from the bottom."

"How hot?"

"Hundred and forty-seven degrees Fahrenheit."

"Did you do it?"

"Sure. Amazing what you'll do when a beautiful girl is watching."

Joel and Manny laughed.

"If the water comes up too hot, it will destroy the crops."

Joel flipped the page and pointed to a line. "Water doesn't get through until thermal energy is fully transferred into electricity and the water is at ambient temperature."

"What tests do you have left?"

"We've done all the tests we can in the lab using an industrial boiler and off-site using our portable lab."

"Which springs did you use?"

"We've had some help from friends in the department of tourism. Now, we need to do our final tests with hot springs. Then we go public."

"You're talking about a worldwide change in land valuations."

Manny said, "All we need is to complete our trials on private land with hot springs." He looked at Joel, who gave a nod, then back at Moshe. "We've also made significant speculations with leveraged options in some desert property at a fixed price. Unfortunately, the recent increase in interest rates has squeezed our purchase power. We don't own any of the land yet. Can't use it for testing."

"Those already in real estate might like this opportunity. Every acre of the desert would increase value by ten or even a hundred times." Moshe paused. "I might know someone."

Miriam interrupted with plates of shakshuka and couscous. Joel scooped up the papers as she placed a gorgeous platter in the middle of the table.

Manny said, "Thank you, Miriam, this looks wonderful." He turned to his guests. "Enjoy."

Moshe took a bite. "I have about a hundred questions for you."

"Absolutely. Joel knows all the details. Go ahead."

As they ate, Moshe launched into one question after the next. Joel walked him through every detail. By the meal's end, Moshe said, "Your research is solid. Numbers are impressive. This looks like the real deal."

Manny said, "You're welcome to visit our lab. See our equipment for yourself."

"I'm having dinner with my uncle tonight night at the Rimonim Galei Kinnerth Resort. I'll chum the waters with him. Tonight, you two will be my guests."

Miriam approached the table with a menu. "Would you like to select a dessert?"

Manny lifted his hands. "We need to celebrate. Moshe, what would you like?"

Moshe looked over the options. "*Ma-aroud*, please."

Miriam looked at Manny. "Father?"

He smiled at his daughter. "Everything on the menu is fantastic. Surprise me."

CHAPTER TWENTY-TWO

Making good time on his brisk walk back to the hotel, Chase called his mother again and spoke with a handful of family members. Sadly, nobody offered anything political connections or ideas. Back at the hotel, he scanned Billy's impeccable workspace—computer lined up perfectly with the desk edge, notepaper on the right side, pen centered on the paper. Chase's disheveled bed where he spent a sleepless night. He sat at Billy's comfortable desk then imagined his hulking torso striding through the door. He couldn't afford another *faux pas*.

He settled back onto his space on the bed with his Bible. Within seconds, he pulled up the passage Rafi had texted. A horned goat flew across the world.

An online Bible commentary revealed several references agreeing on the interpretation of the goat flying across the world historically represented Alexander the Great. Daniel's goat referred to Greece. A request to download incoming images interrupted his reading.

A few clicks later, he found images from Tiffany's drone. He downloaded images of the goat-man. The Hakfar High School mascot was complete with a green coat and cigar. Rudimentary fur covered his legs: half-goat, half-man. A pipefitter had a rougher version without a hat, sport coat, or cigar. Chase saw the Albi Kabab food truck with the logo's smiling face staring back at him. Surprisingly, it wasn't the only restaurant with the logo. One on the south end of town had a character with a blue coat consistent with the rest of their color scheme. Another with a brown shirt matched its legs.

Where did this goat-man start?

He searched Albi Kabab's marketing campaigns. Initially, he only found current ads, eventually he discovered archives from ten to twenty years earlier. Older ads bore the same name, with a simple icon of a steaming plate. He repeated the process for the pipefitter. Ads were few and far between, older ads had a pipe wrench logo. He continued for each business finding the goat-man had appeared only within the past five to ten years. The high school had been founded only a decade earlier. They had never changed their mascot.

He brought up all the images on his screen simultaneously. Took a screenshot. The variety of repeated imagery reminded him of his hometown. The iconic Tiger Hawk image had permeated small-town bars, shops, and schools in Hawkeye country. A local high school named themselves the "Little Hawks," a smaller college adopted the name "Duhawks."

"Could this be a similar lovable copycat? Which came first? School mascot or other logos?"

Zooming in on each one, he saw a clear distinction. The Hakfar High School logo was easily the most professional. The only one with a gif. He ran his search through a translation program so he could scan Hebrew articles in English. A local magazine reported the school's history with pictures of a groundbreaking ceremony, opening for their first day of school. Another article boasted about their first graduating class.

Follow the money. Where do we go from here?

He followed up with other articles with repetitive accounts then stumbled upon a flyer for a fundraiser a year before groundbreaking. They promised to auction off naming rights for various buildings for generous donors. One donor had passed on naming rights and purchased the right to design the school's mascot. Hidden in a long list of benefactors was a simple blue lab flask logo next to the name LabStrength. He dove into their website.

Why would a lab company help start a school?

He dialed Billy. Starting with Rafi's text he explained his search.

"When the school was being built, a company named LabStrength donated some money and purchased rights to design and name the mascot."

"Creative. How much?"

"5000 shekels—about $1500."

"So?"

"Compared to other donations from the event, this was by far the lowest amount, most being 100,000 shekels or higher."

"They found an affordable way to make a big splash."

"A marketing ploy?"

"Where are you going with this?"

"Just following the money. We also have a half dozen or so logos in town with some version of a goat-man. Get this, they all appeared after the school installed their new mascot."

"Probably copycats. What else has the company donated to?"

"Give me a minute." He searched for LabStrength's other donations. "They gave 2500 shekels to a low-income housing project in Jerusalem."

"Did they get something for it?"

"Hard to tell. The article doesn't say." He continued reading. "This is weird. The housing project letterhead has a goat-man on it."

"Hmm. Learn everything you can about LabStrength."

"Oh, one more thing. Daniel 8:5 talks about a horned goat flying across the world. Really weird. Symbolic."

Billy interrupted. "What does any of this have to do with Tiffany and Abby?"

"No idea. Maybe I should look into Alexander the Great or just keep following a weird goat-man."

"Sure."

CHAPTER TWENTY-THREE

As Moshe stood to leave, Joel rose with him. "We look forward to meeting your uncle."

Manny started to get up out of respect for his guest, but Moshe gestured with his hands. "No, please. Stay in your seat. I can make my way to the exit on my own."

Miriam laughed. "I knew you'd find a way to keep him in his chair."

Manny shrugged, "Struggles of the altitudinally over-gifted."

Moshe reached across the table. He shook Manny's hand, followed by Joel's. With a friendly wave to Miriam, he headed toward the exit.

Manny looked at Joel. "Clear your schedule for tonight." He leaned forward to stand.

Miriam gave her father's shoulder a little tug. "Don't leave yet. I need to speak with you about something."

Joel stepped back. "I'll wait for you outside."

Miriam sat in Moshe's chair with her hands folded.

Manny looked at his daughter in surprise, expecting to find a confident young lady who rarely struggled with insecurity. Instead, he saw fear in her eyes. "What's going on?"

"Father," she hesitated, struggling to find her words. "I had a surprising call from Rebekah this morning."

"How's your sister? It's been over a week since I've caught up with her. This weekend we should get plenty of family time. Your mother is looking forward to ..."

"She's concerned. Two American men came to their restaurant this morning asking a lot of questions."

"Why would this bother you?"

"They looked like tourists but were looking for two American women in Beersheba."

"Poor guys. Is there anything we can do to help?"

She fiddled with her fingernails. "They asked about Pantheon."

He shrugged. "Odd. Why were they were asking about the social club. What did she tell them?"

"I asked her the same thing. She said, 'Nothing.'"

He held up his palms. "What's the concern?"

"I don't know."

"You know tourists. They ask about everything." He waved her off. "Hordes of them flock to the Holy Land to popular sites in Jerusalem. Little groups of adventurous ones sprinkle through the country to visit every possible site."

She nodded.

"Tourism brings in billions to Israel's economy every year, over a hundred thousand people are employed strictly to ..."

"Not in Beersheba."

"Nonsense. There's plenty of history in Beersheba. Abraham's well is there."

She shook her head. "Tourists don't go to Beersheba."

"Maybe they were history buffs, Bible scholars, or archeologists."

"Those with extensive academic backgrounds don't ask about Greek culture in Israel."

He laughed. "I once had a British tourist hold a map of Jerusalem up to my face asking where the Parthenon was."

She smoothed the cuticle at the edge of her fingernails in silence.

He sighed. A prolific storyteller, he could entertain people at business meetings or fundraisers. However, with his children, repetitive tales were as effective as a paper map in the hands of a teenager.

Miriam said, "Rebekah also mentioned Yosef was acting funny."

"Yosef? What do you mean?"

"I don't know. She said he had been out a lot recently without an explanation. Something is going on. She sounded worried."

He rested his hands on hers. "I'm sure it's nothing to worry about."

"Do you think you could give him a call?"

"Sure."

She looked at his phone.

"You mean right now?"

"Please."

He picked up his phone. "Call Yosef."

She said, "On speaker, please."

He tapped his screen. Moments later, a masculine voice said. "Abba?"

"Yosef! How are you?"

"Just handling a busy lunch crowd."

"I hear you've been staying busy."

"Just satisfying the hungry masses."

"Your sister said you had some visitors this morning causing some concern."

He chuckled. "She called you, huh?"

"Sisters talk. I'm at Miriam's place right now. She wanted to know what's going on with you."

"Am I on speaker?"

Miriam leaned over the table. "Hey, Yosef."

"Hey, Sis."

She asked, "So, what's going on?"

"Nothing. Just a couple of tourists."

Manny asked, "Why would they be looking for two abducted Americans at your establishment?"

After a brief pause, Yosef continued. "I don't know. I served them coffee on the house. They left a huge tip. Nice fellows."

Manny grinned. "They didn't order a latte or cappuccino, did they?"

"I was surprised. These Americans knew Israeli coffee.

"What did they ask about?"

"Just a few simple questions about some missing girls."

"Anything else?"

"Not really."

Miriam said, "Rebekah said they asked about Pantheon."

Yosef said, "They were poking around the bulletin board. Asked about what we had posted. Harmless."

Miriam shook her head.

Manny held up his hands. "Your sister doesn't get riled up easily. I tend to listen when she's worried."

"Don't worry, Father. I'll keep an eye out for them, but I don't see anything to be concerned about."

"Okay." He looked at Miriam. "Anything else?"

She shook her head.

He continued, "Tomorrow night. Passover. I'm looking forward to seeing you at our place."

"I wouldn't miss it."

Manny pressed the red button and pocketed his phone. "Am I missing anything?"

"I suppose not."

He rose and looked over every patron in the restaurant. Outside, Joel waited in the Midrechov. He gave his daughter a warm embrace then casually ambled through the restaurant back into the sea of humanity as he approached his lead engineer. "We have a meeting tonight."

Joel held up his hand with his fingers crossed. "This is the final step."

CHAPTER TWENTY-FOUR

BEERSHEBA

Chief Valsburg burst through her office door. She stormed between desks crossing the room. The precinct officers avoided eye contact with her. Each of them had more work assigned to them than could be done in regular working hours. Rafi's focus moved from his stack of to-do files to his email when he saw an email from Chase.

> Rafi,
> As you undoubtedly know, the eighth chapter of Daniel is profoundly prophetic. Alexander the Great's conquest is consistent with an image of a flying goat. While I don't see a significant Greek connection in Beersheba, I do see repetitive pictures of the goat-man all around town. This seemed like an odd cultural icon, so I followed the money regarding the goat-man. At a fundraiser for Hakfar High School, a company called LabStrength gave the logo birth in modern Beersheba.
>
> Subsequently, numerous businesses have adopted a version of the image for their business. LabStrength funded at least one of these.
>
> By the way, we found the food truck but couldn't track down the guy inside. He and his boss were in a fight this morning. We're looking for them.
> Thanks,
> Chase

From Avi's bizarre, encrypted note, Chase had found something linking it to a company called LabStrength. *I gave him a scrap from the table. He came back with a viable lead. Not bad.*

Rafi glanced up as Chief Valsburg's settled into her office. No immediate threat to his work, yet she remained a constant reminder to keep his head down.

He read the email a second time. Nothing in it could trace back to him as the source of the inquiry. Using the police's search software, he quickly became well versed with LabStrength's origins, growth, and current economic crisis. The owner won the Negev Award for Community Contributions after philanthropic work. Background checks on their employees lacked luster. Other than a custodian with a lead foot and a marketing manager with a history of domestic disputes with his wife, the office staff was squeaky clean.

We're working in the dark. Avi seems to be the only one who knows what's going on.

An internal email alert appeared on his screen.

Source: Cigarette
Fluid: Saliva
DNA Match: Boaz Sharabi

A few clicks later, Rafi stared at a picture of a man in his late twenties with a ponytail and distinctive scar over his left eye extending over the bridge of his nose. A quick background check revealed unremarkable physical stats: 5'10", 160 pounds. But his presence on Israel's sexual predator list drew Rafi's attention. Usually, this would have an accompanying case number with a link to the details. In this case, he saw no explanation. Rafi navigated into his service record on the military database.

IDF military police logo topped the pdf. Rich in symbolism, a six-pointed star crested by an olive wreath with the Israeli flag stood guard over the military report's rigid formality.

The summary page showed Boaz's photo and military service history. After graduating in the middle of his high school class, he endured four months of infantry training then was commissioned in the Israeli Ground Force. Serving in the 933rd Nahal Brigade as a *Turai* (Private), he manned an outpost during several Syrian Katusha rocket attacks. Nothing abnormal. Rafi found two disciplinary reports. Boaz had been reprimanded for sexually inappropriate comments brought by a female soldier on his base. Familiar enough, these complaints were often dealt with on the field. Routine soldier activity, not exemplary, but he did perform well enough to get promoted to *Rav Turai* (Corporal).

A soldier brought another disciplinary report which resulted in minimal investigation and no trial. At the time, his commanding officer could have easily upgraded the charges to include "Conduct Unbecoming" of a member of the IDF. With limited evidence and no witnesses, they ordered Boaz to undergo sensitivity training.

Rafi squinted. Boaz certainly was no role model, yet this could not explain a spot on the sexual predator list. He clicked on through his performance reports. Average scores.

Then he saw it. In his second year of service, at the Golan Heights, a female soldier accused him of forcing himself on her during a night watch. But she brought it three days after the event allegedly had taken place. She had not gone to a medical provider and had no direct evidence—only her testimony. Rafi scrolled through testimonies from several individuals near the location between three and four in the morning. He noted only slight discrepancies in their descriptions, a disparity of information boosting the testimony's credence. Rafi saw no outside influence or political pressure.

Dishonorably discharged from the army. Placed on the sexual predator list. *This explains the lack of a case number.*

He clicked on Boaz's bank records. Regular deposits from Albi Kabab revealed employment with his uncle, possibly the only job he could get. With identical home and work addresses, Boaz obviously lived at the restaurant. A few clicks later, Rafi familiarized himself with Albi Kabab's financial reports, including moderate success of their food truck service. None of the other three staff members had a stain on their background checks.

Rafi made one final email check and saw Chase's note. Which was more likely? An upright business somehow masterminding an abduction or a guy with a history of sexual crimes who had access to a food truck?

Rafi verified his handcuffs and firearm. Donning his jacket, he headed to his car. He had a viable suspect in the abduction case.

CHAPTER TWENTY-FIVE

Abby listened as a rumble in the distance grew louder. A diesel engine came closer. Tires ground against gravel. A door slammed.

Abby strained to see anything through a stream of light squeezing between the door and the sandy floor. She waved her incendiary laser. "I'll catch his shirt on fire. You find a way to rush past him."

Tiffany leaned forward. "Now we're onto something. I'll push him deep inside the room. Once we're both outside, we lock him in here."

With a glimmer of hope, Abby pointed the laser at the door. "He's coming."

Tiffany bounced on her toes in an athletic stance, she pulled her white hair behind her ears. "Just light the fire."

Latch clicked. Door opened outward. Blinding sunlight poured into their darkness. Abby reflexively closed her eyes forcing herself to focus. The silhouette of a man filled the doorframe. She pointed at center mass. Pressed the button. A red dot appeared on his chest.

He took quick steps entering with precision. In his right hand, a heavy bucket. Abby held her breath, trying to steady the laser. A puff of smoke appeared around the red dot.

It's working! Now, bring the flames.

The man immediately reversed his direction and disappeared. The laser hit the wall. Abby screamed, "No."

The door remained cracked open. Abby could see him again. Aiming at his shirt, she pressed the button.

Smoke rose from the red dot.

Tiffany sprung like a lion leaping towards her prey. She pushed on the door slipping outside with the agility of a dancer. He dropped the object in his hand. Leaped toward her. She spun to evade him. He grabbed her arm, bringing her to the ground.

Abby aimed once again and pressed the button. The red dot re-appeared. She held her breath.

Hurry up. Why isn't this working?

The man swiftly rose to his feet, holding Tiffany in front of him. Abby released the button. He threw Tiffany back inside like yesterday's garbage. An empty five-gallon bucket tumbled in, followed by another heavier object.

Door slammed shut. Entire process transpired in mere seconds.

Abby slammed her hand on the ground. "Wait."

Tiffany turned toward her. "My God! What were you doing?"

"He was ..."

"He was standing right there!"

"The laser ..."

"You didn't do anything."

"... wouldn't ignite."

"What's wrong with you?"

Abby cradled the device in her hands. "There's a lag. When you push the button ..."

Tiffany paced in the small confinement with her hands on her head. "I was outside. Almost there. You only had one job, distract him."

"Maybe his shirt was wet."

"I don't want excuses."

"I'm sorry. I thought it would work." Abby looked at Tiffany's shirt. A dirty imprint of a hand still visible on the fabric. "Are you hurt?"

Tiffany ignored her. She marched around a half dozen times before she released a guttural exclamation. Kicked the metal door. She looked at Abby with clenched fists.

Sunlight from under the door grew stronger as they stood in silence.

Abby looked at the first five-gallon bucket. Almost full of water. Abby put her nose to it. *Odorless*. With her hand, she scooped out a sample and tasted it. *Clean*. Using both hands, she drank a few ounces.

Tiffany turned toward the second bucket, which had tumbled and landed sideways against the wall. A few dark pieces of debris scattered along its opening. She put her nose over it. Inhaled deeply. She immediately recoiled with her hand over her nose and swore. She scooted back until her back pressed against the opposite wall.

Abby approached carefully. From several feet away, the stench took her back to a day where, as a young girl had walked into a bathroom with an overflown toilet. She covered her nose, reached down, picked up the disgusting bucket, and moved it across the room. Though the limited light, she saw remnants of other people's waste littering the bottom. She removed her sweater. Draped it over the bucket, partially quelling the stench. Using a container of alcohol sanitizer, she cleansed her hands.

Tiffany remained statuesque against the wall as Abby investigated the other item he dropped on the ground. She picked up a partial loaf of dry bread. The outer crust formed a firm protective shell. She tore off a small portion. Put it in her mouth. Crunched and swallowed.

"One of the best parts of Israeli food is their amazing assortment of bread." She offered a piece to Tiffany. "This would be the exception."

Tiffany waved her off. "I don't eat gluten."

Abby sat against the wall as far as she possibly could from the septic bucket. She looked at her roommate. "I'm sorry."

Tiffany stood over Abby with her hands on her hips for a long time, both judge and jury.

Abby repeated, "The laser didn't work. I'm sorry." Nothing she could do or say would make it better.

Finally, Tiffany sat down in front of Abby. She held her palms up in front of her. "True forgiveness is when you can say, 'Thank you for the experience.'"

Abby had never heard the saying before. Couldn't be from the Bible. *Is she making up words of wisdom?* She made eye contact. "Profound. I don't deserve your thanks."

"No." Tiffany replied, "You don't."

CHAPTER TWENTY-SIX

BEERSHEBA

Rafi started his Skoda Octavia's engine. Though possibly not the best horsepower for a high-speed chase, he had enough equipment to handle most law enforcement needs—a rifle, shotgun, lights, and siren. His rear seat often housed suspects on the way to the police department for processing.

With Albi Kabab's location tucked into his memory, he drove across town with no need for a digital map. Although Beersheba was not his home area, he knew every inch of this city better than most native residents. In his first month on the job, he became familiar with every neighborhood, every street, and every alleyway. He didn't need his dash-mounted GPS.

He pulled in front of the dreary-looking awning. Parked within an inch of the curb. Stepping inside, he passed between mostly empty tables. Stood at the counter. A young lady said, "Table for one?"

Rafi shook his head. "I've heard you guys make incredible doner Kabab."

She grabbed a menu. "The best in town."

He held out his badge. "I'm Detective Rafi Hadad. I'd love to take time to try it, but today I'm here to meet with one of your employees. I'm looking for Boaz Sharabi."

Her face went pale. She disappeared through a windowless double-hinged door. Rafi followed her. A steamy hot blast of thick hot air hit him as he entered. The aroma of spiced meat overwhelmed him. On the far side of the tiny kitchen, a heavy-set, bearded gentleman wearing a white apron stroked his knife on a vertical column of lamb meat roasting in traditional doner Kabab style.

The young lady said, "Father, someone is here."

He invited Rafi toward him with a wave of his knife. "How can I help you?"

Rafi held out his badge. "Mr. Sharabi? I'm detective Rafi Hadad."

Genuine surprise crossed his face. "What's going on?"

"I'm looking for Boaz."

Mr. Sharabi asked, "What's this about?"

"I'm interviewing several people about an ongoing case. I need to speak with him."

Mr. Sharabi glanced at the young lady. She shrugged. He refocused on Rafi with a vacant stare.

"Sir, it would be beneficial if you could share his location."

The man set his knife down. Wiped his brow with a handkerchief. "He's in the truck."

"Sounds like a spot you'd put a trusted employee. Does he do a good job for you?"

"Good enough."

"Do you have a specific location? I'd like to ask him a few questions."

"He's probably at Ben Gurion University. He'll be back after sunset when business slows down."

"Can you call him for me, please?"

He shook his head. "I'm sorry. He's not supposed to answer."

"I understand."

"We usually park near Ehud Garden at this time of day. The professors and college students are the best customers in town."

Rafi looked at the girl as she pulled out her phone. "Thank you. Can you give me something more specific?"

She showed him her screen. An app showed a map of Beersheba with Boaz's photo in a small circle sitting in the northeast corner of the campus.

"Thank you."

Rafi sniffed a pan of sauteing vegetables. "Smells wonderful."

"What's this about?" Mr. Sharabi asked again.

"I just need to have a few words with him." He nodded at the young lady. "I'll be back for a doner Kabab another day."

Passing through the glass door, he took a deep breath. Fresh air gave a stark contrast to the stifling kitchen heat.

Weaving through congested traffic, Ravi scanned for a food truck. After a left on David Ben Gurion Boulevard, he looked across the corners of Ehud Garden. Backpack-laden students in sweatshirts and jeans scurried along the broad well-manicured passages between perfectly arranged stately four-story concrete buildings. With every parking place occupied, he couldn't spot a food truck.

He drove past the beautiful Salomon Garden. Found a truck clumsily parked in a loading zone. Ignoring the apparent parking violation, he looked at the back of the truck where the fedora-wearing cartoon character smoked a cigar. A line of customers waited patiently on the sidewalk. Rafi wondered if Pavlovian habits factored into his choice of finding a perfect site.

He flashed his badge, cut to the front of the line, and peered inside the window. One young man scooped balls of precious falafel out of the boiling grease and set them on a drying rack. The other worker put finishing touches on wrapping one culinary prize at a time.

An older gentleman holding a briefcase reached up and took the wrapped falafel. Rafi saw the worker's face—dark hair and scar.

"Are you Boaz?"

"Yes, sir. What can I get for you?"

"I'm Detective Rafi Hadad. I'm with the Beersheba Police Department. Looks like you make a mean falafel."

Boaz nodded. "Can I make one for you?"

"I was hoping we could sit for a few minutes."

Boaz glanced behind Rafi. "Can it wait a while? We have quite a line." He made eye contact with a customer behind Rafi lifting his chin.

Rafi shook his head. "Sorry, we really do need to chat now."

Boaz cocked his head slightly to the side. "I'm sorry, I just can't leave the line."

"I expected you to be concerned. I already spoke with Mr. Sharabi. He knows you'll be chatting with me for a bit."

"Why? What's going on?"

"Come on out of the truck. We'll chat for a bit."

Rafi led him to his vehicle and leaned against the hood. "If you don't mind, could you share what you were doing last night?"

"I was at work." His face showed surprise and concern. "Why, what's wrong?"

"Walk me through your whole day."

Boaz rolled his eyes. He explained every detail of getting up, doing daily chores, working at the restaurant. Rafi asked numerous questions, Boaz remained quick with his details.

"Would you mind if I took a peek at your phone?"

He reached for his phone with brown stained fingers. "Is someone hurt?"

Rafi held the phone in front of Boaz's face. The screen unlocked. "Excuse me for a minute."

He tapped on "Settings," "Location Services," then "History." Within a few seconds, Rafi discovered every location his phone had been. Though the "Clear History" button sat easily accessible on the bottom of the screen, it had never been used.

He tapped. A map appeared with blue dots all around Beersheba. Scrolling out, a more comprehensive view showed a solitary dot in the middle of nowhere. The time stamp showed: April 17, 6:47–8:02 p.m. Rafi zoomed in on the parking area where the girls had been taken.

Technology makes my life so easy sometimes.

He took a screenshot of the map at varying magnifications. Sent them to his phone. He pressed print. The printer back at his desk would yield a harvest of two sheets with maps and a series of numbers legible only to IT personnel and detectives. His smoking gun.

Rafi approached Boaz. "Let's take a ride down to the station for a few more questions."

After a quick frisk with his hands on the hood, Rafi opened the back door. Boaz climbed in without objection. Rafi put the car in reverse. The goat-man image on the back of the truck smiled back at him around a cigar in his mouth.

When they arrived at the station, Rafi led Boaz to an interrogation room where he sat alone. He swept a handful of paperwork from his desk and headed to Chief Valsburg's office.

"I found him."

"Who?"

"The guy who abducted the two girls last night."

"I told you to …"

He handed her the DNA report.

"Boaz Sharabi? Never heard of him."

"History of rape allegations while in the army." He slid the other pages across her desk. "Look at his location last night."

She raised her eyebrows. "Bring him in."

"He's in Interrogation Room 1."

She handed back the papers. "Don't waste any time. Find out what he knows."

CHAPTER TWENTY-SEVEN

BEERSHEBA

Rafi dropped into the metal chair, centered a folder on the desk, and looked into Boaz's eyes. "Where are the girls?"

Boaz's gaze darted around the ten-by-ten-foot grey room. A video camera with an illuminated red LED sat in the upper corner. He looked at the large mirror on the wall, then back at Rafi.

Silence.

"Two American girls were taken from the parking site south of town last night. Where are they?"

Boaz's feet shifted beneath the table as his shoes slid across the tile floor. His head cocked to the side like a confused puppy. "I ..." He shook his head. "I have no idea what you're talking about."

Rafi tapped the stack of paperwork in front of him. "I'd much prefer to go easier on you. That just takes your cooperation."

"Cooperate with what?"

"We know you took them. We simply need to know where they are and who else is involved."

Boaz's eyes grew wide. His upper lip retracted.

"If you help us find them right away, it'll benefit you in the long run."

"I ..." He took a deep breath.

Rafi paced the room. Boaz's expression remained identical to when he first approached him. genuine confusion. He pushed away from the table and crossed his arms. "Tell me about the incident in the Golan Heights."

His face fell. "Really? You guys keep going there."

"What happened?"

"You've read the reports. They questioned me about it a hundred times. You know what I said. Why change a true story?"

"Innocent?"

He gave a slow nod. "My word versus hers." He blinked away fluid in his eye before it escaped.

Rafi had seen competent liars hold to their story before but never had he seen a grown man able to conjure tears. "Tell me your side."

"We were on patrol watch together. I said some stupid things, but I never touched her."

"I believe you."

Boaz looked surprised. "What?"

"Doesn't help for me to argue with you, so let's say I believe you. How can we get to the truth?"

"About the Golan Heights?"

"All I care about is last night. Help me figure this out." He placed the phone records on the table. "We know you were there."

He focused on the page. "What is this?"

"Your phone told us everywhere you've been, minute by minute."

"My phone?"

Rafi pointed at the map with the time stamp. "You took a little trip last night. South of town."

"Not possible."

Rafi sighed, "Why?"

"I lost my phone yesterday. I didn't have it with me all day. I found it under my bed this morning. The battery dropped to 1%. I had to charge it in the truck all day."

He's not acting like someone who abducted two women.

"Help me out here. You weren't there. Your phone was. Make it make sense to me."

He shook his head.

"If you didn't take the truck out, who did?"

Silence.

Rafi took a lap around the room. "What I want is to save these two girls. Just tell me if they are alive or not."

Boaz turned his palms up. "I don't know what you are talking about."

"Where were you last night?"

"At work."

Rafi leaned forward. "In the food truck?"

"No. At the restaurant."

Rafi took a deep breath. "Who was there with you?"

"You can ask my uncle. He was all over me last night, treating me like he did my first day on the job."

Rafi remembered Chase's email reference to a fight at a restaurant. "Which could explain why you two were fighting this morning."

"What? How do you know about ..."

Rafi shrugged.

"He accused me of taking the truck out after work."

"Why?"

"He said he didn't want his business represented by a filthy truck. He made me wash it this morning before going out. I missed out on the first hour of lunch rush. He will make me pay for it by taking all the tips I get today."

"Where did you take the truck last night?"

"Nowhere. I was exhausted after closing. When we were finally done, I went back to my room and fell asleep."

Rafi held the phone data in front of him. "This is from your phone. How did you get to the middle of nowhere last night at the same time two girls were abducted?"

He made direct eye contact. "I have no idea. You can ask my uncle. I was at work."

Rafi's internal lie detector kicked into high gear. He had taught countless seminars on interrogation techniques. He could recite chapter and verse in a handful of textbooks on how to tell a lie. Every muscle of facial expression is commanded by a nerve connected to their cerebral processing unit. A person's countenance, posture, and body language all gave pieces to the puzzle. Their choice of words, the order in which they are chosen, everything plays a role. But one-on-one with a subject in the interrogation room, too much information spun around simultaneously to dissect it all. Somewhere deep in his gut, he digested the information.

Something didn't add up. Felt wrong. Plenty of evidence making this pervert appear guilty, but pieces of the story didn't add up. Rafi harbored no emotion. Determined to weed out chaff and discover the truth. He wasn't annoyed, angry, offended, or frustrated. He had been through enough interrogations to know how to get to the truth. He looked at Boaz in a calm, friendly manner. "Let's go back to yesterday afternoon."

Boaz's chin sank to his chest.

Ravi repeated questions in a variety of ways. Later, he requested the exact details in reverse order. Rafi leaned into every supporting wall, truss, and connection of Boaz's story. He pressed to see where his story would bend under the weight of questioning, scanning his face looking for a tell, a tick, or anything to expose the web of lies. Somewhere in the details, there had to be a crack in the wall. He would find it and pry it open. For two hours, they went through the story time after time.

Nothing.

Rafi promised himself he would go back through the video recording of the conversation to see if he had missed anything. For now, this pervert looked innocent.

With evidence this strong, there's no way he's innocent. But still ...

CHAPTER TWENTY-EIGHT

TIBERIAS

Manny Lochotzki turned his black Lexus right on Highway 90 heading south along the western shore of the Sea of Galilee. He passed through the old city with a few luxury hotels on his left. After a sparse region of land, they passed another hotel.

Joel asked, "How many of these does Mr. Elkayim own?"

"About half."

Joel nodded, "What a life. Can you imagine the glorious sunrise views from those upper-level rooms?"

"Keep your eyes on the prize," Manny said. "The only issue at this point is getting access to one of his sites for a couple of months."

The highway drifted further from the waterfront. Manny slowed as he approached the turn then pulled onto a long driveway bordered by palm trees and elaborate landscaping. After a hundred yards, Crown Ben Savoy Resort rose from the greenery like a stately palace. The taller of two buildings, it sat like a fortress overlooking the historic body of water. At the same time, the shorter one lacked nothing in elegance. A circular driveway invited them to pull up, but Manny pulled into the parking lot on the right.

Joel unbuckled his seatbelt. "No valet today?"

"Are you going to pay for it?"

The two men walked confidently past the parking attendant into the hotel. Though a stretch, Manny posed as a guest willing to spend a thousand shekels a night for a room plus an equal amount each evening for exquisite five-star meals.

Manny analyzed the dining area layout as he approached the maître d's stand. He whispered, "Where would the owner choose to meet a guest for a business meeting?"

Joel grinned. "Wherever he wants."

The host, clad in a spotless black tuxedo, waited patiently behind his narrow oak stand. Manny approached. "We're here to see Mr. Elkayim."

He tapped his tablet a few times. "Mr. Lochotzki?"

Manny nodded.

The host said, "Follow me."

He led them past walls decorated with original oil paintings from historic Israeli artists, each one enhanced by museum-quality lighting. Hand-carved crown molding and wainscoting graced every wall. Manny did his best to look comfortable amid the ornate hotel atmosphere.

As they proceeded past tables with elegantly dressed customers, Manny recognized Mr. Elkayim at a burgundy booth in the far corner. He was a huge man—his navy suit filled more than his fair share of the padded seat. His thinning black hair swept straight back with the aid of product. Enormous cheeks eclipsed his ears, and a well-groomed mustache concealed his lip. Next to him, Moshe looked like a small child. Manny greeted them with a smile.

Mr. Elkayim said, "Welcome. Have a seat."

Manny and Joel slid into seats opposite Mr. Elkayim. "I designed this restaurant so I can see everything from this seat." He focused on the activity behind them. "I can view the entire dining room and hotel entryway. The inner workings of our gourmet kosher kitchen, keeping track of every person passing in and out."

Manny nodded his approval.

Mr. Elkayim motioned to the window. "Of course, our guests have an unobstructed view of the Galilee. We've placed every hammock and shaded swinging bench in strategic locations so every guest inside can have an unobstructed view of my private beach."

Manny said, "It's a marvelous place. Your guests enjoy the best of everything."

Mr. Elkayim finally looked directly at them, "Please, take a look at our wine list."

Manny expected a traditional leather-bound wine menu, instead a tablet computer sat next to the centerpiece of freshly cut flowers.

Mr. Elkayim motioned to the tablet. "We customize our wine list based on your particular palate."

Manny quickly answered series of questions about his wine preferences, growing in complexity as they progressed. A list appeared with accompanying images, some of which he had in his personal cellar. "You certainly know me well."

Moshe smiled for the first time. Mr. Elkayim said, "Pick your favorite then hand the tablet to your colleague."

Manny tapped on a modestly priced label.

Mr. Elkayim raised his hands broadly. "The next time you visit with us, a glass of your favorite will be waiting for you in your room or at your table."

Manny bowed his head. "Thank you."

"Don't limit yourself. Feel free to try something else if you prefer. Our selection is extensive."

They discussed local vineyards. Manny wasn't surprised when he heard Mr. Elkayim had personal relationships with the owner of each of them. Their conversation quickly progressed to wine production in Italy and France. Before they knew it, twenty minutes had flown by.

Mr. Elkayim shifted the conversation. "So, Moshe tells me you gentlemen need a place with hot springs for your research."

Manny smiled. "We're on the brink of a major shift in the way agriculture will be done all across the world."

Joel handed a file to Mr. Elkayim. "You should be very proud of your nephew. He has a keen mind for engineering."

Mr. Elkayim shrugged.

"Our geologic research is on the cusp of bringing water into the desert. We can create sustained irrigation in deserts all over the world."

Mr. Elkayim flipped through the files without digesting the material. "Why are you here and not at the United Nations?"

Manny laughed, "The UN has its place for peacekeeping in remote parts of the world. In my experience, truly helping people happens best when done through the markets, not forced by corrupt government programs."

"A true capitalist," Mr. Elkayim said.

"When we do well, the whole society benefits. The solution is in the bottom line. Not only will your property value increase exponentially, but you can be a part of the company which made it happen."

Mr. Elkayim waved an open palm across the table. "What's in it for me?"

"We're looking for two million shekels for a five percent share in our company. We expect significant sales starting at day one and increasing exponentially for years."

"I've heard a lot of pitches and can smell mushroom fodder from a distance." The large man's head swiveled.

Manny placed a folder on the table. "Numbers don't lie."

Mr. Elkayim ignored it. "Your company is founded on water filtration systems."

"A decade ago, I created those filters. They pay the bills while we work on this world-changing technology."

Mr. Elkayim stroked his thin mustache, "Why here? Why now?"

"The geology of Tiberias's hot springs will allow us to complete the final step in our project. We will file for our patents. Deliver the product."

The corners of Mr. Elkayim's mouth raised a tiny bit. "You want to drill holes in my land."

Manny gave a gentle smile with an affirming nod.

Mr. Elkayim looked out the window for an awkward minute. He turned back to Manny. "How much will your work interfere with the operation of my hotels?"

"Everything is portable. We don't need to build any buildings or even occupy any of your structures. Our trucks will only be here a month or two."

A vein appeared in the man's broad forehead.

Manny raised an open palm. "You'll be known as a world changer, a philanthropist—or however you would like to spin it."

Elkayim's body sunk into the chair. "Trucks with pumps and hoses on my pristine land?"

"Only for the short term ..."

Elkayim grasped his wine glass with chubby fingers. "This is a considerable risk."

Nobody said a word for far too long. When he could no longer take the silence, Manny said, "And tremendous benefit when the pumps sell."

"Your filter sales never took off. There is no guarantee for your pumps."

Manny glanced at Moshe, hoping he could infuse life into the conversation.

Moshe set a spreadsheet in front of the large man. "I've pored over the numbers, Uncle Alon. Research is solid."

The large man steepled his fingertips in front of his face. "It's my money. I will not take such a risk."

Manny's mouth went dry even as beads of sweat dripped down the small of his back. He gripped his shaking hands beneath the table edge. Without cash, his company couldn't last another two weeks.

Manny raised his offer. "Ten percent."

Time slowed to a crawl as Elkayim shook his head. His second chin wiggled like marmalade jelly.

Manny darted his gaze back at the owner preparing to launch another appeal. Moshe stood and gestured to his guests. "I'm sorry, my friends. Time to go."

Manny could barely breathe.

CHAPTER TWENTY-NINE

TIBERIAS

Manny burst through the ornate door and followed the sidewalk past the parking lot into a small orchard. He walked between a row of blooming almond trees onto the sandy beach.

"Mr. Lochotzki, sir."

He turned around.

Moshe approached rapidly. "Thank you for the offer, if my uncle isn't on board—"

Joel interrupted, "You weren't much help in there."

"My uncle is a very opinionated man."

Manny turned back to the body of water.

The young man continued, "I'm sorry, sir. Pleasure meeting you."

Manny marched south along the beach, searching the horizon for answers.

Our engineering is sound, our pumps will work. What am I going to do now?

After he passed the beach next to the hotel area, the water's edge transformed into a desert hillside. He pressed onward over crags and brush heading up a seaside hill without a path. A thousand details occupied his mind.

No solutions.

"Manny!" A voice from behind him brought him back to the present. Joel appeared thirty yards behind him. Closing fast.

Not now.

With clenched fists, Manny faced the large body of water. The moon, only a day from its maximum glory, provided sufficient light to sparkle ripples passively rolling against rocks. He looked to his right. A southbound fishing boat brought the waves. On his left, Mount Arbel guarded the region while the Valley of Wadi Haman held ominous clouds. A brisk breeze chilled his face.

Joel pleaded, "Come back. We'll figure this out." Step by step, Joel made his way through the sand, rocks, and undergrowth until he reached Manny's side.

Manny's heart rate slowed. He threw a rock far into the water. The moon's reflection flickered as the ripples made their way across the surface.

Joel stammered, "We'll find another venture capitalist. We can make this work."

Manny turned toward his friend whose bald head reflected the moonlight. "You think we can find another man with unlimited funds, tracks of land, geologically active hot springs, and a nephew who has a thorough understanding of the field?"

"We have to."

"Our last hope for real estate just died."

Joel sat on a flat rock. "I know how much you love the people who work for you. You feel the weight of your fifty employees and their families. You're not alone. We're in this together, whatever it takes."

Manny stared out to the sea.

Joel ignored the silence. "I'll talk with the accountants. Get creative on a line of credit."

Manny pulled out his phone. He swiped until he saw Yosef, his firstborn. Strong, capable, and confident. Their relationship had been strained earlier when he balked at the idea of pursuing engineering like his father. Yosef's artistic nature, incredible work ethic, and love for fine cuisine made him a natural fit for opening his own restaurant. The day he signed the note to financially support Yosef had changed their family dynamic forever.

He swiped again. Miriam started as a social worker in Israel's prison system. She staffed her restaurant at the Midrachov with recently released prisoners. Promising them financial rewards in return for hard work, her strict discipline earned her the nickname "Warden." Her staff required constant attention and soon formed a loyal family. Several employees even lived with her in her tiny apartment.

Manny swiped again. Rebekah had worked for her brother while in college hoping to launch a restaurant of her own. She displayed a faithful servant's heart. With the potential to be the most successful of his three children, she supported her brother, waiting in the wings for him to acquire the capital.

Clouds crept across the sky. Rafi's pledge of a significant portion of the mortgage on Yosef and Miriam's restaurants required monthly payments. Without progress at LabStrength, his house of cards would tumble.

He couldn't sacrifice their futures.

Joel sat on a rock loosely holding his folder. A powerful southbound gust of wind ripped the papers from Joel's hand. They scattered along the rocky crags. Tangled into the brush around Manny's feet.

Ignoring the flying pages, he picked up a rock.

Joel faced him. "Do you know Mr. Haviv Cohen? He ran *Bridal Magazine* with limited circulation. Struggled to get advertisers."

"I know him." Manny stared at the water.

"Three years ago, a local celebrity asked to have him cover her wedding. With a famous actress on the cover, the month's issue went viral. The next month, his subscriptions doubled. He quickly grew to regional prominence. Began covering other high-profile weddings. Soon advertisers clamored for space in his publication. His distribution catapulted. Prices rose. Within a few years, Mr. Cohen purchased other magazines. His publishing house became a household name across the Mideast and Europe."

"What's your point?" Manny turned his gaze north. Just beyond Mount Arbel, the valley of Wadi Haman had doubled in cloud cover.

"What was the secret to his success?"

"I only know him from Pantheon." He threw the rock. Galilee's fierce white caps swallowed it.

"Over the years, you've mentioned a few people from Pantheon whose businesses have skyrocketed. There must be something there—not a coincidence."

Manny fondly remembered being invited to his first Pantheon meetings. They gathered for feasts, garnering favors. Readily reciprocating to anyone in the group, a win-win situation. He had arranged an exclusive deal with the CEO of a company who provided high-tech supplies. Another colleague helped make his initial governmental connections for testing at tourist sites. When they weren't arranging new businesses, conversations revolved around extravagant vacations or politics. Rarely did any of them express any vulnerability with one another enough to show a hint of trouble at their business, heaven forbid any problems in their home life.

Joel interrupted his thoughts. "Marna."

"I'm sorry?"

"A middle-aged woman running an import-export shipping company with six employees. Just a sliver of the market share. She struggled day to day, on the verge of going out of business. Out of nowhere, orders picked up. Within a week, she hired a dozen people to keep up with demand. Sales skyrocketed. Her workforce grew to four hundred strong. Now they're an internationally traded company. She's one of the wealthiest individuals in the country."

Manny tossed another rock. "What's your point?"

"I've never been to the Pantheon meetings, but I have heard rumors of a mysterious power for those who move up the ranks."

"People say all kinds of things. Magic doesn't bring success. Good science and solid business practices do."

"So, how do you explain Habib or Marna?"

Manny said nothing.

"What about those secret ceremonies?"

"How do you know about those?"

"People talk."

"The requirements to be at those ceremonies are intense. I don't know much, but some type of sacrifice is involved."

"What if ..." Joel trailed off without saying more.

"I know." Manny looked at him. "In the back of my mind, I've always wondered."

"What if the rumors are true?"

"Science. Business. All we need."

"Science doesn't have all the answers."

Manny took a step toward Joel. "I've always made my own success. I've never needed to be involved."

Joel raised his eyebrows.

"Fine. Until now." Manny shoved his hands deep in his pockets. "I just don't know about all this."

"You've sacrificed everything for this company, I understand."

"Not everything." He pulled his phone from his pocket. "Not yet."

As Joel turned to head back to the car, Manny stepped toward the shore. The little box in his hand could connect him with anyone in the world, yet it held no answers. A drop of water splattered across his screen.

How could a bizarre ancient ceremony have any real-life impact? If I get involved, will I have to believe in the superstitions, or is it enough to simply participate?

He tapped his wet phone.

A female voice came over the line. "Manny? I'm surprised to hear from you this time of day. What can I do for you?"

"I'm ready to take the next step."

After a pause, the voice said, "Are you not happy with your involvement so far?"

"Quite the opposite. I'm more than happy. I ..." he swallowed hard. "I have an urgent need."

A stretch of painful silence.

"What are you asking?"

"I understand you are the gatekeeper for a solution I need."

"What solution?"

"I would like to participate in your ceremony."

After another long silence. "Call your son."

He looked at the dark clouds over the water, his eyebrows furrowed. "What are you talking about?"

The line went dead.

The wind wrestled against his body. Manny shifted his weight. Drops of water converged on one another as they pelted him. Soaked to the skin, his shoulders weighed down. He had checked in with Yosef only a few hours earlier. He had been doing fine, busy with the hassles inherent in managing a restaurant. Nothing out of the ordinary.

Why would she tell me to call him?

He dialed Yosef's number. When he didn't pick up, Manny tapped the text button.

MANNY: Call me.

Manny headed back to his car with his hands in front of his face to protect himself from the storm.

CHAPTER THIRTY

Chase's laptop crashed to the floor as he rolled over in bed. He sat up and rubbed his eyes. After a minute, he opened his laptop. A photo of Abby smiled back at him. Across the room, Billy remained seated at his desk swiping on his phone.

"Have you been up all night? Two nights in a row."

Billy didn't answer.

God, please protect her.

Chase's leg muscles ached as he walked to the window. The sun, barely above the horizon, punished his tired eyes. After a trip to the bathroom and fresh clothes, he returned to his perch on the end of the bed. Another call to his mother was a déjà vu experience. He hung up and looked at Billy. "What are you working on?"

"Drone."

"Is it still flying?"

"I wanted pictures from Ein Gedi."

"I thought you had her circling over Beersheba."

"LabStrength has a permit for geothermal tests in Ein Gedi every few months. They were scheduled to be there yesterday and today for research."

"You've been busy."

"Why would the government agree to close down a tourist site during Holy Week, the busy tourist time?"

"Tonight, they're going to be in Caesarea Philippi."

"Why those locations? Why those dates?" Chase studied the map on the wall, then placed his left index finger on Beersheba, his right on Ein Gedi. "How far? Forty miles?"

"More or less."

"By dusk, she soared to 20,000 feet, still fully charged."

"Your sister created an amazing machine."

Billy's phone showed a fuzzy video image.

Chase asked, "What are we looking at?"

"Windy."

"Is she still airborne?"

Billy swiped. The screen read:

Airspeed: 32 knots

"Where is she?"

Billy tapped his screen. A blue dot indicated her path in the Ein Gedi region. He tapped again. A photo appeared. A fuzzy image showed an aerial view.

"Elevation?"

Billy swiped right. Rows of white numbers filled columns on the black background. "Ground level. She's in trouble." He looked out the window at the rising sun. "Her panels aren't receiving sunlight yet. Battery isn't charging. She'll crash any second."

"Show me her elevation."

Billy's jaw muscles tensed.

Elevation: 38 ft

Chase grabbed his laptop. "Show me the aerial image again."

Chase glanced at it then pulled up a satellite view of the Dead Sea. His fingers ran across the keys until the image on his screen replicated a satellite image.

Chase proclaimed, "She's about 1400 feet high."

Billy squinted.

"Altimeter reads against sea level. The Dead Sea is 1404 feet below sea level. She has plenty of room."

Billy's shoulders relaxed. He looked at Chase for the first time of the morning.

Chase pulled up a weather report. "Looks like clear skies all day. What are we looking for at this site?"

"Trucks."

"Why would trucks be there?"

"A portable research facility?"

"Seriously?" Chase shook his head. "Impressive."

Billy brought up a video stream. "Any small gust of wind alters her stability. Affects the image."

"Maybe she needs a little time."

His fingers floated across the screen as he gave the drone a few more orders. "There, when she reads a clear image, she'll send it to us."

Chase pulled up a photo of Abby admiring her ring.

How much time does she have?

CHAPTER THIRTY-ONE

Abby spun her engagement ring on her finger. Tiffany knelt on the ground with her eyes closed. She placed her hands on the ground. Raised her hips. With her heels down she locked her knees and elbows with her body in an upside-down V-shape.

Abby looked away. She wished they had some sort of separation or privacy curtain between them. She bowed her head in prayer. *God, you are in control even when I'm not. Please rescue us from this prison. I must get back home. We've planned so many things.*

After a while, she looked back at Tiffany. Still in a V position, but her left leg somehow shot straight above her head. Abby doubted she could get in such a position with a team of people helping her.

Abby continued praying but with her eyes open, wishing for solitude.

In the morning light, she could make out more of the details than before. Lines had been carved into the walls. Score markings of four lines crossed by a fifth repeated on the walls. She stared at the buckets and bread.

God, how long are we going to be here?

Tiffany planted her hands on the ground. Lifting her body by her arms, she hovered.

Abby continued to pray silently.

After what must have been an hour, Tiffany said. "What are you doing?"

Abby opened her eyes. Tiffany had settled into a ball on her knees with her hands extended on the ground.

"Praying."

"To whom?"

"God. You know, Jesus."

"Oh. What are you asking for?"

Abby shrugged. "To get out of here. For freedom. Safety."

"What did she say?"

"She?" Abby shook her head. "Nothing yet."

"As expected," Tiffany stood up, covered in sweat. She reached into the bucket for a few handfuls of water. "I trust everything happens for a reason, even when we're not wise enough to see it."

"You're right. God is in control."

"If a loving God was somehow in control, why did she leave us here?"

Abby pointed out the score marks.

Tiffany ran her hands over the marks. "Dark history in this place."

"They obviously want us alive but don't seem to care about much else."

Tiffany motioned to the bucket. "They plan on keeping us here for a while."

"When he stood here, what did you see?"

"Huh?"

"When the door opened, I concentrated on firing the laser. Didn't see much else."

"I saw the man with a bucket. Just under six feet tall with an athletic physique, not muscular like a bodybuilder, but trim and fit. With sunlight at his back, I couldn't see his face."

Abby asked, "What about the countryside? Buildings? Any clues to where we are?"

Tiffany closed her eyes. "Brown desert landscape with rocks and hills. No buildings or signs."

"Typical desert," Abby said. "We could be anywhere."

Tiffany pointed to Abby's laser. "Worthless."

"He kept moving around. There wasn't time for the energy to transfer into the fabric."

Tiffany paced in the tiny enclosure. "Your ineffective laser and stupid little knife are the only resources we have."

"I wish we had gasoline."

Tiffany stared at the door. Abby extended the loaf of bread. Tiffany declined. Abby held the laser in front of the bread. She remembered hundreds of tests they'd done on various organic materials. "This wouldn't light." She felt a bulge in her pocket, pulled out her hand sanitizer.

Retrieving her sweater from the bucket, she stretched it across the door like a mother holding up a shirt on a toddler. Ignoring the bucket's stench, she tucked one sleeve in a crack in the limestone, gave it plenty of slack, and tied the other sleeve to the doorknob. She cut the sweater into thin strips until the entire back was nothing but fringes.

"Going for a '70s look?"

Abby stood back. "Like kindling for a campfire. Smaller is better." She held up the hand sanitizer. "Accelerant."

Tiffany raised her eyebrows.

With her trap set, Abby placed the small container of alcohol on the ground by the door. She returned to the opposite wall, where she sat down and ran incendiary computations in her head.

"Go ahead and put the alcohol on it."

You think you're so bright. "Dries too fast. There wouldn't be anything left by the time they come back."

"Test it."

Abby waved the laser. "I doubt we have much battery life left."

"You didn't build in a battery meter?"

"We've already concluded it didn't win any awards."

Tiffany pushed on the doorknob. "Why didn't you think of this before you shot at him with your stupid laser?"

Longing for a positive interaction, Abby said "Tell me about your drone."

Tiffany leaned against the door. "Drones."

"You have more than one?"

"Of course. I made two identical prototypes. Only brought one for the competition. And yes, they both have battery meters."

Abby looked at the ground. Remembering Passover, she wished she could attend a service.

God, get me out of here.

CHAPTER THIRTY-TWO

BEERSHEBA

"Passover is in two days. I don't know if we'll find a place for breakfast," Chase said as he followed Billy out the hotel lobby.

Billy looked straight ahead. "Why wouldn't they be open?"

"Passover is the biggest celebration you can imagine, like the Super Bowl and Fourth of July all rolled up in one. Just about everything in this country shuts down. Probably more in Jerusalem than Beersheba."

They walked the street for a few minutes. Most of the establishments were dark with few people mulling about. Chase was please to find a bustling bistro. He followed the host to a small table with wire-backed chairs. When the waitress came, he ordered a kibbutz breakfast. Billy ordered the same.

Chase scrolled through social media posts. Promises of prayer. A few shares. Nothing from anyone outside his immediate circle of friends. "Any news on your end?"

"Nothing productive."

"Prayer chains all across the country are working overtime."

"Great." Billy sighed. "Talk to God."

Chase knew better than to begin a debate. The waiter served eggs, Israeli salad, and various accompaniments.

"Anything from the drone?"

Billy showed a clear image from Ein Gedi.

"Are those trucks?"

"Yes."

"What are the black lines?"

"Hoses."

"How do you know?"

Billy brought up a text thread.

"We tested lithostatic pressures at geologically active sites using portable labs."

Chase said, "What are you talking about?"

"I sent LabStrength's website to my dad. Asked what he knew about geothermal renewable energy. One of his friends gave him this input." He tapped again. An aerial photo appeared with structures identical to the drone's image.

"Where are those images from? They look exactly like the pics from Ein Gedi."

He leaned forward. "My dad told me about a confidential cutting-edge project. He couldn't tell me the company name, what part of the world it was from, or any details.

"Send me the photo."

Billy didn't say anything for a long time. When they had finished their meals, Billy said, "Have you ever lost anyone?"

Chase raised his phone. The image of him sitting with Abby popped up. "Obviously. I've lost her. I need to find her."

Billy's sunglasses slid down his nose. He peered over the lenses with invasive eye contact. "Do you even love her?"

Chase recoiled. "Of course, I do."

"Why?"

"What do you mean? She's everything to me."

Billy pushed his glasses back into place. "After you proposed, posting on social media was a higher priority for you than their safety."

He held up his hands defiantly yet stayed quiet. *How could he make such an accusation?*

"Do you want her back for her sake? Or do you want to sweep in, declare yourself a hero?"

A wave of nausea swept over Chase. He searched for words to rebut his accuser. He had asked her to marry him. *Proof he loved her. She said yes. What else could he do? What else could he say?*

Silence reigned over their space until Chase glanced at Billy's screen.

DAD: Come home.

"What?" Chase put his fork down. "You can't leave!"

"You're reading my texts?"

"You need to stay."

Billy pushed his plate away. "For God's sake, what do you know about what I need or what my dad needs?"

Chase's mouth went dry.

"He's already lost his wife, now his daughter. Do you know what this does to a person?"

Chase sat back in his chair. "I'm sorry, I ..."

"Listen. I want the girls back as much as you do. Probably more. But it's been more than twenty-four hours already. If you're honest with yourself, you'll admit what it means."

Chase said nothing.

"Means there's a ninety-nine percent chance if anyone ever sees them again, it will be the authorities recovering a corpse."

"I thought it was forty-eight hours." Chase looked up. "Or are those stats different in Israel?"

Billy set his jaw.

Chase gave a pleading look. "You can't just give up hope."

"There is no hope."

Billy's phone interrupted their silence. A facetime call from his father. Declining the call, he headed back to the hotel. Chase pushed away his plate and rested his head on the table.

What else can I do to keep him here? What should I do now?

He checked the time. Almost too early to call Rafi.

What he would I do if I were in the states?

Chase pulled up the Beersheba police department on his map. A little far to walk, a ride would be better.

A taxi dropped off a pair of passengers. He leaped to his feet. Waving down the cab, Chase slipped into the back seat. "Police department, please."

CHAPTER THIRTY-THREE

Rafi mentally reviewed the details of his conversation with Boaz. The coffee maker waited faithfully with a promise of hope via caffeination. He filled his cup then checked the holding cell where his suspect slept.

His phone buzzed. A picture of his mother filled the screen. *Not now.* He let it go to voicemail.

A clerk at the front of the building dealt with a loud outsider. Speaking through plexiglass with a speaker, he pressed the button and waved his hand. "Okay, okay."

Out of curiosity, Rafi inched forward. Through the speaker, he heard, "I need to speak with Detective Hadad."

The clerk turned and looked in his direction. Rafi stepped closer until he saw a young man standing alone opposite the plexiglass barrier. Upon seeing Rafi, he began frantically waving to him with both hands.

Chase Johnson?

He stepped closer.

"Detective Hadad, I need to talk with—"

The clerk released the button cutting him off.

Rafi gestured through the window with his palms down. He pressed the button. "Calm down. What are you doing here?"

"I'm sorry to bother you. Did you get my email? I need to know if you've found—"

Rafi released the button and motioned to the clerk, who unlocked the door.

Chase burst through. "What have you found? Are you looking into LabStrength?"

"Slow down." He brought Chase into a private room, directed him to sit. "I haven't ignored you."

"I know. I just—"

"Can I get you something? Coffee?"

"No, thanks. I need to know what's going on."

"I'm talking with a suspect. We're looking into it from every direction."

"Who is your suspect?"

He saw the file tucked under Rafi's arm. The end of Boaz Sharabi's file stuck out just enough for Chase to see the name.

"Can I see his file? What do you know about Boaz?"

He shook his head. "I really can't say anything until I'm done questioning him."

"Why did you send me the Scripture?"

"As I said, I'm looking at it from several directions."

"Seemed like some type of code." Chase looked up at the cameras in the corners of the room. "Is there something you can't tell me?"

He rolled his eyes. "If there were, I wouldn't be able to answer your question, would I?"

Chase looked at him, waiting for more.

"Listen, you've been very helpful. Let me do my job, okay?"

Chase sighed. He wasn't going to get any information. "Okay."

"Don't go too far. We might need further help." Rafi's phone buzzed. *Mom again?* He faced Chase, "I have to get going. See the clerk for a form to fill out before you leave."

"Sure, I'll get out of your way. Thanks for seeing me."

Rafi headed out the door with a phone to his ear. "Shalom."

"You are coming tonight, yes?"

"Of course, Mother. I wouldn't miss it." He found a spot where he could talk in relative privacy.

"Your work. Always your work. You make me think your work is more important than family."

"I'm sorry, Mother. Don't you remember? I've been promoted."

"Detective, I know. How can I forget? You've told me so many times. My little son is now a bigtime detective."

"I'll be there."

"Still no woman on your arm."

There it is. Constant pressure to get married.

"I should have a grandchild to hold."

Here she goes again.

"What are you waiting for? I've brought a dozen for you. You rejected them all."

"In time, Mother." He looked up the hall. A few uniform police officers mulled about. At the front, Chase wrote on a clipboard.

"I've taken the liberty of inviting a guest for you."

He stood up straight, eyes wide. *Not again.*

"You'll love her. She's from a wonderful family here in Jerusalem."

He shook his head. "No. Mom, don't do this again."

"She's younger than you—who isn't at this point?"

I have to do something. "I've invited guests. Please don't invite a date for me."

"Oh, darling, I just want the best for you."

"I'm bringing two American friends from out of town."

"Why didn't you say so, darling?"

"They unexpectedly extended their vacation. Didn't have plans for Passover."

"At least you've remembered your manners. We start at dusk."

"Of course, Mother. I wouldn't miss it."

"You have before."

The call finally ended. Rafi put his hand on his forehead. Chase handed the clipboard back as he opened the door to exit.

Rafi called out, "Hey, can you wait a minute?"

Chase looked back.

"What do you and Billy have planned for Passover?"

CHAPTER THIRTY-FOUR

Manny struggled through another sleepless night. Stories from Pantheon acquaintances ran through his mind. Most were moderately successful businesses with intermittent prominence. A select few had catapulted to meteoric success without explanation.

Had each of them taken a role in the ceremony?

He remembered helping Yosef launch his restaurant. During their first year, they talked on the phone daily. Manny helped him build systems for hiring quality employees. Yosef ran recipes and every major purchase past him. Their relationship blossomed. A proud father, he introduced Yosef to his acquaintances at Pantheon. Great contacts for a young man just starting out.

Recently, the frequency of their meetings had waned. Had he been maturing as a business owner or had he withdrawn because something deeply wrong had consumed him?

When did we last talk business?

He tapped Yosef's number into his phone.

MANNY: I'd love to chat if you have a minute. Call.

Manny's phone announced a Facetime call from Yosef. "Shalom."

"*Erev Pesach same'ach.*"

"What's wrong, Dad?"

"Why do you think something is wrong?"

"For the first time in years, you didn't smile with the traditional greeting."

"We have a little trouble at the office."

Yosef sighed. "I heard."

"What? How?"

"People talk. Anything I can do to help?"

"Not unless you can get me access to active geological land."

Yosef laughed. "Sorry, I'm tapped out."

"I'm in a bit of a pickle."

"Another grant?"

"Not an option. Last night, I called the Pantheon director."

"Really?"

"She just told me to call you. Yosef, what have you been up to?"

Yosef looked away. "You remember when you took me to the Pantheon dinner two years ago?"

"Sure. After Yom Kippur, you were my guest."

"I met your friends."

"That's the whole point of Pantheon. I wanted you to have some exposure for business contacts."

"Haviv Cohen is a fascinating man."

"He's a publisher."

"He's a businessman, just like us. Do you remember when his business went to the moon overnight?"

"I know his story."

"What happened before the event?"

Manny hesitated. "How do you know about—"

"I've been meeting with him."

"Excuse me?"

"He's taken me under his wing as a business apprentice. Shares his business practices with me."

Manny stood up. He wanted to lash out at Yosef for not sharing those things with him. "Is he helpful?"

"Always."

"What has he told you about Pantheon?"

"He keeps his cards close to his chest. All I know is when he jumped into Pantheon with both feet, his business exploded."

"You believe the superstitions? Some type of magical power in their sacrificial ceremonies?"

"Doesn't matter what I believe. I'm just looking at the evidence."

"Like a scientist."

"Mr. Cohen believes it. He participated in something. The next day, a celebrity called him, like some type of magic. He said I could too. So, I asked the director."

"People run businesses. Not magic. One honest, hard-working business owner connects with another. I've been telling you for years—"

"Marna."

"Huh?"

"You remember her import-export shipping company?"

"Are you meeting with her too?"

"Connections," Yosef spoke slowly. "I'm learning as much as I can from highly successful people."

"There are no shortcuts. I've worked hard for every ounce of success which ever came my way."

"I don't have any problem with hard work."

Manny blinked away tears. "Your hard work honors our family."

"Why haven't you taken the next step? You've been sitting on a winning lottery ticket and won't cash it in."

"You're ahead of me." He took a deep breath. "I'm ready."

Yosef's smiled "Let's do it together."

"I'm all in."

CHAPTER THIRTY-FIVE

BEERSHEBA

Rafi checked the address on Yeshayahu Zamir Street as he navigated a narrow cobblestone residential road. He squeezed between tiny sedans driving past conservative homes crammed into the neighborhood like sardines. Each house was walled off from their neighbors with cinderblock or decorative stone barriers. Barely enough space existed to walk between homes.

He parked in front of Mr. Sharabi's property and followed a stone walkway to the door. He peeked through a small window.

A rounded, middle-aged gentleman crept along the living room floor on his knees with a feather and wooden spoon. He pulled a couch away from the wall. Using a candle for illumination, he reached back as far as possible. He swept the entire region, cleaned up crumbs and dust bunnies, stowed them in a paper bag. He pushed the couch back, repeated the procedure on the remaining baseboard. He sat back on his haunches and looked up at the front door.

Rafi gave a polite nod.

The door opened slowly revealing Mr. Sharabi's pale face. "What's wrong?"

"Pesach same'ach."

"Detective, you took Boaz yesterday from my truck. He never came back. You ruined our evening rush. We had a long line. People were leaving. We didn't even cover our overhead."

"I'm sorry. I know it's tough to make ends meet. That's why I'm here. I need to ask you a few questions about Boaz."

"Aye, aye, aye. Fine, come in, have a seat. I have more questions for you than answers." He headed through the living room into a simple kitchen. Setting down his paper bag, feather, and wooden spoon, he pulled two empty cups from the cupboard and filled them with aromatic coffee.

Rafi took a seat in a wooden kitchen chair which sagged under his weight. The large man handed him a cup. Rafi said, "Thank God, coffee doesn't have yeast."

"Just finished up my *bedikat chametz.*"

"Yeast doesn't stand a chance on this day, does it?" Rafi smiled.

"The first step of many." He waved a hand over the kitchen countertop, overflowing with fresh vegetables, lamb, and bottles of wine.

"I'm sorry to interrupt your preparation. Can you tell me about Boaz's work schedule the past few days?"

He stared at the coffee cup. "He's had his share of trouble. What did he do this time?"

"I just need to review his work hours."

"You're asking when he has been at Albi Kabab?"

"Yes."

"He doesn't have an excuse to come in late. He sleeps in the back room. I don't even charge him rent. I just want the boy to pull his life together." Mr. Sharabi sipped his coffee.

"He's lucky to have you in his life."

"Let me think." Mr. Sharabi counted on his fingers. "Monday, Tuesday, Wednesday, and Thursday, every day this week, on time. No problems. He's been doing fairly well the past few months."

"Tell me about Wednesday night."

"What about it?"

"Was he at the restaurant or working in your truck?"

"Wednesday was terrible. I just hired two young guys a month ago. Boaz oversees them. Had them up to speed in no time. I thought they were strong workers, but on Wednesday, they didn't show up for their shifts. They didn't call or text or anything. Just never showed."

"What did you do?"

"Kids these days have no respect for authority."

"How did you manage the restaurant on Wednesday?"

"We had to change everything. We didn't take the truck out. Boaz stayed back. He ran the place."

"So, he was at the restaurant the whole evening?"

"He did an impressive job. Took over the work of two men. We kept up all night. Then you took him. Left me short-staffed again." Mr. Sharabi threw up his hands.

"I'm sorry." Rafi cradled the warm cup in his hands. "Can you tell me specifically about the hours around sunset on Wednesday?"

"You're kidding me." He took a sip of coffee. "Boaz sat customers, took orders, and bussed tables. Without him, I would have had to close."

"Anything unusual about the way he acted that evening?"

"The next day, when I went to load the truck, I found it filthy with an empty tank. He had taken it late doing who knows what. I had him clean and fill it."

"Anything else?"

He swirled he coffee. "He complained about his cell phone being missing, but he had it the next day. I don't know why it's a big deal. I don't let them use it during work. Kids can't live without those dumb things, you know."

Rafi set his notepad on the table. "Can you write down names and addresses of the rest of your staff, please?"

"I thought you just needed to know about Boaz."

"Just being complete."

Sharabi began writing. "I don't know their addresses off the top of my head."

"No problem. Just their names will help."

"What did the boy do?"

Ravi stood up. "Thank you for your hospitality. I'll let you get back to your Passover preparations. I expect Boaz will be home soon."

And I will have to find another suspect.

CHAPTER THIRTY-SIX

Abby drifted in and out of sleep lying on her side with her back to Tiffany. Bizarre dreams of being attacked and hauled into a truck haunted her. She awoke repeatedly to the painful reality of her confinement. Finally, a band of sunlight forced its way below the door. With relief, she sat up and rested her shoulder against the wall.

A collection of score marks stared her in the face. She ran her hands along the lines, a set of five next to a pair.

Will I last a week?

She gazed around at the other marks. Four. Twelve. Six.

Why are they keeping us here?

After dusting off a section of the wall with her palm, Abby opened her Leatherman tool Thick, impenetrable limestone would be challenging to score. The website ad stated, "A tool for every use." She scrutinized the lock on the door.

One could only wish.

Selecting the Phillips screwdriver, Abby pressed it into the stone surface, scraping a line up and down.

Tiffany stood in the middle of the room with her hands in a praying position. She placed her palms on the ground between her feet with her legs straight. Walking forward with her hands she made a V, stayed there for several minutes then walked back to her feet and stood up.

Abby continued. A line began taking shape.

Tiffany continued her full body motions, oblivious to Abby's scraping.

A hundred passes back and forth.

Eventually, Tiffany sat on the ground, covered in sweat. "Day two."

"Today is Good Friday."

"What's good about it?" Tiffany took a few sips of water. "You should get up, walk around. We need to stay limber, be ready."

Abby continued scraping. "I planned on visiting someone in Jerusalem today."

Tiffany stood with her hands on her hips. "You didn't tell me."

"I didn't tell anyone. I have an invitation from one of the other contestants at the engineering fair. He has family in Jerusalem. When he heard we would be in town but didn't have plans, he invited us to their family Seder."

Tiffany gave her a questioning look.

"The traditional Jewish Passover celebration is a big deal all across Israel."

"Oh."

Abby continued scraping. "I'd hoped to surprise Chase. He lives in the moment. I thought he'd love it."

"Seems about right."

"The only way I can be spontaneous is to plan a surprise."

"Were you going to invite Billy and me?"

"Absolutely. I hoped we all would be able to go." Abby gave a shy smile. "I thought I'd go out on a limb."

"Quite generous of them to offer the invitation."

"The Jewish tradition includes being extraordinarily hospitable." Abby stopped scraping. Running her finger along her scored line she compared it to the others.

Tiffany continued stretching.

Abby's hand felt natural wrapped around the Leatherman tool like a carpenter wielding a hammer. She started in on a second line, parallel to the first. "They say a Seder is amazing. Everything is so meaningful from cleansing their house of yeast to how they prepare the food, the games, and activities—it's all rich with symbolism."

"Yeast?"

Abby nodded. "In the Bible, yeast is symbolic of sin. The physical removal of yeast is a reminder to repent and turn from any sinful behavior. Bread, pasta, cookies, pretzels, anything leavened has to go."

"How?"

She stopped scraping. "They traditionally scour the whole house in the weeks before Passover. The night before, they go over every corner by candlelight using a feather and wooden spoon. They call it the bedikat chametz. A deep spiritual practice, symbolic of cleansing yourself."

"Do Christians get rid of yeast?"

"No. Maybe we should."

Tiffany sat against the opposite wall. "He's not much of a planner, is he?"

"Who?"

"Chase."

"He's more of a fly-by-the-seat-of-his-pants kind of a guy."

"He asked me for advice on your ring, you know."

"When?"

"During the engineering fair. He showed me three pics on his phone. Asked which one was the best."

"Really?" Abby shook her head. "He must have snuck off. I had no idea."

"We barely knew each other. Why would he trust my judgment?"

"Maybe he figured since you were a professional female, you'd have good taste."

"Pretty naïve."

Abby stopped scraping. "Chase is a free spirit. He called me once at nine o'clock on a Friday night. Asked if I wanted to go camping. I told him I would be free in two weeks. He and his buddies were going that night!"

Tiffany shook her head. "You can't run your life by the seat of your pants."

Abby shrugged, "He does."

"Did you go camping?"

"Of course not. I had plans."

"Simply doesn't work."

"Works for him."

Tiffany wrapped her arms around her legs. "You seemed surprised when he asked you to marry him."

"Absolutely."

"Did you want to get married?"

"Of course." Abby ran her finger along the unyielding rock surface.

Tiffany stared at her waiting for more.

"Well, sure. He's great. Spontaneous, fun, good looking, and smart."

Tiffany prompted, "But ..."

"I have plans," Abby sighed. "I'm going to finish my master's degree. Start my career. I had planned to get married later. I'd have kids. Go part-time. Work two days a week."

"You're an idealist."

"No, I'm a planner."

"Did you want a white picket fence too?"

Abby pointed at the ground. "An underground fence for our yellow lab."

"Of course." Tiffany scoffed. "You plan everything. Control every detail. You're such a hypocrite."

Abby dropped the Leatherman tool. Held out her hands defensively.

"I thought you were pleading to God for help?"

"Huh?"

"You pray for hours on end, pleading for some god to save you. You act all self-righteous. Saying God is in control."

Abby recoiled. *What brought this on?*

"You say some cosmic force has a plan for your life. Yet, you plan every detail. Trying to control every tiny aspect of your world as if your god doesn't exist."

Abby's hands fell to her lap.

Tiffany headed back to the water bucket. "I trust everything happens for a reason, even when we're not wise enough to see it."

Abby knew dozen responses to such critiques. She tried to formulate a counterargument but couldn't.

"It's like we're standing at the foot of a mountain with many paths to the top. You're taking one path. Jews are on their path. I'm taking another. We'll all get there."

Abby started scraping again. The crater deepened.

CHAPTER THIRTY-SEVEN

BEERSHEBA

Rafi hunkered down at his desk after finishing an interview with each person on Mr. Sharabi's list. He wrote brief reports for his interviews, then checked the time. The drive to Jerusalem would take ninety minutes, possibly longer with holiday traffic. He couldn't be late for another family event. With an hour to spare, he looked through Boaz's record once again.

How could a guy with a DNA match for a cigarette at the crime scene have a rock-solid alibi?

Mr. Sharabi wants him to be successful, but he didn't give the feeling of covering for him. Rafi's internal lie detector didn't make a peep while they spoke.

I need to know the rest of his story.

He ran a search of Boaz's known associates. Background checks on his work colleagues, and family members came up empty.

What about his army buddies?

Rafi opened Boaz's military files and dug in. Previously, he had focused on the criminal proceedings. Skimmed the rest of it. This time, he highlighted every person involved in the criminal case, everyone in his unit. All the people he ever trained with. An extensive list.

He ran the batch of background checks. Discovered quite a few soldiers who had been in trouble when they had returned to civilian life. Though robberies, domestic assault, and embezzlement excluded them from being role models, they didn't seem to connect to the missing girls. He also looked for individuals Boaz trained with or were living in Beersheba. Since most young men moved back home after their service, the number of known associates living nearby included nearly a hundred percent of those on his list.

Rafi looked through Boaz's military record again. Perused a list of other men in his unit. Of the twenty young men who trained together, he wasn't expecting to recognize many names. His gaze fell on the name Yosef Lochotzki.

Where did I see that name recently?

He ran a quick search. Yosef owned a local restaurant. Searching Lochotzki, the LabStrength logo appeared on his screen.

Chase looked into the flying goat. He followed the money to LabStrength.

Rafi reread Avi's email. He confirmed Chase's research. LabStrength had been solely responsible for the goat-man image.

Could there be a connection between Yosef and the abductions?

Yosef and Boaz served in the same unit at the Golan Heights. Yosef testified against him. Otherwise, Yosef's file was pristine. Pure as the driven snow.

Something doesn't feel right.

Rafi wanted to sit down for an extended interview with Yosef. Search his residence. Go through his computer. However, since Yosef hadn't done anything wrong, Rafi had no justification for looking further on him. He wasn't even in contact with someone who had committed a crime. Legally, he had nothing.

He did have a friend who wasn't limited by the same legal constraints.

He composed an email.

Avi,

Remember when we talked about owning a restaurant someday? I know you've been to a place here in Beersheba called The Ben Yehuda. We should visit it together, troublemaker.

Rafi

He sent the email then second guessed himself.

Too cryptic? Would he look into Yosef?

Rafi remembered some of the cyphers he and Ani used. He opened a Bible website. A quick search revealed a Scripture in Genesis which said, "I am Yosef." He didn't have to read the rest of the passage to know it pointed a finger at one person. He tapped in Ari's number.

RAFI: Genesis 45:3

ARI: On it.

CHAPTER THIRTY-EIGHT

BEERSHEBA

Chase strode through the Leonardo Negev Hotel lobby full of hope and anticipation.

A Seder in Jerusalem would be Abby's dream come true.

Opening the door, he watched Billy remove a final page from the wall and place it on a generous stack of paperwork on the bed with a jump drive on top.

Chase chuckled, "What's this? Is the jump drive like a cherry on top of all your work?"

Billy's shoulders, though gargantuan, drooped in a way Chase had never seen before as he packed his suitcase.

Chase asked, "What's going on?"

"I have a plane to catch."

"You're kidding me, right?" Chase thrust his hands in the air. "We're making progress."

Billy's temporal veins bulged as his face flushed. He pointed at the jump drive. "My research. You have everything. My plane leaves Tel Aviv in a couple of hours." He checked his watch then brushed Chase away. "I barely have time to get through security."

Chase announced, "They arrested a guy last night. Won't be much longer."

"What are you talking about?"

"They have somebody in custody right now. The DNA matched to a guy named Boaz Sharabi. They are about to find Abby and Tiffany."

Chase blocked his path. "You can't get on a plane."

"The detective didn't send us an email. I don't have any texts either. You're full of it."

"I know it doesn't sound right. I don't understand why he didn't tell us. I spoke with him myself. They have the guy! They will find out where the girls are real soon. You can't leave."

Billy's forehead grew horizontal lines. "Out of my way."

Chase explained his unplanned trip to the police station, every detail from the clerk to his conversation with Rafi. He relayed the DNA match. How it had to be their guy. He concluded with Rafi's invitation to the Seder, locked eyes with Billy. Repeated his appeal to stay.

Billy sat at the desk. "Fine."

"Good." Chase breathed a sigh of relief. "I can't tell you what your decision means to me."

Billy's face no longer carried the anger it had a minute earlier. Instead, the bags under his bloodshot eyes showed a textbook image of sleep deprivation. "How long until you hear from the detective again?"

"I'm not sure, later this morning?"

"Tell me more about this Boaz guy."

"I don't know much." Chase tossed his phone on the bed. Extended his hand like a peace offering.

Billy ignored the handshake.

"We've been invited to a Passover Seder."

Chase's phone buzzed. Though every instinct in him drew him to the shiny object, Chase refused to break eye contact. Billy looked at Chase's phone and rolled his eyes. He put his computer back into his bag, zipped it, and in a smooth athletic motion, slung it over his shoulder.

"What are you doing?"

Billy said, "Look at your phone."

RAFI: He's not the guy. I released him.

Chase's mouth dropped open. He held his breath as he swiped. He stared at the pale screen, hoping it would change. Nothing. He wished for something to hang on to.

Billy grabbed his luggage. Stood face to face with Chase. "Get out of my way."

Chase's world sank into oblivion. His shoulders drooped. He stared at the carpet as Billy slipped past him into the hallway. Disappeared around the corner.

Why would Rafi release him?

"I need your help." Chase sprinted down the hall.

"You're wasting your time." Billy pressed a button. "They're dead."

Chase slipped into the elevator. Assumed proper elevator etiquette, side by side in silence. Like an obedient puppy, he followed Billy to the parking lot without a word.

Chase looked over the seat. "Where's my inflatable mattress?"

He sat behind the wheel. "In the room. I checked out of the hotel. If you're staying, book a room."

Chase suddenly remembered Şeker Bayrami circling overhead an obscure Israeli town. "What about Tiffany's drone?"

"Duplicate. App is on the jump drive. Do whatever you want."

He pulled away.

CHAPTER THIRTY-NINE

BEERSHEBA

Chase looked around the hotel room. The desk and dresser were pristine, almost sterile. The coffee maker had been wiped down like a maid service had refreshed it for their next guest. Billy had even made the bed.

Chase picked up the stack of papers, separating them by topic, making piles for Mt. Sinai, human trafficking, and organized crime. None of those topics had loose ends ready for him to pull. He saw a page labeled "DNA testing."

Was Boaz Sharabi really the DNA match? Why did Rafi let him go?

He looked up his address scrawled it on a legal pad. In frustration, he shoved the page aside. He came across a handful of printed photos of Abby and Tiffany which Billy had made to hand out to people asking if they had seen the girls. Tiffany's image fell to the bedspread. He held Abby's photo with both hands. Confusion turned to dread as he touched the image.

He could feel her warm embrace. Imagined the satisfaction of conquering the impossible.

She can't be dead. I'll find her.

After finding a home for each page, he stepped back to organize his thoughts. Billy's perfectly made bed became his workstation. Before long he covered it with loosely organized pages.

The printed goat-man image caught Chase's eye. He remembered the back of the truck at it pulled away. If only he had followed it.

A page referring to LabStrength brought Chase back to reality. He reviewed their scheduled off-site research at Ein Gedi, Ein Herod, and Caesarea Philippi, then asked himself, *What do those places have in common?*

He opened his laptop. Typical tourist site information told why people visited the places. A story from the Bible revealed what happened in each location. Green lush tropical foliage dominated his screen with beautiful images of people standing next to streams. Google Earth images of each area clearly showed each as an oasis in the desert. A few clicks later, he realized each also had a spring coming out of a rock.

Is water from a rock common in Israel? Anywhere in the world?

As he stepped back, he realized all three were government-controlled historic sites. He rechecked LabStrength's schedule. En Herod's dates had long since passed. Ein Gedi today, Caesarea Philippi scheduled for Sunday. He needed to look at images of trucks and hoses they had garnered from the drone.

Drone! I have to do something with it.

He looked for the jump drive. He'd left it on top of the papers.

Where is it?

He shuffled the pages frantically over the bedspread. He pressed down on the pages, scattered across the king-size bed. He dropped to his hands and knees. Searching the floor. His heart rate picked up.

Where did I put it?

He checked his pockets. Ran his hand around the bed frame along the wall. Reaching in between the bed and nightstand with two fingers, he felt it. He struggled for a bit, then pulled out and kissed the magic device. After inserting it into his laptop, a window opened with a dozen folders organized alphabetically. The file labeled "drone" took him to twenty more files. He downloaded the app on his phone. Read through the other files. The app controlling the drone was written on the base of basic video game programming.

No wonder it's so easy to fly. Tiffany is a genius.

He opened the drone's video stream. Saw an image just like one Billy had shown him. Three trucks gathered in a desolate region upstream of the green area. Hoses thick enough to be seen from a thousand feet drew a line from the trucks into what must be the spring opening.

What are they doing?

Without a plan for the drone, he set her altitude to 22,000 feet. When it started climbing, he refocused on the jump-drive files. He sorted through plenty of articles from Billy's dad about geologic research. These data-driven engineering papers made great bedtime reading for the chronic insomniac. He dove into the comprehensive discussion on hydrostatic and lithostatic readings. Though renewable energy and desert irrigation were foreign to him, with his inner nerd in high gear, he digested the new information, like drinking from a firehose.

When he came up for air, Chase saw a stack with the name Boaz Sharabi.

Who is this guy? Why did Rafi let him go? Why would someone live at a restaurant? I need to know more about him.

He looked up the restaurant's website. Closed.

A visit wouldn't hurt.

A knock on the door interrupted Chase's solo dialogue. He had lost track of time. Through the peephole, he saw a housekeeper next to her cart of cleaning supplies and towels.

Dang! Billy checked out. I'm not supposed to be here.

He opened the door. Before he uttered a single syllable, a flurry of Hebrew words spewed at him in rapid succession. She pointed her finger at his chest, then at her watch. Kept yelling.

Chase held up his hands defensively. "Okay, okay, let me grab my stuff."

Her chatter continued as she left her cart and hurried down the hall. Chase ran to the bed. Scooped up pages like autumn leaves. Stuffed his dirty laundry into his suitcase. A knock rattled the door.

"Shalom."

A man in a dark suit with perfectly groomed hair stared at him. Just behind him, the housekeeper stood next to her cart, shaking her head in disappointment. He said, "Our records show you've already checked out. Can I help you with your bag, sir?"

"No, thank you. I'll be just fine." Chase felt like a child being scolded. He headed to the elevator. The manager followed him to the lobby, where he resumed his post behind the service desk.

Well-dressed men and women bustled through the lobby, all with plans to go somewhere with someone. They had schedules to keep, people to be with. He checked the time, still several hours before he needed to leave for the Seder with Rafi's family.

Plenty of time to find out more about Boaz. He considered booking a room, but not at the prices here. Hostels were more his speed. He enjoyed the bargain basement cost but also the wide variety of fascinating people he met. He often struck up conversations with fellow students or tourists from many countries who surfed hostels with little money and rarely with a plan.

He would look into a place to stay later. He saw a bellhop take baggage from another patron then store it in a locked room. He considered storing his luggage. Though carrying it around with him would be a hindrance, he wanted the freedom to go wherever he wanted. He left with bags in tow under the guise he had a plan. Once on the sidewalk, he focused on finding Boaz.

CHAPTER FORTY

Chase marched toward Albi Kabab, hoping for inspiration. On the way, he did another quick social media check weeding through the continual flow of well-wishers. The response rate had slowed, posts sounded more like condolences. The streets were as tranquil as he had seen since arriving in the country six days earlier. Every business was closed. Checking his phone every minute or less like a nervous tic, Chase hoped for any new information to help find Abby.

He stopped in front of Albi Kabab, looked in the window. Tugged on the locked door in frustration. He slipped into a narrow alleyway. Albi Kabab's back entrance was littered with cigarette butts. Confident in whose DNA they contained, he tested the door with a bit of a tug. Locked.

He knocked gently. Waited. Nothing.

He gave a silent mental shout-out to an old roommate from college who held lock picking competitions to pass the time. He hoped enough skill remained for a simple deadbolt. He jerry-rigged a lock-picking set using a couple of paperclips from the bottom of his bag. Severely out of place with his luggage, he surveyed the alleyway repeatedly as he fumbled with faltering fingers trying to manipulate the pin and tumbler. After ten minutes, he managed the lock without being discovered.

He entered the dark room, closed the door, and waited until his eyes adjusted to the limited light. A clean, deserted kitchen. Straight ahead, the restaurant seating area held no interest for him. On the right, a stuffed pantry. His gut reminded him he hadn't eaten for too long. In the opposite direction, a nondescript door, closed.

Holding his breath, he grasped the doorknob. Empty. Chase flicked a light switch. Surveyed the dingy grey ten-by-ten-foot room. Reeking of stale cigarette smoke, Boaz's room was a tribute to male sloppiness. Dirty apron on the small cot. A pair of boxes partially full of clothing against the wall. Couple of shoes next to the boxes. Small television on a cooler by a six-pack of beer, a handful of empties, and a carton of Noblesse cigarettes. Charger cord on the floor next to paperwork—cell phone bill, a nightclub receipt, and a few bank statements not worth bragging about.

Not the home of a criminal mastermind. At best, a recovering addict. At worst, a criminal lowlife. Could he be involved with such a high-level crime? Chase was in trouble if finding Abby depended on Boaz.

He left the room untouched. Headed back toward the alleyway. His mind ricocheted from the DNA test to every one of Rafi's statements, including the email and cryptic text. His rapid footsteps fueled his cerebral processing.

He knew something was amiss with the flying goat, but what?

He turned the knob. Glanced in either direction into the alleyway before heading back the way he had come in. With his suitcase in tow, he stuck out like a sore thumb. Keeping his head down he traipsed back toward the sidewalk. With only a dozen yards to go, a sedan's rumble drew his attention.

A small black sedan drove by slowly with the windows down. At the driver's seat, a man removed his sunglasses. Looked directly at him.

I've seen him before.

Chase watched him speed into the distance. He slipped onto the sidewalk making an attempt to not look suspicious. After a block, he turned again to avoid being seen if it returned. He filed through the faces he had encountered in Beersheba. He knew the face. He had seen him up close.

Yosef, from the Ben Huda Grill. Why would he be here?

CHAPTER FORTY-ONE

Chase tried to create space between him and Albi Kabab. He headed north on Yitzchak I. Rager Boulevard, replaying the brief scene in his head.

Why would Yosef be at Albi Kabab?

On his right, behind an unkempt row of shrubbery, he saw a public park.

The only public gathering place open on Passover eve, young families bustled about without thought of the holiday. Probably Protestant. Chase found an open bench under a date palm tree, plopped his belongings on the ground next to a vacant seat. Relaxed in full view of a modern plastic playground. Young children climbed the staircase with enormous effort. They hurled their diminutive bodies down a spiral slide, landed on the grass, and ran back to the beginning just to start the process all over again.

Chase looked over the quaint park. He figured he could stay there until Rafi picked him up. After texting Rafi his location, the internet gave him information about the Passover meal and the symbolism of the traditional Seder plate. This is much more than a simple family dinner.

Maybe this isn't a good idea.

A small white sedan stopped at the curb.

Rafi leaned out the driver's window. "Where's Billy?"

Chase shook his head. "He went home."

"I'm sorry to hear that. You still coming?"

Chase shrugged. "I don't know. I feel like a fish out of water with the thought of attending your Seder."

"Nonsense. We've been bringing gentiles to our Seder for years—don't worry about a thing." He helped him with the luggage. "Come with me."

Chase noticed his trendy new suit. He looked at his wardrobe choice—slacks and T-shirt woefully inadequate. He opened his suitcase, pulled out a wrinkled dress shirt, sport coat, and tie.

He motioned to Rafi. "Give me a minute," and hurried to a nearby public restroom.

He struggled to secure his tie. The last time he had worn it, he had won a first-place award at the Tel Aviv scientific competition. An insignificant part of his distant past. So much had happened since then. The career-bolstering award now barely made a blip on his radar.

Chase walked back with his arms out. "Better?"

With a quick nod, Rafi headed north on Highway 406.

Chase said, "Billy was convinced they're already dead."

Rafi clenched his jaw.

Chase asked, "Is it possible?"

"Abduction cases are tough. At this point, we don't know why they were taken or where they are. But we do know something. They have been taken by bad men with some type of complex plan and a fair amount of resources. I won't stop looking."

Chase stared ahead. The smooth highway cut a path through the harsh desert. "Why did you release Boaz?"

"I didn't have a choice. He had a solid alibi."

"He was the DNA match from the cigarette, right?

"Correct. His phone puts him on site. But I spoke with his employer, then visited his coworkers. They all vouched for him in different versions of the same story."

"You believed them?"

"I've interviewed thousands of people. I can sniff out a lie pretty easily. None of the four people I interviewed knew I had conversations with the others. They all came up with realistic, convincing versions of the same events. Boaz worked that night. I believe them. A cigarette, a missing phone, those things can be manipulated. There is no way Boaz could have been at Mt. Sinai on Wednesday night."

They rode in silence, passing the Duda'im Forest. Chase continued, "You sent me on a bit of a wild goose chase with the texts. What did you think of the info we dug up on the goat-man image?"

Rafi said, "You're better than a team of interns. LabStrength convinced the school to use the image as a logo. A few other businesses started using it. Now the goat man image is everywhere."

Chase nodded. "Manny Lochotzki's company."

Rafi asked, "You know him?"

"He's a businessman and philanthropist. What about his son, Yosef?"

"He was in the army with Boaz, with a spotless record."

"I saw Yosef at Albi Kabab."

"Why were you there?"

"I visited to see if Boaz had anything which could lead us to Abby."

Rafi turned toward him. "When?"

"This afternoon."

He raised his right hand. "You can't do that kind of thing. What did you say to Yosef?"

"We didn't speak but made eye contact."

"My word." Rafi raised his voice. "You must leave police work to the police. You may have ruined this investigation."

"I'm sorry, but I'm running out of options."

Rafi stayed quiet for a few minutes. "Maybe your ill-conceived and poorly timed visit might be useful."

"What do you mean?"

"Listen, I have limitations. I would have spoken to Yosef if I could link him to the crime, but I can't. He hasn't done anything. I have no reason even to question him."

"So, you're just ignoring this?"

"Not at all. I had a friend check him out for me."

"What kind of friend?"

"The kind you want on your side. He works for the State Department. Doesn't have the type of limitations we have as police."

As they entered Jerusalem, Chase recognized some of the landmarks. "Abby looked forward to spending time in Jerusalem. She wanted to see King David's tomb, Hezekiah's tunnel, the Cardo, and Rabinovich Square."

"We can see the whole region from my parent's house. The history never gets old."

"I'll bet the Golden Dome is beautiful at sunrise."

"A scar on the face of Jerusalem."

Chase looked down. "I apologize."

"We prefer to focus on the Western Wall."

"Of course—the temple site."

"It'll be hectic today. Passover is big business. Hundreds of thousands of visitors come from all over the planet. They pay premium hotel rates because we're the center of the religious world." He looked at Chase. "Most people don't stay in hostels for $23 a night."

How did he know this? He must have looked into me pretty profoundly to see how much I paid for a hostel. "What else did you find when you looked at my bank records?"

"I know you didn't go cheap on her ring." he winked. "One can only tell so much about a person by scanning their accounts, school transcripts, résumés, and social media. I still barely know you."

They drove up a narrow street, past a large stone windmill into a neighborhood with stately homes made of stone lined up next to one another like soldiers linking shields. Chase gawked at the buildings, a style of construction he had never seen before. Each home had ornate stone with an artistic edifice. The neighborhood looked like an impenetrable city with defensive turrets in the walls.

Chase looked up. "Looks like a castle."

"As you say in America, home sweet home." Rafi pointed to the most prominent building on the road and parked among dozens of small sedans. "We're about fifteen minutes early. This will be a first for me."

"Beautiful neighborhood."

"It's one of the newer homes in Mishkenot Sha'ananim. My family built it in 1860. When they constructed this area, there was no law and order. Outside Jerusalem's walls, they defended themselves."

Chase took a photo.

"Oh, one more thing. I should have told you before. No electronics once we go in the house. Shabbat begins at sunset tonight and continues all day tomorrow."

"Would you make an exception for me?"

"Listen, I'll be checking in regularly. Shabbat law allows for me to do so. I'll be discreet. Only check for things related to her case. I'm sorry, but I just can't have you looking at your phone when you're with my family."

Chase asked, "Can I make one final check?"

"Sure," Chase confirmed the drone soared at a comfortable 22,000 feet, hopefully all set to make it through another night. He swiped through his standard apps, then stowed it.

Rafi said, "All the way off, please."

Chase hadn't turned his phone off in years. He stared at the device, trying to remember how.

Rafi did his own survey before closing his phone. He held his hand over Chase's phone. "Wait. Don't turn it off." He pulled forward. His facial musculature strained under pressure.

Chase shook his head. "What are you doing?"

"You can't be here."

Rafi tossed his device to Chase as he drove past the windmill back to the main road. "See for yourself." A texting app showed Chase's photo followed by paragraphs of Hebrew characters.

"What does it say?"

"My friend put a trace on Yosef's phone."

"I thought you couldn't do those kinds of things."

"I can't but the State Department has a different set of rules. You need to be on the next plane."

"No."

"Listen. This is a message from Yosef to an untraceable burner phone. Contains everything I knew about you before you came here—your résumé, banking information, social media, and contact numbers."

"So?" Chase shrugged.

"This is high-level information."

"I don't have anything to hide."

Rafi pointed at the bottom of the screen. "This is an assassination order."

CHAPTER FORTY-TWO

Chase's mouth gaped. "They want to kill me?"

"They're tracing your location right now. You're not safe."

His hands shook as he fiddled with his phone. "I'll turn it off."

"Not yet. Let's get you out of here first." Rafi flipped on his red and blue flashing lights. Weaving through the tight traffic.

Chase felt as though all the air had been removed from his lungs. "Means we're getting close."

They continued through congested traffic past a few stoplights before they stopped on the side of the road at a five-point intersection.

Chase tasted bile in the back of his throat. "Why would they care about me unless I was on the verge of finding out something which would hurt them?"

A stoplight allowed a stream of pedestrians to cross the busy street. Men in black suits, broad-brimmed black hats, with the fringes of their tzitzit hanging from their shirts, moved calmly toward their destination while sedans, busses, and vans waited.

"Do it now."

Rafi stared at the device in Chase's hand. "Press the power button for five seconds, then slide right."

Rafi pressed a button. A siren blasted from his car. He slipped between a minivan and a Smart Car managing a U-turn in the middle of traffic.

Chase gripped the dashboard. "What are you doing?"

"You're off the grid now."

"So, I'm safe?"

Rafi slowed. Turned off his flashing lights. "I had you disappear in the middle of traffic, so there would be no way to tell which way you would go next."

As they parked in front of the castle once again. Chase said, "Thank you."

"Stay here tonight. Tomorrow, I'll take you to the airport."

"We're close. You can use this to arrest Yosef, right?"

Rafi held up his palm. "My friend can get information, but he can't make the arrest. I can only make an arrest with lawfully gathered information."

"I didn't know Israel had to adhere to similar laws as—"

"You're safe for now." He checked the time. "I'm late again. Right now, I have to get to the house. We'll talk it through after dinner."

Chase's head was spinning.

Rafi killed the engine. "I know this isn't the best circumstance to enjoy a celebration, but you must keep this to yourself. We must set everything aside for a bit. Not a word of this while we're with my family. Understand?"

Chase nodded.

"Let's go."

They entered the front door, the vaulted ceilings, ornate paintings, marble floor, and grand piano impressed Chase. A hand-carved wooden door opened to a kitchen next to an elegant dining room. Chase felt like he had entered a museum, except it overflowed with people, every one of them talking over one another.

Rafi positioned himself, so he could see his whole family. "Attention, please, I brought a guest tonight." Conversations died down. All eyes focused on him. "I would like to introduce my new friend, Chase Johnson, an award-winning engineer from the United States."

He grabbed a nearby glass of wine, held it high. "Pesach Samech!"

Cheers went up throughout the house.

Many returned to their conversations while others approached the newcomer to shake hands. Rafi stepped back as an older gentleman gave Chase an embrace then moved on. A young woman did the same. In a flurry of activity, they greeted countless olive-skinned brunette Israelis.

"Rafi darling, you made it. Late, of course, but at least you're here. Come in. Your brother has been here for a while." The short, wide woman with thick black glasses and short-cropped black hair turned to Chase. "This must be your friend. An award-winning scientist?"

"Good evening, Mother." Rafi kissed her on the cheek.

"Come, darling, you must be starving." She led them to a table covered with hors d'oeuvres. "Eat, eat. Your aunt and I made everything. You must try them all. Everything is fantastic." She placed three deviled eggs on a plate, tossed on some matzohs, scooped a spoonful of a yellow-green dip covered with olive oil, and set it in Chase's hands. "You'll love this spinach dip with hummus. I made it myself."

A few seconds later, she was caught up in conversation with another family member then disappeared into the kitchen.

Chase whispered, "I didn't expect all this."

Rafi said, "You're doing fine, but your accent could use some work."

Mrs. Hadad clapped her hands at the kitchen doorway. "Come, come everybody. Time to sit."

She led them into the dining room and stood by an expansive mahogany table. In the middle of the table sat four bottles of wine, a plate with matzohs, and a sterling silver cup. On a sideboard, a row of wine bottles awaited. The family gathered in a whirlwind of words Chase couldn't comprehend. Rafi guided Chase to a chair between himself and Mrs. Hadad. They brought the Seder plate containing a bone, an egg, horseradish, apple relish, and celery. With a graceful motion, Mrs. Hadad placed it on the table.

She waved her hands at Chase. "Everything is symbolic, deep with meaning. If you have questions, ask away." She pointed at a skinny preteen across the table. "Asher will explain everything to you as we go. Won't you, darling?"

Rafi sang a beautiful Hebrew song, poured wine, and passed the bottle. Without prompting, each person dipped their vegetables and ate.

Chase gave Asher a curious look.

Asher whispered, "Dip it in the saltwater. Represents Pharaoh's enslavement."

Mrs. Hadad corrected, "It's not a secret, darling. Speak up."

He assumed a stage voice. "Tears of slavery. You know, like when Mom makes me scrub the char off her pots and pans." Laughter rolled across the table.

Rafi took matzoh from the middle of the table and broke it. He wrapped half of it in a napkin and gave the piece to Mrs. Hadad who waved it over her head as she scooted out of the room. She returned laughing. Playfully pointed at each of the children, she declared, "You'll never find it!"

Rafi smiled at the youngest family member. "Kobi, I believe you have something for us." Kobi sang a short song, then they opened their leather-bound Haggadah books and began reading.

Asher leaned over to Chase. "Do you know the Passover story?"

"Burning bush, ten plagues, Red Sea, Ten Commandments."

"Perfect. Looks like we're done already."

Rafi said, "We tell it a little slower, with lessons applying to our world today." After more storytelling and singing, they each made a sandwich of matzoh and horseradish.

"Suffering under Pharaoh." Asher held up the matzoh. "Like when Dad makes me wash all the windows."

Mrs. Hadad sprang into action with steaming platters of spicy fish, chicken soup with meatballs, brisket, a lamb stew, rice, cooked vegetables, and a fresh salad. Not an inch of room on the table for another dish. The service converted to a dinner party within seconds. Together, they filled plates, and shared stories.

When the dining period waned, Rafi looked around the table and tapped his wine glass. "*Zazim Tzafun*?"

The children sat up straight.

Rafi said, "*Yalla!*"

All the kids darted in the direction where Mrs. Hadad had gone with the matzoh. Chase whispered to Rafi, "Like an Easter egg hunt."

Asher yelled with delight as he formally presented the wrapped matzoh to Rafi, who rewarded him with a bag of candy. Once again, each of them took their seats, and Rafi picked up the matzoh, broke off a little bit, and passed the remainder to his left. They each took a small piece.

Asher looked at Chase. "Afikomen. The symbolic memorial of the Passover lamb."

Rafi pointed to a cup of wine in table's center. "For the prophet Elijah." He nodded to Asher who ran to the front door and swung it open.

Rafi closed the meal with Barech Grace and Hebrew songs. With wine glasses in the air, they all stood. "Next year in Jerusalem!"

They broke into a party with games and conversations in every corner of the home. Even the family poodle wore a yarmulke as he picked up scraps under the table.

Rafi led Chase to the back porch where he sat at an onyx table. "Does celebrating Passover cause any conflict with your religious beliefs?"

"Not at all. As a Christian, I can worship arm in arm with my Jewish brothers and sisters in a synagogue. We worship the same amazing God."

Rafi looked at him curiously. "But you don't celebrate Passover."

"True, we focus our celebration on another major event on Passover—April 3 in the year AD 33 when the Romans killed a certain man on a cross."

Rafi nodded.

"At twilight, as the priests slaughtered Passover lambs at the Temple ..."

Rafi looked up. "A coincidence."

Chase shrugged, "An obvious parallel between the Passover and Jesus's sacrifice for sins. Once and for all."

Rafi turned toward him. "Tomorrow, you are getting on a plane."

"Not without Abby."

"As soon as you turn your phone on, they will find you. You can't hide. They'll track you on traffic cameras with facial recognition."

Chase returned to the railing. "They want me dead. Abby is still alive."

"You will buy yourself a plane ticket with my card. Reimburse me when you get home. You need to be out of the country before they can find you."

"I've been resourceful so far. Let me find them."

Rafi folded his arms. "How can you hide without any money in a culture you don't know and find girls who have been taken by organized criminals?" The grandfather clock in the living room announced the ninth hour. "Let me show you to our guest room. In my father's house, there are many rooms. If it weren't so, I would have told you."

Chase recognized the quote, but coming from a Jew? He kept his thoughts to himself. "Very gracious of you."

Rafi showed him a small bathroom, then pointed to an empty room across the hall. "Our bomb shelter. Israeli law requires one in every house built after 1991. We could have gotten an exception, but my mother had it built just to be safe."

Rafi led him to the spare bedroom with an adjoining bathroom. "Bathroom light will be on all night." He pointed at Chase's pocket. "Leave your phone off."

"I wouldn't think of turning it on. Not safe."

Rafi shook his head. "We'll talk in the morning."

CHAPTER FORTY-THREE

Abby held the hand sanitizer gently between her fingers. Gave it a little squeeze. With the cap closed, it bulged out on both ends, a catalyst waiting for the right time. She ran a finger along her cardigan, sacrificed for their rescue, with an ear tuned to any distant sounds. Ready for their captor to return, she focused on the door. She silently vowed never again to miss an opportunity. Hour after hour, she listened for a vehicle, footsteps, or any movement at all as she remained near the door, ready for action.

Their captor's first visit replayed in her mind—creak of ancient hinges, red dot on his black shirt, his swift motion, buckets.

Will he return with more bread and water? Will the laser work? What will happen to us if …

She refocused, listening for sounds in the distance. While attending college, she'd joined a Christian group dedicated to memorizing long stretches of the Bible. Accustomed to committing hordes of material to memory in her studies, her intellectual muscle operated in spades. Abby rehearsed those lines like an actor preparing for a lead role. By the time she graduated, she had grafted entire books of the Bible into her heart.

Abby closed her eyes.

"And we know that for those who love God all things work together for good, for those who are called according to his purpose."

Oh, the irony.

How could any of this be used for good?

Abby forced herself to continue. Another verse took center stage as she mouthed the words in silence. Then another. Some passages came easily, rolling from her memory like ordering a popular dish at her favorite restaurant. Others seemed hidden through a cruel filter of time.

When the flow of words halted, she dropped her head between her knees concluding a prayer.

"God help." This time, her words only reverberated against the stone walls.

Tiffany said, "You've been praying for a long time."

Abby opened her eyes. Tiffany's glare penetrated her.

"I'm not saying prayer is wrong. You get in life what you have the courage to ask for."

"Actually, I wasn't praying."

"What have you been doing all this time? Were you having some sort of mouth spasm or something?"

"Reciting Scripture."

"How is reciting an old document going to help?"

Abby thought for a minute. "We're not alone. Plenty of people in the Bible were wrongfully imprisoned. The authorities threw Joel in prison even though he had done nothing wrong. They tossed Jeremiah in a cistern where he sank into mud. Even Jesus and some of his disciples were locked up."

"So, you recalled stories of miraculous rescues?"

"There are some of those, but I didn't really focus on those."

"What then?"

Abby took a risk, "Do you know the story of what happened the night Jesus was arrested?"

"They nailed him to a cross."

"The following day, yes. But first, they threw him in a prison cell in the basement at the high priest's house." She looked around the room, "A place a lot like this."

"What's your point?"

"Jesus's emotions reached a dark place. He likely recalled the words of Psalm 88:

'I am a man who has no strength, like one set loose among the dead, like the slain that lie in the grave, like those whom you remember no more, for they are cut off from your hand. You have put me in the depths of the pit.'"

"That gives you comfort?"

A tear ran down Abby's cheek. "Tiffany, I don't want to be here. I want to go home. But when I take a step back and remember how Jesus suffered because he loves me, my perspective changes."

Tiffany gave the bread to Abby.

Abby held it. "Do you pray?"

"Of course," she said. "Each mind conceives god in their own way. There may be as many variations of the god figure as there are people in the world."

"Do you mind if I pray for us?"

"Go ahead."

Abby closed her eyes. She asked God for divine protection. To be released. With her heart on her sleeve, she prayed for the police to find clues to their location. To come open the door. Or for their escape. Continuing in a spirit of prayer, she poured out her heart then concluded, "Amen."

When she opened her eyes, she saw Tiffany standing ramrod straight with her palms together at her chest in a namaste pose.

Abby refocused on the door.

Bring it on.

CHAPTER FORTY-FOUR

They want me dead.

Chase stared at the dark oak beams lining the guest room's ceiling. The generalized rumble of family members settled as they retired for the evening. Chase lay on the bed as he replayed Rafi's command to be on the next plane.

The previous evening, Chase's digital footsteps had gone into the heart of Jerusalem, where his phone became a ghost. Someone who wanted him dead would have to follow him. They would never imagine he would be in the home of an Israeli detective. Nobody could find him. But what about the coming days? How could he remain in Israel looking for Abby and stay safe?

I'm right.

He jumped up and paced the small room.

What am I right about?

He dumped paperwork from his backpack onto the floor. His phone fell on the stack of pages, a lifeless paperweight. He focused on the information in the giant pile of paperwork. Though his sporadic style contrasted to Billy's precision, it worked to get his mind churning. He shoved aside the pages about Boaz. Chase needed information about the man who wanted him dead. What did he know about him? Ben Yehuda. LabStrength. A connection with this goat-man and Pantheon. He recalled everything he could. Heavy on information. Light on conclusions.

Hours went by slowly.

If I go home without finding them, how could I live with myself? Especially when I'm right.

Chase retrieved a prepaid debit card from his wallet. An image of an elderly couple graced the front of the card. His grandparents had given it to him when he graduated from college. Though he had permission to use it however he wanted, Chase cherished it, vowing to use it only in an emergency.

He lay back on the bed, his thoughts drifting to the drone. Miles away, it circled in the skies above Ein Gedi, an inconspicuous area near the Dead Sea, gathering no new information, just surviving the night.

What new information could it uncover? Would it do any good to send it back to Beersheba? What about Caesarea Philippi?

Chase laid out the crisp freshly printed pages on the floor. Though new to geological research before now, he became familiar with the terms, sites, and results of their extensive testing. The springs fascinated him. Each location grew on him like a friend he longed to visit.

On the paper map, he found Caesarea Philippi in the northeastern corner of the country. He had never heard of this small town in the hills about two and a half hours away. He shuffled through the pages. Found nothing. Chase longed for unlimited access to information he had become accustomed to. He jotted down the city on a list of potential areas he needed to learn more about. He couldn't rest. Silently he cursed the stagnant Shabbat. He needed the internet.

How long has it been?

He opened the window. He extended his arm with his palm facing the sunrise, one finger's width every fifteen minutes, around 6:45.

He stuffed the papers into his backpack. Descended into the living room. Mrs. Hadad busied herself at the stove. "Good morning, darling. How did you sleep?"

"Very well," he lied.

She thrust an empty coffee cup into his hands. "Cream and sugar?"

"Thank you."

Though the kitchen busyness didn't rival the previous evening, early risers proved to be just as extroverted over coffee as they had been over wine and matzoh. They encouraged him to eat. Before long, he had a plate covered with eggs and fresh fruit. He listened to the constant flow of words from every side.

How much caffeine had they had?

By the time his plate was half empty, he had heard several versions of the Hadad clan history. Rafi entered the kitchen wearing khakis and a black T-shirt. Grabbing a cup of coffee, he motioned to Chase. "Let's have breakfast on the porch."

Chase excused himself, scooped up his plate, and followed Rafi. "What do you know about Caesarea Philippi?"

"I'll get you to the airport this morning. We can check flight availability when we get there. They have several departures which can get you to safety."

"I need to stay."

"And do what?"

"They're alive. I can help."

"How can you survive?" Rafi rubbed his index finger and thumb together in the classic sign for money. "You can't go to an ATM. They'll find you in an instant. How much money do you have on hand?"

Chase pulled out his prepaid debit card. "This has a thousand dollars on it. Can't be traced to me."

Rafi shook his head. "What would you do?"

"I'll search from Dan to Beersheba until I find them. Starting with Caesarea Philippi. LabStrength is focusing there."

"Don't be ridiculous. You stick out like an American tourist."

"I'll blend in like an American tourist here for Easter."

Rafi walked to the railing. The sun's rays reflected off the beautiful historic city.

Chase said, "Abby and Tiffany are alive."

"I agree."

"I'm not going home without Abby."

"You've been resourceful, but I just don't know how you can help while staying safe. How will you get around?"

"I'll rent a car, get out of Jerusalem. Stay away from Beersheba. Those are the only places they know I've been." He joined Rafi at the railing. "I'll stay at a hostel in a small town."

Rafi leaned against the railing.

"I need to find out what LabStrength is doing in Caesarea Philippi. I'll follow breadcrumbs from there."

"Breadcrumbs?"

"You know, like in the children's story Hansel and Gretel ..." Chase trailed off seeing Rafi's blank stare. "Never mind. I'll follow one clue to the next. I'm going to do this."

Rafi crossed his arms.

"I'm not getting on a plane."

"My chief tied my hands," Rafi said. "I'm limited on what I can do in this case. Maybe with your help and a little more information from my cryptic friend, we can find them."

Chase hugged Rafi. "Thank you so much."

"Don't touch your cell phone. Stay away from anything with a camera, traffic lights, ATMs, security gates."

"Okay." Chase looked at the city's light traffic. "How can I get an Uber without my cell phone?"

"There are no Ubers in Israel." Rafi took a long sip of coffee as he looked Chase in the eye. "Take my father's car."

"*What*?" The unexpected generosity took Chase by surprise.

"Follow me." Rafi led him down a set of stairs. "My father recently passed away. We plan to sell his car but haven't gotten around to it yet."

"Oh my. I'm so sorry for your loss."

Rafi waved him off and continued to a carport where a pristine silver Audi Q5 waited. "It's five years old with a bunch of miles. This should get you around just fine."

"No. I can't take your family vehicle."

"Take it."

"No. I can't take your—"

"Not an option. You're taking the car since you won't get on a plane."

Chase caught the key Rafi grabbed from a hook by the door. "Thank you."

"You probably threw out my card after you put my number in your phone." Rafi gave him another business card. "Stop at an electronics store. Purchase a burner phone. I'll have my phone on if you need to reach me."

Chase raised his eyebrows, "Even on Shabbat?"

"If your donkey falls into a pit on Shabbat, do you not go into the pit with him and get him out?"

"I can't believe you're doing this."

"If you have concrete evidence I can use legally, I'll be there with plenty of reinforcements."

"I'll do everything I can."

"Find them."

Chase gave Rafi a brotherly hug, slipped behind the wheel, and pressed the "Start" button. The powerful engine purred.

CHAPTER FORTY-FIVE

Manny rubbed the worn armrest on his favorite recliner. He replayed the scenario in his mind a dozen times. Taking solace in how his family could sleep in after the traditional family Seder and the late night, he settled into reading the news on his tablet.

Yosef appeared in the kitchen. "Shalom."

Manny held his index finger over his lips. He didn't want to wake the rest of the family. He quietly retrieved two travel mugs from the top cupboard, filled them with a fresh brew, handed one to Yosef.

He whispered. "Let's take a walk."

Manny cringed at the creaking ancient doorway. Made a mental note to oil the hinges when he returned home. Yosef latched the iron gate behind them as they headed out for a stroll down HaMagid Street through the German Colony. Built for horse-drawn wagons, the narrow stone-walled street struggled to accommodate small cars now cruising the passageways. At the street's end, they turned right onto a road equipped with the modern luxury of a sidewalk.

Yosef said, "Do you want to head over to the Old City?"

"Not today. Let's just enjoy a relaxing walk around our neighborhood."

"I always enjoy Emek Refaim Street."

Manny took a sip of his coffee. "Let's not sit down today. In a city with a million people, it still operates like a small town. Everyone knows everyone's business."

Yosef ducked below an overhanging olive branch. "What was the first thing you did for Pantheon?"

Pleased with Yosef diving right into the topic, Manny answered, "Years ago, I received an invitation from a friend to a social event. Being a guy who towers over the room, I couldn't hide. The director shared her concern of Pantheon getting too much attention in our local press. News about a pagan god who lives in a mountain, travels by rivers, and demands blood is never good for a reputation."

"I remember."

"Sounded like nonsense to me." Manny sighed. "She just asked me to normalize their image."

"She gave an engineer a marketing job?"

"She gave a businessman a business job. I found a cheap, easy way to choose the logo for a high school."

"I remember being surprised you did marketing for the school. I didn't know it had anything to do with Pantheon."

Manny nodded. "We had plenty of blowback on year one. When a local hair salon ran with their version of the image, it was smooth sailing from there."

"I remember Albi Kabab, the plumber, and others. How did you get all the other businesses to adopt the goat-man into their logo?"

Manny smiled. "People either loved it or hated it, but they couldn't ignore it. A great way for them to get attention."

Yosef asked, "Did it help your business?"

"Word spread when I helped found the school. I gained a reputation as a philanthropist."

"Excellent."

"My mission succeeded. The image is commonplace, the director feels we can put it on anything now. Nobody cares."

Yosef turned left. They strolled between stone apartment buildings. "What else have you done for the director?"

"Not much."

"Really?"

"When she found out my research included various geologically active sites, she asked me to schedule time at Caesarea Philippi as well."

"What for?"

"I never asked. I don't know the secret handshake or anything. Sure, I know they exist, but I'm there for business contacts, not superstitions."

"Until now."

Manny hesitated. "Things have changed."

In the distance, a few people walked by an overgrown Judas Tree with its purple blossoms crowding over the sidewalk. Yosef dropped his voice, "Tomorrow, we will step up big time."

He looked at his son with concern. "Start from the beginning. What have you done?"

"As I said before, I've been meeting with Mr. Cohen for a while. A few months ago, he suggested I might benefit from stepping up in the same way he did."

"Why didn't you ask me?"

"I did. Over the past couple of years, I've asked a bunch of times. You always refer to it as superstition, so, I let it go."

"Why didn't he run it past me?

"He did. Don't you remember?"

Manny recalled a casual conversation with Mr. Cohen. "He brought up the idea of me participating, but I poked fun at him."

"He took it as a no."

"So, you pursued it with Mr. Cohen?"

"He set up a lunch meeting. Just him, the director, and myself. I told her about my business struggles and how I admired Mr. Cohen's success."

"How did it go?"

Yosef stopped. "She's magnetic. Listening to her was inspiring."

Manny faced him. "What did she say?"

"She talked for a long time about the power resting in Pantheon. Beyond the surface, deep within the earth. When we're centered with the power within, strength flows through us."

"Did she talk about a magic power?"

"Not at all. She explained spirituality by saying if you are on a ship going nowhere, eventually you must jump out of it into nothingness. Only an individual can jump, not a group. Groups are nothing but people huddled together because of fear of nothingness."

"Profound. What does it mean?"

"The energy body acts as a bridge connecting our physical and spiritual bodies. For us to influence the transformation of body and mind, we must transform the energy flow through sacrifice."

"How does this help us?"

"Sounds mysterious. If you want to know more, I journaled my thoughts. Took notes on all the meetings."

Manny motioned for them to keep walking. "I didn't know you still journaled."

Yosef nodded. "Helps me process."

"What's the bottom line?"

"Power will be released in mysterious ways after your sacrifice is complete."

They turned a corner onto Emek Refaim Street where perfectly groomed trees lined the cosmopolitan business region. proceeding left past a closed newsstand, they continued through the comfortable neighborhood.

"How many times have you met with her?"

"We've been together quite a bit recently."

They continued walking. Manny didn't know what to say next. His son had advanced far ahead of him.

Yosef motioned to a table for two at Burger's Bar. "I know the owners of this place. Closed for Shabbat. I'm sure they wouldn't mind if we took a seat for a minute so I can show you something."

Manny looked around. He supposed it wouldn't hurt to sit at the sidewalk table. He asked, "Have you already been through some type of ceremony?"

"There's something she did to prepare me. Let me do for you what she did for me."

"Okay."

"Think of where you are in life. What lies next. There are multiple paths ahead. What do you want?"

"You know the answer."

He drained his coffee. "Humor me."

Manny looked into the distance. "The final piece of research will show my pumps work. The whole package will be sold together."

"Great. With your success, what happens next?"

"Geothermal energy powers irrigation in desert lands. LabStrength will be at the center of all of it."

"What else?"

"I'll be able to make payroll."

"And how does it make you feel?"

"Amazing."

"Now think long term. Imagine radical success a year from now. Paint a picture for me."

"Everything changes." Manny could feel his mood shift. "I've paid off a bundle of loans, Helped Rebekah start her business." The tension in his shoulders lifted. He smiled for the first time in a long time.

"Describe the feeling you have right now."

"Peace."

"Anything else?"

"I can't tell you the satisfaction I'll have when it comes to fruition."

"You can't always control your circumstances, but you can control your response to them. When you obtain mastery over your feelings, your actions arise from a positive place within, your potential is unlimited."

Manny's squinted at his son. "Is this the director talking or you?"

"Just hold onto this feeling."

"Okay."

"What would you do to be able to have such success? To wrap your arms around the things you just mentioned?"

"At this point, I'd do anything."

"Okay, now let's look at the other side. How many people would be hurt if you do nothing?"

His shoulders grew heavy once again. "My staff would lose their livelihood. Not just them, but each one has a family depending on them."

"Your family depends on you."

"This would be devastating on a lot of fronts."

"Collateral damage would be extensive."

Manny turned toward Yosef. "I can't let that happen."

Yosef's voice remained firm but soothing. "On the other hand, if you're successful, how many families would benefit?"

"If we can change the face of agriculture in the world ... millions."

Yosef planted his hands on the table. "So, if you do nothing, many will be hurt. If you have great success, millions will benefit. Let me ask you this, is it worth a small amount of collateral damage to achieve benefit for millions?"

"Absolutely."

"Go back to the feeling of your success. Capture it." Yosef pulled out a small notepad from his pocket pen. "Write it down."

Manny gave an inquisitive look.

"I'll wait." He set a red candle on the table. Held a lighter to the wick.

Manny wrote:

Research complete. Patent. Sales. Desert irrigation. Millions benefit.

Yosef nodded. "Good. Those are facts, accomplishments. Now move on to how it makes you feel."

Manny dropped his pen. "I don't understand."

"You were just there. Go ahead. Write down your inmost feelings then summarize all of them in one word."

Manny closed his eyes, set his hands on his lap. With a quivering chin and tears running down his cheeks, he picked up the pen.

Family.

Yosef nodded. "Perfect."

Manny tapped the paper. Smiled at his son.

Yosef pointed at the first line, "These things need to happen." He moved to the next line. "For this." He took the paper, folded it three times. "You've written your heart's desire. There's power on this page."

Yosef reached into his pocket and produced a golden octagonal locket charm hanging from a sturdy gold chain. One side held an embossed image of the goat-man, like a perfectly preserved ancient coin. Not the cute smiling face with a cigar and fedora they had plastered all over Beersheba. Instead, it held incredible detail of a fierce man with a powerful body, horns, and goat-like legs. Manny couldn't look away.

"May I?"

Yosef nodded.

Manny reached for the ancient artifact. Heavy for its size. Sturdy construction. Turning it over, he saw words he didn't recognize. He felt a little ledge on one side and hinges on the other. Pried the two pieces open with his fingernail.

"How old is this?"

"Place the paper inside."

He took the folded page carefully set it within the charm's confines. Closed it.

Yosef blew out the candle. Poured molten wax along the edge. He placed the pendant in Manny's open hand. Covered his hand with his own.

"Inside, your dream is alive and well."

Manny no longer paid any attention to the pedestrians passing by. Yosef took the chain. Slipped it over his father's head until it rested at his chest. He reached into his shirt and brought out a similar amulet, also sealed with wax. The sun reflected off the gold with a blinding effect.

"You've also done this?"

"A symbol of my commitment to Pantheon."

"What did you write in yours?"

"My heart's desire."

Manny gripped his pendant in his hands. Warm. Too much heat to be just from the molten wax.

Is it giving off heat?

"What's next?"

"I don't know all the details. Mr. Cohen's testimony and Marna's experiences speak for themselves. When we participate in the sacrifice tomorrow, something takes place at a deep level."

Yosef's sheer determination impressed Manny. "Right."

"A powerful spiritual event." He held the pendant between his fingers. "The desire of our heart comes true."

CHAPTER FORTY-SIX

CAESAREA PHILIPPI

"Stay hidden. You're not safe."

Chase barely realized he had said the words out loud. He glanced at the new flip phone and his cell, both sitting on the passenger seat. A sign announced Caesarea Philippi. He made the turn.

His drive had begun with a tired brown landscape with occasional lifeless underbrush, reminiscent of the Arizona wilderness without cactus. As he neared his destination, naturally growing Ficus and olive trees in well-groomed orchards flourished with aggressive irrigation. He considered LabStrength schedule for the night of the abduction.

Will I be able to get close enough to see anything? Would the tourist area be shut down for research under the ruse of maintenance?

He passed buses and countless vans exiting the tourist site. Open to the public. He entered the tourist area parking lot. Settled for the only available parking site quite a distance from the gate. He dug through his paperwork to find LabStrength's research schedule. Double-checked the dates. They were indeed scheduled to be here, but what about the trucks, pipes, and hoses?

Are they doing research? What am I missing?

He walked through the parking lot to a path leading to a gate. Lush greenery surrounded the trail like a tropical paradise. Chase scanned for cameras, finding none until he reached the gate. With his back to the camera, he stepped up to the counter, held up one finger, and slid the clerk a 50 shekel bill. She gave him a brochure, ticket, and a receipt.

"Are you from Iowa?" The question came from a group of young adults wearing Arkansas Razorback T-shirts and hats.

He glanced down at his shirt. "Yeah."

He motioned to the scenery. "It's beautiful here, isn't it?"

"Yes. Yes, it is."

Another young man in the group looked at him inquisitively. "Where's the rest of your group?"

"I'm alone."

"You're touring Israel by yourself?"

"It's a long story."

"Are you familiar with this place?"

Chase shook his head.

"Are you doing a self-guided tour?"

He shrugged.

The young man said, "Join us."

"I can't intrude on your group."

"No trouble. Especially for a fellow Midwesterner." He extended his hand. "I'm Arthur."

Chase shook it then stepped back. "I shouldn't intrude."

"We're just walking along and listening to our guide" He pointed to a tall, slender blonde woman. "Olga knows everything about the history of Israel. You'll love her."

A microphone curled around Olga's neck and rested in front of her mouth. She whispered, but Chase couldn't hear anything.

"Here, take one of my earbuds." He offered Chase a tiny speaker on a plastic-covered wire. "Without this, you'll never really understand the history of this place."

Chase inserted the earbud and listened to Olga's lecture. "People read the Bible completely differently after they experience this place. Listen carefully, it might change your life."

Chase walked alongside Arthur as the group moved forward.

Olga continued, "In the first century, Caesarea Philippi was a busy city. Over here, you can see a path heading up the hill and a sheer cliff next to it. Where you are standing right now may have been the busiest part of town. This small creek provided their water supply, flowing directly out of a large cave into the Jordan River." They passed by a pool where the water exited through a gentle waterfall through the ancient ruins of a Roman city.

Arthur whispered to Chase, "Seems like this would be a great place to live."

Olga continued, "Roman influence dominated this town. Well renowned for its pagan activities."

Arthur raised his eyebrows. "Maybe not."

As they walked along the paved sidewalk, Olga explained, "This is a city Jews would never visit. They were commanded to keep themselves separate from the world of idol worshipers. Caesarea Philippi embodied the definition of evil. They would never come here."

They stopped at the cliff base with a large cave. Up a path, several doorways had been carved into the hillside.

Olga said, "Go ahead, explore the area. You can take your headphones off. I'll restart in ten minutes."

Arthur and his friends walked up a series of hand-carved steps to the cave. He looked up. "What do you think? Seventy-five feet high?"

"At least."

Sectioned off by a guard rail with a light chain, the chain was off limits. Chase peered inside, not able to see well, but he and Arthur hopped over the chain with ease. Looking behind them, they saw nobody seemed to take notice. Easily ten degrees cooler inside the forbidden cave. They followed stream deep within it. As his eyes adjusted to the dim light, he crouched down by the spring origin and saw crystal-clear water bubbling up between rocks.

Chase felt darkness.

It's my fault. I shouldn't have left her. I can't do anything right.

He wandered around the darkness wondering if Billy had been right.

Maybe. Probably. Certainly.

He sat on a rock next to the spring. Took a deep breath. Somehow the air felt lukewarm, humid. The stone he sat on seemed to have warmth in contrast to the coolness of the cave.

What am I doing? She's already dead.

How could he be so brazen and arrogant to think he could make a difference? He didn't know what to do. In a foreign country with customs which he didn't know or understand.

He wanted to get up and head back out but couldn't move. Somehow, he knew they would never find Abby.

Nothing he did would matter.

Hopeless.

No reason to take his next breath.

He felt a tap on his shoulder. Arthur said, "Come on. Let's head back."

Chase forced one foot in front of the other. After a dozen steps, it felt cool once again, then he saw the entrance. Light brought renewed life. As he made his way back out onto the path, sunlight bathed his face with warmth. He could breathe again.

What was I thinking? If she was dead, they wouldn't have given the assassination order. She's alive. I need to find her.

The group sat down on a circle of benches in full view of the cave Chase had just exited. Arthur handed him an earbud. Olga began, "In Matthew 16, we see the discussion they had right here in front of this cave." She opened her Bible. "Now when Jesus came into the district of Caesarea Philippi, he asked his disciples, 'Who do people say the Son of Man is?' And they said, 'Some say John the Baptist, others say Elijah, and others say Jeremiah or one of the other prophets.' He said to them, 'But who do you say that I am?' Simon Peter replied, 'You are the Christ, the Son of the living God.' And Jesus answered him, 'Blessed are you, Simon Bar-Jonah! For flesh and blood has not revealed this to you, but my father who is in heaven. And I tell you, you are Peter and on this rock, I will build my church, and the gates of hell will not prevail against it.'"

Olga pointed at the cave. "What's over there?"

A girl held her hand up. "The sign calls it 'The Gates of Hell.'"

"Right. Romans built an ancient pagan temple inside this large cave. They called it the Gates of Hell. They worshipped the god Pan right here."

The Gates of Hell is a place?

Olga said, "Good Jews never visited this place. His disciples must have been shocked when he brought them here. Pan is a god who lived deep in the earth. Traveled along rivers. They considered this place to be special because a river flows out of a cave. Therefore, they built the temple here."

Arthur said, "Sounds weird."

Olga replied. "Just wait till you find out what they did. High priests made sacrifices to Pan every spring. They threw a virgin from the cliff. Watched as she landed. If her blood flowed into the stream, they took it as a sign the sacrifice would be accepted. They would have a good year. If her blood flowed away, Pan had rejected their sacrifice."

Chase gripped the bench.

Could the ancient cult still be active? They took Abby just so they could ...

Arthur nudged him. "Are you okay?"

Chase stood up. The earbud pulled away along with Olga's continued historical narrative. He walked toward the gate. Passed through a gift shop. He couldn't imagine purchasing anything to remind him of this place. Back at the parking lot, he leaned against the car's hood.

I need more information. Images from the air.

The drone circled a hundred miles south. To program it to come, he would have to turn on his phone.

I'm not giving up my position. Nobody who wants to find me would recognize this vehicle. I'm safe for now.

He slid behind the wheel. With at least a two-hour drive from anyone who wanted him dead, he tapped the screen at a record pace. He programmed the drone to fly to Caesarea Philippi, circle overhead, and stream video to his phone. Starting the melodious engine, he headed back the way he came.

He turned his phone all the way off again. Hopefully still safe.

CHAPTER FORTY-SEVEN

Jerusalem. A city replete with cameras and at least one person known to be hostile to him.

Not acceptable.

Where can I go?

Alone with his thoughts, Chase turned south on Highway 90. The temperature rose steadily as elevation decreased. A vast, intimidating desert replaced the sparse vegetation. Periodically, large green highway signs announced directions to upcoming cities in Hebrew, Arabic, and English. He pressed a couple of buttons on the vehicle's GPS.

The highway wound for miles through the arid region until he saw a large body of water.

Where am I? The Dead Sea?

He pressed on the map and saw water labeled, "The Sea of Galilee."

The sun was directly overhead in a cloudless sky, a perfect seventy degrees, and a breathtaking view of the lake. Perfect day except no Abby at his side. Not a single vessel stirred the water. Chase imagined what a lake of similar size in the United States would look like on a Saturday after Good Friday. Open-bow boats would be pulling tubes and skiers, large white yachts would be tied up next to one another playing music. But here, on this beautiful freshwater lake, on Passover's Sabbath of, silence reigned.

He recalled a handful of stories when Jesus taught in the city.

Abby would love to be here.

She had looked forward to this trip for months. Her laser seemed to be an afterthought compared to the time she would spend in the Holy Land. Galilee was her top destination—where Jesus had walked, taught, and healed people.

Chase couldn't imagine heading home with her being held captive somewhere nearby. Possibly a stone's throw away. He had to find her.

The town of Tiberias caught his attention. He had heard of it—should be large enough to have a place for him to stay. Far enough from Jerusalem to be safe. His thoughts returned to Yosef.

If only I could spend a little time inside his head. Or inside his home.

He wiped the moisture from his eyes. Dialed Rafi.

He answered on the first ring, "Shalom."

"Rafi, I need to know where Yosef is."

"Probably with his family continuing the celebration."

"Can you check, please?"

"Sure." Quick fingers sounded over a keyboard. "Where are you?"

"I'm coming up on the city of Tiberias."

"Perfect."

"What? Why?"

"I hoped you'd go there. Easily the best place for you to be, far from anyone looking for you. There's a hostel where you can stay. I'll book a reservation in your name.

Text you the address. Just go to the desk. They should be able to help you."

"Thank you."

"What did you see in Caesarea Philippi?"

Shivers went down his spine. "That's a spooky place with a dark history."

"Any connections with the missing girls?"

"I don't know. Probably not. I never want to go back there again."

"He's with his family."

"What?"

"Yosef. I had my buddy check just now. Yosef is with his family in the German Colony in Southern Jerusalem."

"Good."

"Don't assume you're safe. He may have guys working for him who can be upon you in a few minutes if you expose yourself."

"Right."

"What are you going to do now?"

"I'll head to the hostel, then keep digging."

"Keep your head down."

"I will."

Chase ended the call. When Rafi's text came, he entered the address into the car's GPS and followed the blue line to Tiberias. Leaving Highway 90, a quick left and then right brought him to a small strip mall which contained the hostel. Fortunately, coffee shops were prevalent in the surrounding area.

The hostel's first floor boasted a glass edifice with support columns, the top two floors a simple whitewashed cinderblock.

With youthful vigor, Abby had arranged the trip on a shoestring budget. Comfortable with hostels, they enjoyed bare-bones places. Of course, they rarely had security cameras. With nobody around, Chase looked around. On the counter, he found a small key safe labeled with his name on a post-it note.

He flipped open the safe's plastic cover. Noticed a keypad. He needed to enter a code.

What would Rafi use?

He found the phone number for the flip phone. Entered it. The old-fashioned mechanical lock clicked.

No electricity on Shabbat.

The safe sprung open. Inside, a key sat on top of a simple hand-written receipt for room three. With his luggage in tow, he quickly found the minimalistic room with three black metal bunk beds with moderately clean mattresses.

He spread out his thin sleeping bag.

Yosef wants me dead.

He recalled seeing him the previous day.

Something isn't right.

He zipped up the suitcase. Headed back to his car and entered Yosef's address into the GPS.

CHAPTER FORTY-EIGHT

Chase drove down Yohanan ben Horkansos Street. In this section of town, the Audi stood head and shoulders above anything else. On his left, electrical lines crept across the outside of a cinderblock, three-story apartment building. On his right, small sedans sat in front of a row of tiny homes. The protective wall, outer court, and entrance to homes were all encompassed within a cozy covered portico.

Chase approached Yosef's door with paperclips in hand. With a few flicks of the wrist, he conquered the lock. His heart pounded as he swung the door open.

Silence.

The house couldn't have been more than six hundred square feet. Primitive art and posters gave the white walls a dorm room feel. He rummaged through the items on the love seat, coffee table, and bookshelf. Kitchen held no surprises. Entering the bedroom, he combed through the dresser.

Nothing interesting.

Chase scanned through Yosef's wife's belongings. Then into the bathroom before returning to the small living room when he saw another closed door.

Probably just their bomb shelter.

He turned the knob. Flicked on the light. Empty except for a small white table covered by a black runner and a dozen half-burnt white votive candles arranged in a semicircle. The clean table held a black notebook. Behind the table, a hand-painted mural of a goat-man covered the wall from floor to ceiling. A fantasy image in a forest with sunrays piercing through the lush overhead foliage illuminating the goat-man's muscular chest. Glistening sweat dripped from his arms. His fur-covered legs supported him in regal fashion. His face held a hardened expression of determination. Long spiraled horns curled around the sides of his head. In his right hand, a double-edged sword, a warrior ready for action. Chase stared at the mural. Skillfully drawn artwork stood in strikingly contrast to anything else in the home. He snapped a handful of photos.

He picked up the notebook and thumbed through the pages. Hand-written Hebrew entries organized by date.

Could this be Yosef's journal?

His heart rate increased. A journal could speak volumes. Just needed a translator. With the small leather book in his hand, he raced back to his vehicle.

Chase drove to the east side of town with a keen eye on his rearview mirror, looking for anyone following him. Shielding his face whenever he neared a street busy enough to have a traffic camera, he made multiple erratic turns. Doubled back on his path. Fully convinced nobody had been following him, he pulled over and texted Rafi.

CHASE: Found Yosef's journal, need help translating.

He followed the text with a few photos of the mural and journal.

Within a few minutes, Rafi called. "What were you thinking?"

"What do you mean?"

"You agreed to keep a low profile, stay safe. How could visiting Yosef's house be considered 'laying low?'"

"I stayed away from cameras. Nobody was there."

"You know I can't use anything from his journal. You stole it."

"It's better than not having it. I just need to know what it says."

Rafi hesitated. "Fine. Take a photo of a page or two. I'll look at it."

Chase opened the book, took an image of two random pages in the middle, and sent it to him.

After a moment, Rafi said, "He's talking about a meeting with someone named Mr. Cohen. Yosef had to fire an employee. This guy gave him some coaching on how to do it in a way to maintain staff morale."

"What else?"

"I'm just reading what you sent me."

"Please read the whole thing. There must be more in here."

The line went dead.

Chase immediately called him back. Voicemail. He had no message to leave.

CHAPTER FORTY-NINE

Sunday morning at four o'clock, Chase lay still with his eyes wide open. A full moon shining through the hostel window lit the bedside clock. He ruminated over every image, map, website, and statement they had collected throughout the week.

There's nothing I can do about it right now.

A deep breath, eyes closed, he hoped to escape into peaceful slumber once again. Didn't happen.

What am I missing? How can we find the girls? What else can we do?

Reluctantly, he draped his legs over the edge of the bed and sat up—instinctively reaching for his phone. A dead weight, he left it, and exited the room. With no goal or destination in mind, he walked north along highway 90. Within a few minutes, Tiberias's streetlights faded into the distance, and the full moon brought the only illumination. Cool, dry air and peaceful solitude brought a welcomed change. To his right, the Sea of Galilee reflected moonlight.

After about a half-mile, a turnoff on the left looked attractive. His feet left the pavement and moved briskly along a dirt road as he marched up a hill, away from civilization. The road narrowed then became nothing more than a goat trail with steep switchbacks. The path continued through arduous inclines. Chase's heart rate increased as the altitude rose. With no idea what lay ahead, he continued onward.

Eventually, the trail seemed to lead straight up a cliff. He secured his feet into position on the rocks one step at a time—limestone ledges served as handholds. The moon provided enough light to avoid falling sixty feet into a gorge below. With confidence in his ability and not a fleeting concern for safety, he crested the summit. He estimated he had conquered a thousand vertical feet and made it to the top.

Top of what?

A few paces on the flat terrain revealed a rock with a broad flat surface, making a chair facing east, a perfect view of the Sea of Galilee. Perfect place for a well-deserved rest.

Surely, this far off the beaten path couldn't be a tourist destination.

Abby would love this sunrise. Maybe not getting up so early. Perhaps not the climb, but she would like the view.

What have I missed?

As the morning's first rays began to creep over the horizon, Chase saw the dark, steady rim of the mountainous landscape on the opposite side of the Galilee. Directly East, though still below the horizon and not yet visible, the source of light began to reveal itself. A precursor to the coming brightness, an orange glow appeared. He looked straight up into the sky. Countless dark, shapeless clouds slowly traversed the atmosphere.

His heart rate settled while endorphins released in his climb continued their impact. He considered returning to Tiberias when something stopped him. Morning rays illuminating the eastern horizon grabbed his attention. Light shouted with joy, a forerunner for the coming sun. Like a vast chorus across the horizon, the night transformed into a showcase of colors. A few minutes passed. The yellow orb burst above the hills. A thousand wispy veils of mist formed a divine prism, scattering the sun's white rays into the brightest mixture of colors he had ever witnessed. Pink merged into orange as it spread toward the west, shifting to indigo and deep royal violet. In addition, the flat, calm Galilee waters doubled the beauty with their reflection.

Chase longed to capture the image forever. He regretted having left his phone. Every piece of vegetation sparkled lavender in the glory of the sunrise. Even the lichen, ordinarily invisible on the limestone surface and completely ignored, took on a bright violet illumination.

His mind drifted to the simplicity of the scenery—hillside, rocks, and water under a gorgeous sky. He thought about all the Christian tourist sites in Israel. Every one of them had been commemorated with a church built over the site and looked completely different from how it appeared in Jesus's time. Yet, at this location, nothing had changed in thousands of years. The view Chase beheld could very well have been precisely the same as it had been since Jesus walked on the Sea of Galilee.

There's no way I'm the first to see this.

A voice said, "You're right. You are not."

Chase looked to the left and right. He was alone.

Who said that?

He looked down the mountain. Capernaum's ruins lay a few miles away along the vast sea. Jesus spent extensive amounts of time there, his home base. He preached, healed the sick, and taught. Escaped from there early in the morning to pray. Chase remembered the words of

Mark 1:35, "Very early in the morning, while it was still dark, Jesus got up left the house and went to a solitary place where he prayed."

The voice came again, "You're sitting in my chair."

Chase started to get up. The voice said, "Stay there. Enjoy what I made for you this morning."

He appreciated how the expansive sea repeated the morning sky's vibrant colors. The horizon began to merge into a deep orange.

"I came here early in the morning to pray. My Father and I spent many hours in this very spot."

Chase felt a warmth he had rarely experienced.

"I enjoyed being with him here. Just he and I."

Chase closed his eyes, enjoying Jesus's presence.

"Keep your eyes open. This is yours, a gift for you this morning, but it won't last long."

Chase confirmed nobody else had the privilege of enjoying this view. The sun, clouds, and sea joined together singing of God's glory. The sky molded its appearance from one superb composition into another as the sun rose inch by inch. Eventually, his mind drifted to the girls. His heart pounded.

The voice said, "Journal's last five pages."

While the subject had shifted, the voice hadn't changed. Still him.

Journal?

Chase had tossed the small leatherbound book across the passenger seat after his frustrating conversation with Rafi.

"What will I find?"

Silence.

"What do I do with the information?"

Silence.

Chase raised his voice, "What else?"

Silence.

The painted sky slowly dimmed as remnants of his spectacular experience lingered. As cloud cover burned off, the heavens settled into baby blue around a yellow sun, and the morning glory had ended.

Chase rushed back down the steep path anxious to get back to the journal.

CHAPTER FIFTY

Abby heard a rhythmic rattle like a muffled percussion instrument. Tiny footpads made quick contact with the sandy surface. A lizard ran inside, footsteps louder without the door's muffling effect. He crawled up the wall. Stopped just above Tiffany's head. The drumming ceased, then picked up again as he ventured on. They had a pet, a silent companion to spend time with them before the creature left them just as it entered.

Abby's stomach grumbled. She took a few more handfuls of water trying not to think about how her body would respond to the confinement or lack of sustenance.

Is it time to make another score mark?

A diesel engine rumbled outside.

"Tiffany, get up."

She rubbed gel into the sweater's fringes. The engine noise grew louder. She double-checked the sweater's position. Pressed a finger to her lips. Abby aimed the laser and waited.

Let's do this.

The engine shut off. A door opened then slammed shut. One set of footsteps.

A shadow appeared under the door.

Tiffany whispered, "Do it."

Abby pressed her thumb firmly, aiming at the lower central portion of the alcohol-soaked strips.

A key entered the metal lock.

Blue flames appeared on the fabric.

It's working.

Her thumb continued with steady pressure as she moved the laser to the left side of the sweater. Another section ablaze.

The lock clicked.

She moved the laser to the right. Another flame born. Three sections of fire converged and blossomed into a blue-orange blaze about two feet high.

As the door swung outward, flaming fabric swept up and out of the room. A partial silhouette of a man appeared. Burning material wrapped around his arm. He reflexively jumped back swiping the fabric away. Alcohol gel remained on his skin. Blue flames spread across both forearms.

Tiffany darted across the room. She dove through the doorway, landing with a tuck and roll outside. She broke into a sprint. Abby followed her out the door wide open. Running to freedom. Tiffany had already made it to the base of a small rocky path leading up a hill. The trail zigzagged between boulders the size of picnic tables with switchbacks making the way reasonable for a normal stride. Tiffany ignored the path, jumped on a large rock. Using her forward momentum, she launched over a gap onto the next boulder like a parkour athlete. Landing with perfect balance, she vaulted her way over the complex bundle of obstacles arriving at the truck.

Abby sprinted and watched Tiffany's progress.

Impossible.

Abby followed Tiffany's route to the first boulder. She tumbled against the rock like a crash test dummy. She tried to climb but slipped back to her starting position once again. She settled for the zigzag path Tiffany had ignored.

Behind her, grumbling sounds followed by heavy footsteps inspired her to pick up the pace. At the first switchback, she looked back. The man ran at her while frantically patting his arms.

Tiffany reached the boxy-looking truck. Climbed into the driver's side. The engine rumbled to life. She yelled, "Run, Abby. You can make it!"

Abby's heart pounded. She ran as fast as she could.

Tiffany yelled, "Faster, he's coming."

Keep moving.

She rounded the turn. Her reluctant legs continued one step after the next. Everything seemed to be moving in slow motion like a dream. Tiffany looked back at her from the driver's seat. Only a few feet from the parking area, a strong hand grasped Abby's wrist. In one fluid motion, he twisted it behind her back. She bent forward wincing in pain, hair draped over her face. She managed to make eye contact with Tiffany. "Go!"

Tires spun. Tiffany lumbered down the desert road.

The tension on Abby's arm eased, but she remained pinned to the ground with her hands painfully tugged behind her back. The man tied a pair of zip ties around her wrists as her face rubbed across the sand. He stood her up, spun her around. Desert all around her. No signs of civilization anywhere. He pushed her down the path toward a heavy metal door where she stopped.

A cave?

Pressure on her back forced her inside. She tripped. Landed on the dirt floor where she skidded to an inglorious stop.

The steel door slammed shut like a stone rolling across a grave.

CHAPTER FIFTY-ONE

JERUSALEM

"What happened to the Christian boy? I haven't seen him since yesterday."

Rafi cringed. *I can't tell mom about Abby and Tiffany.* "He left."

"You let him go? You didn't show him around Jerusalem?"

"He's a grown man, mother."

"An American in Jerusalem with nobody to help him? How could you be so inhospitable? Where are your manners?"

"I gave him the keys to Dad's car."

"Your father's Audi? You let a young boy drive around in his high-powered machine? He'll get a speeding ticket for sure."

"Seemed like the right thing to do. He'll return it soon."

She pinched him on the cheek. "You're a good boy. You make me proud."

"Of course."

She grabbed another platter, continuing the never-ending process of food preparation. "Today is Easter, you know. Those Christians love to talk about Jesus rising from the dead. Thousands of them carry crosses down the

Via Dolorosa. They go to the Garden Tomb. Make sure he sees those particular sites. He will love it."

Rafi shrugged. He knew the Garden Tomb well from a homicide case he had worked on years earlier. They had tracked a suspect all around the Old City, then he disappeared. They couldn't find him for hours, so the police department put out an announcement with his photo. Numerous security teams entered the image onto their facial recognition systems. Then a guard at the Garden Tomb called. He bought a ticket and disappeared into the crowd. A single exit through a gift shop was under constant video surveillance. Rafi found him hiding inside the open tomb.

If Chase turned on his phone at the Garden Tomb, he could be bait. We could catch Yosef, however I'd need legal standing to look into him.

He kissed his mother on the cheek before slipped to his room with his laptop. Reviewing Garden Tomb's blueprints, he finalized his plan and dialed Chase.

"Hello?"

"Chase, listen. I have a plan to catch Yosef."

"Rafi, I need to tell you what I learned this morning. Our answer is in the journal."

"Chase, stop talking. Listen to me."

"I'm sorry. Go ahead."

"Come to the Garden Tomb right away. Can you be there in half an hour?"

"Sure, why? What's going on?"

"Just be there on time."

He hung up then punched in another number.

AVI: I need Yosef's location. ASAP

Rafi pulled up the Garden Tomb's blueprints and imagined how they would conduct a service in such a tight location. The tomb would be front and center. They would set up a pulpit with a small sound system, possibly two hundred people in attendance. He picked a spot where he could sit behind Chase with a full view of the crowd and his back to the wall.

When Chase turns his phone on, will Yosef come inside? Will he wait in the parking lot with plans to assault him later? Would he hire someone else to do it?

Usually, an operation like this would require at least five officers and hours of planning. Rafi had written up dozens of similar proposals then brainstormed a dozen ways they could go south. Together his team made plenty of changes before he submitted a plan to Chief Valsburg. This time, if he requested officer support for a sting operation for a guy he had no legal right to arrest, on a case she told him to shelve, it wouldn't go well. He was on his own—with the help of an impetuous distractable tourist.

Using a police officer's privilege, he bypassed the online ticket office, and acquired two tickets to the sold-out event.

Rafi's phone vibrated.

AVI: German colony since yesterday afternoon.

Let's set a trap.

CHAPTER FIFTY-TWO

JERUSALEM

Rafi zipped through the busy Jerusalem roads like a career cab driver. Pulling into the Garden Tomb's parking lot, he squeezed between buses. A swarm of people from every nationality and culture filled the lot.

In the far corner, he saw Chase crouched down behind the Audi's steering wheel. He parked next to him.

Chase cracked the window. "Are we safe?"

"Yes. Give me a minute." He walked to the entrance, politely showed his badge, and asked to see the head of security. After explaining their situation, Rafi gave him a copy of Yosef's photo along with his business card. "Text me as soon as you have anything."

They scanned the photo. Agreed to use facial recognition software to alert them if Yosef's image came up.

Rafi returned to his vehicle and retrieved a black sport coat, a fedora, and a fake grey beard. "Put these on."

Chase waved a black leather book in his hand. "Read the last five pages, please."

"Fine." Rafi slipped the book under his arm. "Let's get you inside, then you can turn on your phone."

Chase donned the hat and coat then viewed himself in the car's window adjusting the beard. "This looks ridiculous. Why do you want me to dress up like this?"

"People don't pay attention to older men. Don't worry, nobody will recognize you." He surveyed the parking lot. "We're short on time. Let's get in there." He tossed the black book on the dashboard. After giving Chase's outfit a final check, he headed in.

Though not a large location, the Garden Tomb historic site appeared much more expansive than its footprint on the map. Tropical plants created an artistic display of pines, ficus, and fig trees. A intricate wrought iron guardrail kept visitors on the stone path, where they would generally meander around the site with a professional guide. Two thousand years ago, rocks had been carved out to receive the body of Joseph of Arimathea. A large round stone sat rolled back displaying the empty tomb. Today, a large crowd gathered at the grave to celebrate.

A worship leader in skinny jeans tuned his guitar while several band members waited behind their microphones. A staff member placed a humble wooden pulpit a few yards left of the tomb.

Rafi chose a seat with his back to the wall and commanded Chase to occupy the seat directly in front of him. Just a few yards away from the tomb, he would take advantage of the full hundred and eighty degrees of sight from his vantage point.

He leaned over to Chase. "Do it."

Chase pressed the button. His phone slowly came to life. His eyes seemed to ricochet from the stage to the back row and back again.

"Relax."

Chase continued to look side to side, constantly shifting in his chair. "Settle down. He'll be here soon. I'll be all over anyone who moves."

Rafi checked his phone. Nothing.

After the music died, an elderly man in all black walked to the lectern. A black yarmulke attempted to tame his wispy, long, white hair blowing in the gentle breeze. His white beard waved over his slender chest. His deep brown eyes peered around the group assessing his guests for their level of interest. He raised his hands and commanded their solemn attention.

"My name is Mordecai. I was born and raised a few miles from here, right in Jerusalem."

A Jew speaking at an Easter service?

"I'd like you to join me on a journey through promises. Some of these promises take faith to believe. They placed Jesus's body in this grave on April 3, AD 33. Those facts are recorded in multiple historical sources and take no faith to believe. What happened next changed the world forever."

Rafi listened to the Jewish preacher while he scanned the crowd.

"Salvation is from the Jews. God made a covenant with his chosen people. The prophets made predictions about their coming Messiah. He would be a prophet like Moses, preceded by Elijah, a willing sacrifice, born in Bethlehem, ending up in Egypt. The foretelling doesn't stop there: he would be called a Nazarene, perform miracles, come riding on a donkey, be the object of a murderous plot, be betrayed for thirty pieces of silver, and then resurrected." Mordecai went through Scripture and provided references for each claim.

Rafi had studied the Old Testament since childhood, but most of what the preacher said came as a surprise. He checked his phone, no texts or calls had come in.

After speaking for about ten minutes, Mordecai said, "Did you notice how so far in our Easter morning discussion, I haven't even touched on the New Testament?"

Rafi had expected to hear about Jesus's crucifixion and resurrection. But had been familiar with all of it from the Old Testament, except the thirty pieces of silver.

"In the book of John, Jesus said, 'Destroy this temple, and in three days I will raise it up.' Jesus was talking about his body, a clear statement predicting he would rise from the dead. Now listen, if anyone predicts he would rise from the dead, then does it, believe him."

Mordecai stood before the empty grave. "After Jesus walked out of this grave, he used the same Old Testament Scriptures I quoted to explain to his disciples what the Scriptures said about him. Let me ask you this. Can you be a believer in the Messiah without knowing Jesus?"

Of course, we're waiting for the Messiah to come.

Rafi had been in conversations with Christians all his life who condemned Jews if they wouldn't believe in Jesus. He cringed in anticipation.

"Of course. All Jews believe the Messiah is coming. An honest evaluation of the Scriptures in light of history inevitably points to Jesus as Messiah. The only difference between the Old Testament and New Testament is the New Testament tells us the name of the lamb."

Rafi surveyed the area as he listened.

Mordecai grabbed a tiny wooden cup. "During our Seder meal, we share the Afikomen. A piece of bread to represent the slaughtered Passover lamb." He motioned to servers at either end of the crowd. They distributed bread and wine. Rafi gracefully declined. The preacher continued, "Jesus, who walked out of this grave, is the Passover lamb."

Intrigued by the message's simplicity, Rafi watched the Christians eat and drink.

When the singing returned, his phone vibrated with a call from the Beersheba police department. He let it go to voice mail. A second later, a message arrived from the clerk at the triage desk.

HEADQUARTERS: Call me.

I'll deal with that later.

The singing resumed. The crowd stood. Rafi put a hand on Chase's shoulder, a clear indication for him to remain seated. The people stood. Some swayed with their hands raised. A few danced. Anyone concealing a weapon could be ready to take aim.

A security nightmare.

Chase asked, "What's wrong."

Rafi motioned for him to relax. Nobody looked in their direction. After a few minutes, the music ended. They closed in prayer. The crowd began to disperse.

"Time for plan B. Let's go find him."

Chase's face went pale.

Rafi put a firm hand on his shoulder. "When the crowd is almost gone, we'll head out. I'll be within an arm's length. Don't make eye contact with anybody. Do exactly as I say."

As the crowd thinned, Rafi decided the remaining women, teenagers, and hipsters did not pose a threat. Grasping the back of Chase's shirt, he guided him through the gift shop.

"Just look down."

Pedestrians flowed out from the gate to busses, vans, and cars into the parking lot. Only one person swimming upstream. A stocky bald man with a dark jacket and medium build looked directly at Chase from thirty yards away.

Bingo.

"Walk slowly. When I tap your shoulder, drop to the ground."

Rafi stayed directly behind him with his pistol in his right hand and a stun gun in his left.

Chase slowly took one step after another, closing the gap.

Fifteen yards.

A handful of people mulled around between them and his target.

Rafi didn't take his eyes off the bald man, waiting for evidence of a concealed weapon. Chase continued his slow pace forward.

Five yards.

The man didn't have a blade or gun drawn. Both hands rested at his side. Rafi was confident he would win the match if he exposed any type of weapon.

He firmly tapped Chase's shoulder, who dropped leaving nothing between Rafi and the bald man. The man's eyes remained fixed on Chase as he went down. Rafi lunged forward. He thrust his stun gun into exposed skin on his man's neck with the button pressed. He fell like a brick. A woman next to them screamed. The crowd dispersed, leaving the three of them alone. Rafi stood over him, scanning the crowd for a second attacker.

None.

Confident of their safety, Rafi swiftly applied handcuffs and searched the bald man. He took a combat knife from his right hip and a pistol from his left shoulder harness.

Chase squatted down. "That's not Yosef."

Obviously.

Rafi found identification in his back pocket. "This guy probably works for him."

"Does this mean ..."

"No. You are not safe."

"Are you going to arrest him?"

"I'll bring him in on charges of possession of an illegal firearm and intent to do bodily harm."

"Kidnapping?"

"Possibly, if we can find evidence to link him to it."

The man's front pocket held a burner phone. Rafi held it up. "This will be helpful."

"I'll bet you'll find Yosef's number on there."

Rafi looked around the parking lot. "You can't stay in this city. You can't come with me."

"Where can I go?"

As he marched the man over to his car, Rafi answered a call on his phone.

He turned his back to Chase and spoke in Hebrew.

Chase said, "What's going on?"

Rafi hung up. "They found Tiffany. Haven't seen Abby yet. Get in the Audi, follow me to Beersheba."

CHAPTER FIFTY-THREE

Zip ties dug into Abby's wrists. Sitting with her hands behind her, she struggled to find a remotely comfortable position. Nothing seemed to work. She pressed her shoulder against the wall managing to stand. No comfort in any position. She had no chance of reaching the Leatherman tool in her pocket. She paced as her laser lay helplessly on the ground. After a few minutes, she sat down next to it and, with winces of pain, managed to stuff it into her back pocket.

God, give me another chance to use this.

She oscillated between sitting and pacing, hoping for a creative solution to the pain in her wrists. Passing by the water bucket, she regretted not having drunk more during the morning. Though she reached new levels of creativity with her positioning, the water level evaded her reach. The bucket, still a quarter full, mocked her.

What are they going to do to me?

Abby dug through her memory, hoping to find something to bring solace or peace.

I was looking forward to a life with a brilliant, spontaneous man. Life with Chase promised to be full of excitement. We were going to have kids. Get together with friends and families for bonfires.

She pondered how each of the twelve disciples finished their journey on earth. Peter crucified upside down. John boiled in oil.

I don't want to die.

She mentally turned the onion skin pages of her Bible. She recalled Jesus's final words to his disciples:

"You will be my witnesses in Jerusalem and in all Judea, and Samaria, and to the ends of the earth" (Acts 1:8).

This passage brought to memory a lesson of Greek etymology. The word for witness was '*martuers*,' base for the English word martyr. Jesus started his ministry saying, 'Follow me.' When he passed it on to the next generation, he commanded, 'Come and die.' Jesus instructed them to tell everyone about him and live the way he modeled. Abby knew if any of them died in the process, it would not be a surprise.

Jesus already saved me. Who am I to ask for more?

Her thoughts evaded her defenses. She remembered the life stories of Jim Elliot, John Wycliffe, William Tyndale, Dietrich Bonhoeffer ...

I don't want to die. Dying doesn't solve anything. Living does.

In desperation she cried out, "God will never give us something more than we can bear."

A silent voice inside her said, "Show me that verse in the Bible."

She hung her head. *I know. Not there.*

The voice said, "Finish the race."

Immediately she recalled the Apostle Paul's words to his protégé, Timothy: "I have fought the good fight, I have finished the race, I have remained faithful (2 Timothy 4:7).

No. I don't want to be okay with dying.

She searched her mind for a way to reconcile death. God left heaven. He came to earth in flesh. Nothing we could ever do could repay what he has done for us. We give him our everything. When we commit our lives to him, it is a response to his call to come and die.

She heard a vehicle in the distance, quieter this time. Wheels ground against the sand as it pulled to a stop. Two men spoke quietly in Hebrew.

Footsteps.

The door creaked open. Sunlight blinded her as the silhouette of two men approached. Strong hands wrenched her arms. She planted her feet on the ground.

"Stop," Abby said.

They took her to a small black sedan and opened the trunk.

"Wait," she protested.

Her shoulder pushed down. Her face dug into the smelly carpet, they forced her into the small trunk and slammed it shut.

CHAPTER FIFTY-FOUR

BEERSHEBA

With the bald, would-be assassin secure in his back seat, Rafi made the trip in little over an hour. On the corner of HaAtsmaut and Herzl Streets, a food truck was illegally parked in front of the police station.

Chase left the costume in the car and waited at the entrance while Rafi transported his prisoner to an interrogation room. The clerk gave Rafi a small scrap of paper. Hastily written in feminine handwriting:

> I was kidnapped from Mt. Sinai on Wednesday. Held in a cave in the desert and escaped this morning. Contact Billy Rawlings.

The clerk directed him to a small conference room off the main hallway. Rafi knocked then slowly opened the door. Wrapped in a blanket, the disheveled white-haired girl sipped from a water bottle. Crumbs from a vending machine snack sat on the table in front of her.

He quietly asked, "I'm detective Rafi Hadad. Are you hurt?"

She shook her head.

"Good. I'm sorry for what you've been through, glad you're safe. We've been looking for you."

"Your clerk doesn't speak English."

"Can you tell me what happened?"

She looked away. "I don't know much. We were taken. I escaped."

Rafi remained expressionless. "How did you get out?"

"Abby lit a fire. I ran to the truck."

"Good. Did Abby escape too?"

"I waited. The guy grabbed her. I wanted to help. He would have overpowered me too. Neither of us would have escaped."

"Is she still alive?"

"Yeah, she was fine when I left. I'm so sorry. I didn't have a choice."

"Tiffany, you've done nothing wrong here. I appreciate your help. We want to catch the guy and find Abby. Do you know who took you?"

She threw up her hands. "I have no idea. A strong guy in a black shirt."

"Okay, thanks. Every detail helps. Were you in a building?"

"A small cave. It had a door."

"A cave! Where?"

"Out in the desert. Who puts a door on a cave?"

"Excellent, this help. Did you drive the food truck here?"

She nodded. "I wasn't very nice to Abby back there. I hope you can find her."

"Can you trace back the roads you came from to help us find Abby?"

"I'll try my best. I drove winding desert roads for a long time before I made it to a road."

"Which way did you travel?"

"I don't know."

"Do you remember any road signs?"

She closed her eyes. "When I finally reached a paved road, I saw a sign which said Beersheba, 22."

"Good. We're making progress."

"Can I go with you? Maybe I can see something familiar."

"Absolutely. Let me get a few officers to help."

"Can I talk with my brother now?"

"Sure." He dialed Billy on his cell and handed it to her. Stepping into the hallway he saw Chase waiting at the front door.

He leaned over to the clerk. "Buzz him in."

Chase stormed through the door. "Where is she? Is Abby okay?"

Rafi held up his hands. "Cool your jets, man."

He flew down the hall, checking each window. "I need to talk with her."

"Not right now."

He saw her through a window and grabbed the doorknob. "She can help us find Abby."

Rafi put his hand on top of Chase's. "Stop. She's talking with her brother."

Rafi firmly removed Chase's hand from the door, positioned himself between the door and Chase. "Imagine what she's been through. We don't know the extent of her trauma."

"So?"

"This will take some time to do it right. She needs to feel safe. Calm. So she can help us."

"Then start asking her questions."

"I have. They were held in a cave in the desert."

"A cave?"

"Sure. Residents have used caves in these wilderness areas as private storage facilities for thousands of years. Many have doors."

"So you know where Abby is."

"We know where to start looking."

"It's my turn."

"No."

Chase tried to grab the door again. Rafi blocked him.

"You need to wait somewhere else."

Rafi led Chase into a nearby room where he sat and rubbed his hands on the Formica table.

"We'll find Abby. I know the area south of town well. Riddled with hundreds of caves. People use them for storage. She could be in any one of them."

Chase's eyes lit up. "Would a drone help?"

Rafi shook his head.

"Do you have satellite coverage?"

"Not in the desert."

Chase pushed back from the table. "We have to do something!"

Rafi stepped back. "You need to calm down. Take a few minutes and get yourself together."

He left Chase alone, locking the door behind him. He checked in with the clerk. "Did her conversation with her brother reveal anything noteworthy?"

"No."

He printed out a photo of the bald man in the interrogation room then gave a gentle knock. "May I come in, Ms. Rawlings?"

"Fine."

He set a fresh bottle of water in front of her.

"Thank you."

He repeated the questions in a different order. Had her break the story into pieces. He asked her to tell it backward, hoping to jar a memory.

She provided more details of Abby lighting the fire. Using her knife. Nothing leading to her location.

He produced the image of Chase's bald attacker. "Does this man look familiar?"

Tiffany shook he head.

Rafi showed her a photo of Yosef. "Have you ever seen this man?"

"No."

"Thank you. A couple of our officers will take you on a bit of a drive in the hopes of finding something familiar."

He went to his desk to dial the shift supervisor. They arranged for two officers to work with Tiffany on a long shot attempt to find Abby. By the time he hung up, orders had already been relayed. Help was on the way.

Rafi heard muffled yells. A door rattled back in the hallway. Chase shook the doorknob, pounded, and yelled for help.

Rafi opened the door. "Settle down."

Chase said, "What are you doing?"

"My job. Now let me work."

"What did she say?"

"Abby is still alive."

He stepped up to Rafi. "Did you look at the last five pages?"

"What are you talking about?"

"The journal. What do the last five pages of the journal say?"

He shook his head. "My word, you're like a dog with a bone."

"Where did you put it? You need to translate the last five pages."

"Sit down."

Chase obediently sat.

"If I translate those pages, will you promise to leave me alone? Let me get back to finding Abby."

Chase held his right hand over his chest. "Cross my heart."

Rafi retrieved the journal from his car. Pulled a plastic chair up to the table.

I can't believe I'm doing this.

"Fine." He scanned a few pages in the middle. Journal entries appeared to be about a half-page long. He flipped to the last five pages. "This is an entry from two weeks ago."

Chase looked on energetically.

Rafi read a few lines. "It's Yosef talking. He goes on about a meeting. He has committed to the sacrifice." He stopped reading.

Chase said, "What do you see?"

Rafi read:

Director provided a key to the cave.

Rafi pointed at the page. "We've got the cave's location." He texted the details to the officers.

"Keep reading."

Rafi scanned the remainder of the page. "A reminder to bring bread, water, and a waste bucket. The rest of this entry is vanilla."

"What else?"

Rafi flipped back to the first few pages of the journal.

Who is the director?

He found the first date they met, a lunch meeting with the director and Mr. Cohen. He went back through page by page, trying to determine the director's identity. Yosef either intentionally had been hiding the person's identity or honestly didn't know it.

Chase asked, "What are you doing? The last five pages are all we need."

Rafi looked at him. "Why are you so insistent on this?"

"Just trust me, please."

He found the spot where he left off:

Start looking early. Could take a few days to get a girl.

> Get two if possible. Food and water until Sunday.

> Pay two Albi Kabab workers to not show up for their shifts. Take Boaz's phone. Leave some of his cigarette butts at the site.

"Oh, God." Chase stood up. "That explains why we found Boaz's DNA at the scene."

"And why his alibi checked out."

"They set him up."

Rafi turned the page:

> Sunday go to CP early for the sunset sacrifice. My life will change forever.

Chase paced again. "CP? They're still using Caesarea Philippi."

Rafi checked the time, Five o'clock. "I'll cancel the search south of town."

Chase's jaw dropped. "Sunset is about seven."

"It's normally a three-hour drive. Not today."

273

CHAPTER FIFTY-FIVE

BEERSHEBA

Rafi revved the engine. Turned on his flashing red and blue lights. He turned north as he dialed the chief. After four rings, it turned over to voicemail. He left a message. "Chief, this is Hadad. We have an emergency situation with the abduction case. I'm heading to Caesarea Philippi. Need immediate backup."

He called the shift supervisor. Relayed his updated information on Abby's position. They arranged a SWAT team from the Golan Heights to meet them in Caesarea Philippi.

He glanced at the gas gauge and made a quick calculation. He wasn't sure they would make it. Close.

He tossed his phone to Chase. "Send a text to my friend Avi. Tell him to call me ASAP."

Rafi wove between light traffic until he reached the freeway where he pushed the pedal to the floor. Slipping precisely between blurred vehicles, he buried the speedometer.

"Be careful."

"Smooth road, powerful engine, we'll be there in no time."

Chase waved the phone. "Your friend Avi."

"Put it on speaker."

Chase pressed the button.

Rafi said. "Shalom, troublemaker."

"You've been a busy boy."

"I need a big favor."

"Sounds serious."

Rafi passed a sedan. "There are ancient tales from the weird place up North. You remember Caesarea Philippi?"

"Some god who lived in a cave?"

"That's the one. They also talk about sacrifices."

"Sure."

"Human sacrifices."

"The abduction case?"

"Yes. Avi, the ancient ceremonies are still going on. They are real. Going down tonight at sunset."

"What evidence do you have?"

"I'll send you the last five pages from a journal. Everything you need is in there."

"This is not a secure line."

Rafi tightened his grip. "I don't care. We don't have time."

"What do you want me to do?"

"I'm out on a limb here. I need someone up the chain for support."

"I can contact Commissioner Ovadiah Altschul but will need evidence."

"I'll send everything you need."

"Do you need backup?"

"I've requested a Zaka team from Golan Heights."

"Perfect. I'll be there too." The line went dead.

Rafi set his phone on the center console, rechecked the time. Chase was already in the process of taking photos of the last five pages of Yosef's journal and forwarding them to Avi.

Chase asked, "What's Zaka?"

"An international emergency response team. Like 9-1-1 in your country, but more intense. As a country under constant threat from neighboring countries who hate us, Israel has experts in everything from antiterrorism to body recovery."

Chase turned away. "You didn't have to be so explicit."

Rafi's grip on the wheel tightened as he passed a handful of small SUVs. "Best in the world. They have all the tricks of the trade."

Chase grabbed a backpack from the rear seat, set it in his lap, and patted it like a prized poodle. "Have I told you about my project I presented at the Tel Aviv Engineering Fair?"

CHAPTER FIFTY-SIX

CAESAREA PHILIPPI

Manny's heart raced as he entered the parking lot. He passed numerous parking slots for buses, and pulled up next to a small collection of luxury sedans near the entrance. Thankful for Yosef's bold initiative, he felt as nervous as a schoolboy. The increased elevation and cloudless late afternoon drive brought cooler air, but Manny still found it hard to breathe.

What am I doing here? I don't have any choice. Trust Yosef.

He grasped the golden locket. Still warm.

What is the power source for this device?

The engravings mesmerized him. Everything important in his life was sealed within the golden amulet. He kissed it, tucked it under his shirt, then stepped out of his car and punched in Yosef's numbers

MANNY: Where are you?

YOSEF: Cave

Manny found the path through tropical foliage leading to the historic site. He slipped past the vacant ticket kiosk to an open area in front of the cave. About a dozen men and women bore semi-formal attire. They had black robes draped over their arms, obviously preparing for a religious ceremony. Yosef waved as Manny approached.

"Abba, welcome."

"Shalom."

Yosef shook his hand before turning toward the director. Her long black hair shone in the evening light. Her sharp facial features and demanding brown eyes commanded his respect. She looked at Yosef. "You had some trouble this morning?"

"Thank you for sending your guy to help."

She turned to Manny and folded her hands. "The ship of religion is futile. Eventually, you must jump out of it into nothingness." She placed a hand on each of their shoulders. "You are two individuals joining together. In you, there is no fear of the nothingness."

Yosef said, "An honor to serve." He gave Manny a nudge.

Manny parroted, "An honor to serve."

She continued, "Have you prepared?"

Yosef pulled the pendant from under his shirt then stood with his hands folded in front of his waist.

The director looked at Manny. He mimicked Yosef's motions, letting the warm metal object hang in front of his chest.

She looked up at him. "What's inside?"

Manny held it between his fingers as if to open it.

She touched his hand and scowled.

He watched it fall to his chest. "My dreams."

"Specifically."

Manny looked at Yosef, then back at her. "Research. Sales. Desert irrigation ..."

She held up her finger. "One word."

Manny swallowed. "Family."

She grasped his hand and gave an affirming nod. Turning to Yosef she said, "You did well." She held both of his hands in hers. "Not only did you step up to the next level, but brought your father along as your apprentice, a rare occurrence."

Yosef bowed his head. "He's ready."

She released his hands and faced Manny. "What do you know about the object you behold?"

He held it in his hand gently. "Represents Pantheon."

"What do you see on it?"

"The Pantheon logo."

"You eased this logo into our society with wisdom." She nodded. "We haven't forgotten what you have done. You made the first step years ago. We've been waiting."

"The time has come."

She pointed to the locket. "What you're holding is precious beyond belief."

"I'm honored."

"Do you know how many of those exist in the world?"

"No."

"Take a guess."

"Through the years, maybe a thousand?"

"Pure gold, forged in ancient Dan, with the power to connect to the realm beyond." She grasped the charm around Manny's neck with her left hand and Yosef's with her right. "Only two have ever been made."

Manny had no words.

With a bit of tug, she forced them to stand close together with a profound intensity in her eyes. "All year, they are secured in a safe inside a locked cave deep within the holy crypt. Removed once a year, a week before the ceremony."

Manny looked at Yosef, who seemed incredibly calm.

"Normally, the director wears one while the candidate wears the other." She looked at Yosef, "Because of you, tonight we have two candidates." She turned to Manny. "Your son has inspired me to make an exception."

Yosef said, "Will it still work? I made every effort to get two sacrifices, one for each of us, but—"

"One sacrifice is sufficient for two of you." She released the pendants. "The power does not come from me, young man. I am but a humble servant. Soon, you shall see the full extent of his power."

Manny touched the gold amulet. Hot. Not to the point of bursting into flames, yet too hot to touch. He considered the physics behind what he felt in his hand. He longed to open the hinges and run tests on the metal.

She faced the cave. "You sacrifice to him who lives in the mountain and travels by water. If accepted, your lives will change forever."

Yosef bowed his head. "An honor to serve."

She turned to Yosef. Grasped his hands in hers. "By pledging submission to Pan, you will be greatly rewarded."

Yosef said, "An honor."

She peered up at Yosef with a motherly manner, then released him. Her small cold hands flanked Manny's hands as she gave an intense gaze. He couldn't move a muscle.

"By pledging submission to Pan, you will be greatly rewarded."

He averted his gaze, glanced at Yosef, then back at her. "An honor."

"Our window approaches." She checked her watch. "Where is the sacrifice."

"In my car."

She handed him a small black duffel bag. He unzipped it, pulled out a long satin black gown, and gave it to his father. He reached into the bag. Pulled out a short hoodless white dress.

Her voice deepened, "Go."

Yosef briskly headed back to the parking lot, followed by Manny, who texted Joel.

MANNY: Pantheon holds the solution. Breakthrough starts tonight.

He caught up to his son. "I hope you know what you're doing."

"If we get this wrong, people will call us a cult. However, if we get it right, at this time, in this place ..." He looked confidently at his father. "For the next hundred years, people won't have to work on your birthday."

CHAPTER FIFTY-SEVEN

Chase leaned towards Rafi's shoulder to see the gas gauge needle.

Empty. Or at least very close.

He looked at Rafi. "Do you think we'll have enough gas? How much further?"

"You're a nervous talker, aren't you?" Rafi decelerated as he approached the turn to Highway 65.

"What do you mean?"

"You talk nonstop when you get anxious." Rafi cut an aggressive path like a formula one driver. "I've heard more about your inflatable mattress, Abby's laser, and Tiffany's dang drone than I ever would have imagined."

Chase waved the phone in the air. "If you'll let me turn this on, I can get aerial footage from Caesarea Philippi right now."

"I still don't understand why you programmed it to go there."

"I don't understand it, but I had a hunch something must be going on."

"What good would a drone do?"

"You'd be surprised." He looked up at the cloudless sky. "The conditions are perfect. What do we have to lose?"

"Fine, do it."

Within seconds Chase viewed a thousand-foot image of green foliage, roads, and a couple of buildings. He pulled up the map. Evaluated the drone's oval pattern.

Where is the horrible cave?

"What do you see?"

"I need a second." Chase flipped between windows. The drone's performance remained outstanding. He struggled to aim the drone to see inside the cave. "I don't know what kind of images we'll get in these wind conditions." He reprogrammed the drone's pattern and modified the settings pushing for greater clarity.

"You finally have something relevant to tell me, and this is when you choose to quit talking?"

After a few minutes, with the drone in position the cave opening came into view. "I see people in graduation robes."

"Odd."

"Most of them are gathered in front of the big cave, but two are heading another direction."

"Which way?"

He watched two people disappear into a forest of greenery.

"They were going back to the parking lot when I lost them under the canopy."

"Track their progress. Pick them up on the other side of the trees."

Chase zoomed out continuing his surveillance.

CHAPTER FIFTY-EIGHT

Caesarea Philippi

Manny followed Yosef to his car and donned the black robe. His slacks were visible beneath the hem like a middle-school boy during a growth spurt. Yet, he appreciated the extra layer in the cool evening air. Yosef stood behind the trunk looking dapper with a perfectly fitted robe.

He looked at his father with burning intensity. "Before we take the next step, I will step back and review one more time."

Manny made quick circles with his finger. "Get on with it."

Yosef held up his palm. "Why are we here?"

"Isn't it obvious?"

"I need to hear you say it."

"Family."

Yosef pointed his finger at Manny's chest. "If you do nothing, how many people will be hurt?"

Manny shook his head. "We've been through this."

"How much collateral damage will there be if you don't take drastic action, right here, right now?"

Manny took a deep breath. "Tremendous."

"And if you have success, how many people will be saved?"

"Millions."

Yosef pointed at him with both hands. "Are you willing to sacrifice one to benefit millions?"

Manny closed his eyes and nodded.

Yosef continued, "This isn't for you or me. For the family and the tremendous good your business will provide to millions."

Yosef handed him the white robe. Opened the trunk. Inside, a girl lay on her side with her hands behind her back.

Manny took a step back. Stood ramrod straight. He looked over her head at Yosef and grasped the pendant. His hand burned. He didn't move.

Family.

Yosef swept her up on her feet. She screamed, "Get off me!"

Manny thought of his daughters. They weren't much older than this girl. How could he do this? What would this make him? He shrugged away the thought.

His mind turned toward Miriam at the restaurant. Then remembered his many debts. His dwindling accounts. He needed to proceed.

Manny stepped in and grabbed her tight.

Yosef nodded at him then said to the girl, "You can make all the noise you want. There's nobody here to help."

She kicked him in the shin. He forced her belly against the car. "Stop."

She twisted around, brought a knee to his groin, then broke into a run heading to the open space of the parking lot. Undoubtedly no track star, she struggled to put a few yards between them.

Yosef sprang on her like a lion chasing a gazelle and took her down hard. She struck her head on the pavement.

Motionless.

Manny knelt next to her. She was breathing.

"Not what I had in mind, but it works." Yosef helped get her to a sitting position. Slipped the gown over her shoulders. "We need a vibrant, aware sacrifice, so we can't sedate her."

He concealed her face with a black hood. Tossed her over his shoulder.

"She'll wake up any second."

Yosef said, "Pantheon has a rich and glorious history. In ancient days, people lined up to give their daughters for this."

Family.

"The benefits we receive are not just for us. All the blessings will also be granted to her family in spades."

"I understand."

"As we head over, I'll go over a few more details of what is required for the sacrifice to be accepted. When we see the director again, the two of us are bound in silence until it is complete."

Manny followed Yosef as he confidently headed toward the cave.

CHAPTER FIFTY-NINE

Avi's face appeared on Rafi's phone again. Chase tapped the speaker button.

Rafi said, "Shalom."

"Where are you?"

"Heading north, close. Tell me you have good news."

"Good and bad. The good news is those pages from the journal convinced commissioner Ovadiah Altschul to hear me out. I'm working on getting SWAT there."

"How soon?"

"Within twenty minutes."

"Not quick enough."

Avi said, "I'm doing my best."

Rafi replied, "We have live drone footage of Caesarea Philippi. This is going down now."

"How did you manage to get a drone?"

"Later. I'll send you what we have."

The line cut off.

Chase immediately sent Avi still shots of the cave.

CHAPTER SIXTY

Manny saw nine figures in black gowns at the cave entrance. Yosef approached carrying his burden. Without a word, the director picked up a backpack, left the group. Led them up a path. They followed obediently, carrying the girl over rocks and brush. They marched through a wasteland where every plant and non-living thing seemed to have intent and capability of doing them harm.

Manny realized their vow of silence had begun.

A trail led to a set of carved steps attached to an elevated stage. Ancient engravings adorned the ten-foot-wide octagon's periphery. In the middle, Pantheon stared up at him in expectation. A detailed carving of hairy goat legs, muscular human torso, menacing face, and curled horns filled the polished surface.

The director pulled a thick yellow candle from her bag. She lit it, then planted her toes at the cliff's edge. With the candle at her waist, she looked down for a moment before slowly raising it above her head. From below, voices brought forth a slow and steady chant. Manny furrowed his brow at the monophonic mantra. He peered over the edge at eight candle-laden robed figures gathered around the stream.

The director set her candle on a circle carved into one of the corners. She lit and placed seven more candles with care. She directed Manny and Yosef with his burden to the platform's center facing one another. Standing on the goat-man image sent chills up Manny's spine.

Her voice was a bullhorn. "The energy body acts as a bridge connecting our physical and spiritual nature."

The girl began to struggle in Yosef's arms. He set her down between them, facing the cliff. Manny grasped her right arm while Yosef secured her left.

With reptilian quickness, the director grasped Manny's gold pendant. Her crimson eyes peered into his soul as a wave of nausea tumbled through his abdomen. Drops of sweat ran down his back. As dry heat rose from the platform, his breaths seemed to be void of oxygen. His knees buckled. He concentrated only on staying upright. Yosef remained at attention like a soldier.

How is he standing up?

She grasped Yosef's amulet. He bent forward in apparent pain.

I can't take this much longer.

Chanting from below grew louder. Musical motifs woven together in a dirge.

The director's voice took on a depth well below her natural physical capability. "For us to influence a transformation of body and mind, we gather tonight in this hallowed place to honor the one who holds the power."

The golden chain on top of Yosef's black robe gave off a warm yellow glow. The luminous metal increased in intensity as it reached his collar and disappeared behind his neck. His eyelids drooped, he rocked as sweat dripped off his chin.

She bellowed, "We have the privilege and opportunity to transform energy flow. We connect our spirit with his. Water, light, and spirit, unite!"

Light escaped between her knuckles. She released the adornments. They fell to the men's chests glowing like lanterns. The acapella harmony from below rose as Manny's body undulated like an ocean wave.

I can't stand much longer.

She raised her hands to the sky. "We call on our Lord, the great and mighty Pan."

Manny's feet felt like they were on fire. He shifted his weight to escape the heat. No relief. Molten yellow wax flowed into the carvings like water. They began to give off the same yellow hue as the pendants framing the platform with brilliance. Wax flow progressed inward. Streams connected. Luminosity doubled. Under their feet, the creature's left hip glistened. Within seconds, leg hairs flickered like a thousand tiny lamps. Radiance advanced into the torso, face, and horns. His eyes burned like beacons. The entire body emanated eerie incandescence.

Yosef stared ahead. His weary face, illuminated from the glow, looked like he had taken a beating.

The director removed the girl's hood. "Oh, mighty indomitable Pan, we stand on this holy ground bearing a worthy sacrifice and humbly request an audience with your majesty."

A scorching gust of wind punched Manny from behind and flew upward. The girl's white covering sprung up as her ponytail lifted like smoke over a fire.

The director said, "It's time."

CHAPTER SIXTY-ONE

Rafi drove tight lines through torturous turns as Highway 99 closed out the final mile to Caesarea Philippi. Chase remained glued to his screen, desperate for a clear image from the drone. On a night when the moon wouldn't rise for another few hours, he struggled to get a clear picture. He flipped between routine video, night vision, and thermal enhancement as he focused on the four people at the cliff top.

Standard video image showed a bright white girl and possibly a few others. Night vision gave a dark green image showing four individuals. Thermal image revealed a brilliant white column from the cave all the way through the cliff top.

Thermal must be malfunctioning.

He switched back to the regular video and noticed bright yellow lights on the floor.

There must be LEDs built into some type of stage.

The girl in white had a black hood over her head. The short person behind her reached up, ripping off the hood. A sandy blonde ponytail fluttered then somehow rose straight into the air. He zoomed on her wide eyes and open mouth.

"It's Abby!"

Rafi said, "What's going on?"

This really is the Gates of Hell.

The image destabilized as if a windstorm swept over them. "Get to the cave! It's happening."

Rafi made another sharp turn at incredible speed. Chase pressed a button on the backpack. Tiny green lights flashed in a series around the base. Fully charged. Sensors working. Latches intact.

Rafi sped through the parking lot, bounced over the curb and through the gate. The car barely squeezed between tropical underbrush as they careened along the sidewalk to the cave entrance. As they skidded to a stop, Chase leaped from the vehicle and sprinted.

CHAPTER SIXTY-TWO

The platform was like a stovetop to Abby's feet. She shuffled her weight from one foot to the other. Soles of her shoes offered little protection. With her hood stripped from her face, she struggled to figure out where she was. Her arms were immobilized by a strong man on her left who looked ill. The tall one on her right held himself up with her arm. In front of her, out in the dark, a vast expanse of nothingness.

What's going on?

She bent her knees, pushed back, and let out a scream. "Help!"

Where are we?

Over the men's robes, glowing necklaces swayed. An eerie light shone from below. Something seemed to press in on her skull from either side. She brought her shoulders up for protection. Twisting from side to side.

An oven-like whirlwind rose from below. Her white dress flapped all around.

"Let me go!"

Her cry rose to the heavens. The men neither acknowledged her nor made eye contact. Some type of writing around the periphery of their bizarre stage shone in a deep shade of saffron. Hoofs, animal-like legs, and man's body. A wild-eyed creature with horns, alive under her feet.

"Get me out of here!"

In the distance beyond the stream, red and blue lights flashed. Someone was running toward them.

CHAPTER SIXTY-THREE

As the girl struggled, the director bowed low until her forehead rested on the ground. Her arms extended forward in a child's pose. Motionless. Palms on either side of the glowing goat-man's menacing image.

Manny's heart raced. Bile bubbled up in the back of his throat. The world started to spin. No longer did he care about projecting the image of a man in command of his faculties. He focused on Yosef. Shoulders slumped over amid the scorching tempest. Bags had formed under red-rimmed eyes, his right eye completely closed, the left struggled to remain open. A young man in his prime who usually projected the image of strength and determination looked like he was near death.

As Manny's vision tunneled, the director disappeared. He couldn't see the cliff edge. His grasp on the middle of the girl's arm slipped. His body lurched forward. His hand stopped at her elbow, where he regained control. Sapped of strength, he held fast to her arm with both hands, leaning on her simply to remain upright.

The director spoke from her bowed pose. Her words reverberated. "We humbly offer this sacrifice."

Yosef stepped forward, his left leg at the precipice, his right planted behind the girl. Manny tried to mirror his position but stumbled. He almost slipped off the cliff to his death. He summoned every ounce of remaining strength to catch himself.

The director commanded, "Now."

Manny tried to lift the girl from the platform to launch her. His legs gave out. He collapsed on his knees. He barely managed to give her a shove over the brink. Combined with whatever force Yosef could provide, she moved across the boundary. Her glorious descent began.

Her white robe slipped out of sight as he collapsed. His face made impact onto stone. He vomited, gathered himself then looked at Yosef. Struggling to support himself on his hands and knees, the amulet hung between his neck over the glowing rock surface.

Manny touched the pendant. His skin sizzled. He pushed it away.

Will our sacrifice be accepted?

CHAPTER SIXTY-FOUR

Chase sprinted to the circle of chanting figures in front of the cave. He looked up and, for the first time, saw his precious Abby on the cliff edge. She had scolded him for doing far less dangerous things than standing in such a precarious position. Her wind-blown hair stormed furiously as she struggled between two men.

This can't be happening.

He tossed his blinking backpack into the circle of chanting figures. Bounced and settled next to the stream with lights flashing.

A scream came from above. He looked up. Her body careened forward and tumbled head over heels off the precipice.

Time slowed to a crawl.

The backpack roared. Wind rushed into it, snuffing out the candles the robed men and women held. His mattress began to reveal its form.

As Abby reached the halfway point, the life-saving cushion taking shape. To Chase's horror, he could see she would miss the device by several yards. Nothing existed between Abby's falling body and the rocky surface. He had thrown it short. The rocks which had taken the lives of thousands of innocent girls would claim one more.

A high-pitched wail once again came from the backpack. An additional blast of air thrust outward. The inflated contraption moved across the rocky surface and slipped under Abby's falling body. She collapsed into the nylon cushion like a ragdoll.

Chase pushed his way through the thin fabric. As she settled onto the rocky surface, overlapped sections of nylon folded over trapping air like a pillow under her head. He knelt next to her, slipped his arms under her back, and gave a gentle squeeze.

"Abby, you're okay!"

She curled into the fetal position and sobbed.

He brushed her hair from her face. "I'm right here."

She covered her face with her hands, breathing erratically. The nylon structure was in the process of deflating all around her.

Chase embraced her. "I'm so sorry."

"I thought—"

★★★

Rafi followed Chase into the circle of robed worshipers with his sidearm drawn. "Get on the ground, all of you."

The hooded figures remained stationary. The activity around the magic mattress consumed their attention. He raised his voice. "Get down on your knees. Put your hands behind your head."

They cast furtive glances in silence at one another then moved in unison surrounding Rafi.

The odds were not in his favor. Rafi knew he could take down just about any person one on one. Still, their oversized clothing prevented him from evaluating whether they had weapons. He stepped back, trying to find a position to engage them all together.

One of them calmly said, "Now."

They positioned themselves around him. Within seconds, they surrounded him with choreographed precision.

He aimed at the closest pair. "Back up. Get down, or I will fire."

The duo dropped to their knees. They placed their hands on their head. Rafi quickly looked side to side, hoping for a similar response from the others.

A blow to the back of his head took him down. A strong hand wrenched his pistol from his hand. Something heavy pressed him into the solid surface.

From the cliff top, he heard a familiar female voice. "Get rid of those two. Bring her back up. Our window of opportunity remains."

CHAPTER SIXTY-FIVE

Mighty hands landed on Chase's arms and shoulders. Within a second, they had him on the ground with his face pressed against the rocky surface.

Abby flailed in the middle of flattening fabric. Two men restrained Rafi twenty feet away. A large, hooded figure picked Abby up and slung her over his shoulder like a ragdoll, heading out of sight.

One of the men held a pistol at Rafi's chest and looked up at the cliff, waiting for orders.

A female voice came from above. "Is that you, Rafi?"

Rafi looked up. "*Chief Valsburg*?"

"I told you to let this go. You are a talented young man. You would have gone far if you had learned to follow orders."

"You told me to ignore the kidnapping, so you could do this?"

"This is bigger than you, the police force, bigger than all of Israel."

The gun man said, "What do you want us to do with these two?"

"Kill them. Dispose of their bodies deep in the crypt."

He raised his gun to Rafi's head.

Suddenly, six men in black military uniforms with automatic rifles and riot gear swept in. "Drop the weapon."

The man with the gun dropped the weapon. The SWAT team took them down in an instant. They apprehended each of the robed individuals and secured them. A few minutes later, a black-haired man in jeans and a black jacket walked up to Rafi and helped him to his feet.

Rafi said, "Nice entrance, Avi."

"You didn't give me much of a head's up."

Rafi pointed at the trail. "There's one more, heading up with the girl. Three at the top."

Avi called to one of his team members. "Grab him." Three men started running.

Rafi said, "Ringleader is upstairs, a real troublemaker."

"Let's go."

Avi and Rafi started jogging. Chase followed a few yards behind.

At a hairpin turn halfway up the trail, two soldiers restrained a man face down on the ground. In contrast, another soldier knelt beside Abby, who sat on the dirt with her face in her hands.

Chase knelt next to her. "I'm so sorry."

Rafi pointed up the trail. "Three more."

Two soldiers joined Avi and Rafi up the path. After a few steps, they suddenly stood face to face with a robed woman confidently walking alone down the trail.

Avi pointed his weapon at her. "You're under arrest."

She brushed aside the three men and walked right between them. "You have no authority to arrest me or any of my Pantheon brethren."

Avi grabbed her arm. "I'm sorry, ma'am."

"I'll have you court-martialled."

Avi applied handcuffs. "You're under arrest."

"On whose authority?"

He pulled a small tablet from his jacket pocket. Police Commissioner Altschul's face appeared. A deep male voice said, "What's going on, Avi?"

Avi held the tablet in front of his face. "Commissioner, we have Chief Idit Valsburg."

The commissioner said, "Idit, you and I are going to have a long conversation."

"Sir, I'd be happy to talk with you. Apparently, a young man I trusted as one of my best detectives has accused me of something preposterous."

"I'm not so sure." He held his phone up to the screen. "Some journal entries have revealed quite a bit of information. Plus, your actions tonight have been quite revealing."

"I'll be happy to come to Jerusalem and meet you in your office first thing Monday morning."

"I don't think so."

Avi turned the tablet around. "Thank you, sir. I don't want to take any more of your time."

The commissioner said, "So, this is the Pantheon group you told me about?"

"Yes, sir. They've been busy at the Gates of Hell."

"Human sacrifices?"

"Murders. I can't imagine all the rituals which have taken place here through the ages."

"Show me the area."

Avi panned the camera across the cliff, creek, and deflated mattress.

"Any casualties tonight?"

Avi zoomed in. "They made one attempt, but Detective Rafi Hadad intervened."

"How?"

Avi pointed the tablet's camera at Rafi. "He saved the girl's life with some type of emergency inflatable mattress."

"Impressive. I want a full report on my desk in the morning."

"Absolutely."

The commissioner ended the call.

Rafi looked up the trail. "Where's Yosef and his father?"

Avi's team leader pointed west. "They fled into the wilderness."

Rafi looked at Chase. "Your drone has night vision, right?"

Chase tapped on his phone.

Rafi held out his hand to Abby. "It's a pleasure to finally meet you."

Abby shook his hand.

Avi said, "Introduce me to your friends."

Rafi motioned with his hands. "Avi, this is Chase, the magic mattress inventor, and his fiancée Abby Radcliffe."

Chase stared at his screen. "Found them about a quarter-mile north."

Avi said, "Already?"

Rafi laughed. "He's truly resourceful."

CHAPTER SIXTY-SIX

Manny did his best to keep up as Yosef ran across a rocky path. From the cliff edge to the brush-filled wilderness, down a hill to thick vegetation, they ran. After ten minutes, Yosef stopped next to a wall of boulders. Manny caught up and bent over at the waist with his hands on his knees.

"Where are we going?"

"We have a long night ahead. What type of physical condition are you in?"

Having just run more in a few minutes than he had in years, he could barely speak. "You have a backup plan?"

"They'll call for a canine search crew and be all over this area." He looked farther down the hill. "I have plenty of tricks up my sleeve between now and then."

"Give me a minute."

Yosef checked his watch. "Take two."

Manny took a knee. "I can't believe I compromised so much."

Yosef shook his head. "We had to step up. With the sacrifice comes so much benefit."

Manny's voice cracked. "She was Miriam's age."

"How many people would be hurt if we didn't—"

"Enough." Manny turned away from his son. "I've done a poor job rearing you as a son. Supporting you financially wasn't ... you've inherited my greed. I've failed you as a father. Now I must pray for forgiveness."

"I parked a car a few miles away. We still have—"

"No. I can't outrun my conscience."

"Abba, there's no need, no time for this self-abasement."

"Quiet." Manny heard footsteps behind him.

Suddenly bright lights pointed at him as commanding voices boomed, "Get down on the ground."

Within a few seconds, Manny felt handcuffs clamp his wrists together.

★★★

Rafi peered over Chase's shoulder as the drone footage showed thermal images of four men surrounding two men on the ground. He turned to Avi with a thumbs up. "Under control."

Avi nodded.

Rafi called the Beersheba station supervisor. Gave a brief report. He approached Avi with his arms crossed. "How did you know?"

"Know what?"

"Daniel 8:5. Follow the money. You sent the riddle pretty quick. Almost like you had it ready and expected me to reach out."

"I have a special interest in this case."

Rafi looked at his friend's left hand, still void of a wedding ring. "I understand."

"I have special access from my station at the State Department.

"You never stopped researching Laili's case, did you?"

"I've gone down dozens of rabbit trails. When I stumbled on Pantheon, I obtained a list of every member. I scanned thousands of emails. Listened to countless calls."

"You knew about Manny and Yosef?"

"Just pieces of the puzzle but no actionable evidence."

"So, when I reached out—"

"This time of year, it doesn't take much to get me on edge."

"When you used the word troublemaker ..."

"A hunch. I wasn't sure of any of this. You followed my hints well."

Rafi looked at Chase. "I had help."

Avi said, "Everything changed when you sent the journal."

Rafi nodded in Chase's direction. "He's like a dog with a bone."

Avi continued, "I don't care how you obtained it, but your information gave me an audience with the commissioner on short notice."

Chase grinned. "A miracle."

Avi's phone vibrated. Rafi watched as he checked it and smiled.

Rafi said, "I haven't seen you smile like that since ..."

He looked at the screen.

Stay safe.
Love you.

Rafi smacked him on the shoulder. "You've been holding out on me. Who is that?"

Avi grinned. "I'll introduce you to her soon."

★★★

Just down the hillside, two officers escorted Chief Valsburg to the parking lot. Rafi had caught up with them when he addressed the officers. "Can I have a minute?"

They nodded.

He stood in front of her. "You've been doing this all along? Did you really think you wouldn't pay the price?"

Her eyes darted from side to side. "In this space, works of faith have eternal ramifications."

"As Torah says, 'Justice, justice you shall pursue.'"

The corners of her mouth raised slightly as she looked at the cave. "There's more to faith than you could possibly understand."

He grabbed her restraints and turned her back toward the officers. "Take her away."

CHAPTER SIXTY-SEVEN

In the parking lot, Chase and Abby watched Tiffany's drone slowly circle overhead. He tapped his phone a few times, and it flew to the road before turning back. "I'll reduce the speed. Get ready to catch it."

The machine dropped to a foot above the ground. As it approached Abby, it rose to waist-high right in front of her. She grabbed the hull with both hands bringing its record-breaking flight to an end.

His phone buzzed. "Hello?"

"Congratulations. I heard y'all were successful."

"Billy?"

"Yeah. Abby's safe too?"

"Word travels fast."

"Tiffany called me from the station."

"I couldn't have done it without you."

"Sorry I bailed on you."

Chase didn't know what to say.

"You did some nice work over there."

"Thank you."

"No problem."

"Let's keep in touch."

"Will do." The call ended.

Chase looked at Abby. "That's a surprise. I thought he'd never talk with me again."

"What are you talking about? I thought you two were friends."

"With Billy?" Chase rolled his eyes. "A lot has happened in the last few days." He handed her his phone. "You should call Tiffany."

She shook her head. "I don't think so."

"She'll want to hear from you."

"I doubt it."

Chase's phone showed a call from an unknown Israeli number. He took it on speaker. "Hello?"

"Chase?"

"Yes, who is this?"

"Tiffany."

Chase said, "I'm so glad you're safe."

"Thank you. Listen, I just heard Abby is okay. Bless her heart. Do you know how I can get ahold of her?"

Abby waved her hands. Chase ignored her. "Sure, she's right here."

Abby reluctantly took the phone. "Hello?"

"Abby, I'm so glad you're okay."

"You too."

"I wish I could have ... I'm sorry I left without you."

"I understand."

Tiffany said, "Listen, I might not have been my best self this week."

Abby stared at the phone.

"You have a quiet strength which comes from somewhere I don't understand. You have something I thought I had." After a moment of silence, she said, "I guess what I'm saying is I'd like to get to know you better."

Abby's eyes widened. "I suppose."

Tiffany continued, "I'm on a flight tomorrow afternoon."

Abby said, "I don't have plans."

"That's a first."

Abby laughed. "I guess it is."

"Maybe we could get some good Jewish bread tomorrow morning for breakfast before I head out?"

Abby smiled. "Sounds like a plan."

CHAPTER SIXTY-EIGHT

ONE YEAR LATER

IOWA

Chase paced in a small room outside the foyer of the Evangelical Free Church with a small group of close friends. His phone buzzed in his pocket.

"Hello?"

"Shalom, my friend."

"Rafi, it's good to hear your voice."

"I just wanted to congratulate you on your big day."

"Hasn't happened yet. She still has a few minutes to back out."

"If Abby planned it, you could guarantee it will go as smooth as silk. You two will be very happy together. I'm sure you'll keep her on her toes."

"No doubt."

"How is she doing?"

"Fine."

"Listen, what she went through may have lasting effects." His voice was empathetic. "Things like this don't just go away."

"You're right," Chase sighed. "Our counselor has been helpful for both of us."

"And?"

"Abby's a strong, resilient woman. There is no forgetting what happened, but the sharp edges have smoothed down over the past few months."

"Good to hear. Hey, next time you're in Israel, let me know. I'll give you a proper tour."

"Likewise, if you are ever in the States, come for a visit."

"Can I join your family for Easter?"

"Absolutely."

Someone tapped Chase on the shoulder. "It's time."

"Ceremony's starting. Thanks for calling."

Chase joined the group of young men wearing tuxedos huddling at the door. "Let's do this."

As the door swung open, he stepped out and saw his mother waiting in a full-length dress. Extending his elbow, he escorted her down to the front row while a beautiful melody played in the background. Abby had transformed her home church into the wedding chapel of her dreams.

Chase smiled at the crowd of impeccably dressed family and friends as he took his position center stage next to the minister who would preside over the ceremony. A select group of Chase's friends in dress shirts, suspenders, and slacks ushered the other VIPs to their seats. Five groomsmen escorted an equal number of bridesmaids in long, paneled dresses adorned with lace trim. At the altar, they separated and formed lines on opposite sides of the stage.

A three-year-old girl in a pink princess dress waited at the back of the sanctuary. With coaching from her mother, she ambled down the aisle, periodically dropping pink flower petals from her basket. Her older brother followed with a pillow in his hands, carefully protecting the gold rings. He stopped numerous times along the way, picking up petals and placing them in his pocket.

With the cast in position, the pianist struck a chord. The back door swung open. Backlit by the doorway Abby appeared in a picture-perfect moment, radiant in beauty. Her ivory dress extended along the floor. A veil graced her wavy locks as she held a bouquet. Her mother stood. The entire church rose in response. Every eye in the building fixed on the bride as she moved elegantly forward.

For Chase, only one person existed at that point in time, everything he wanted in a friend and soulmate. He would be lucky to have her as his wife.

As she reached the front, a baritone voice boomed. "Who gives this woman to be married to this man?"

Abby's father's voice cracked. "Her mother and I."

Chase and Abby joined hands facing the pastor. He opened a small leather-bound book. "Marriage is joining two lives on the rock-solid promise of God's love."

Chase gazed into Abby's eyes as the pastor spoke about love and commitment. "Jesus brought his disciples to a city called Caesarea Philippi. He sat them down in front of a prominent temple, the Gates of Hell."

Abby's mouth dropped open. Chase squeezed her hands.

"Through a few questions, Jesus taught them he is the Son of God. The lesson ended with a promise to Peter he would be the rock for the church. Even though they were at a dark place with a temple with a terrible name, Jesus concluded with the promise the Gates of Hell would not overcome his church."

Abby's bright eyes remained fixed on Chase's. Her face wasn't flushed, her hands weren't clammy.

He whispered, "Are you okay?"

She gave a slight nod, the corners of her mouth raised slightly.

The pastor continued, "Today, I'm going to extend his promise to you as a married couple. Yours will be a lasting marriage, and the Gates of Hell will not overcome it."

Dear Reader,

This novel is the result of our family trip to Israel. A few years ago, we joined a group of friends and traveled from one Biblical destination to the next for ten days.

Amazing.

At Caesarea Philippi, our pastor sat us down on benches near the dark and ominous cave. With a Bible in one hand and his notes in the other, he said, "This place changed the way I read the Bible."

The Gates of Hell is not a concept. It's not the doorway to the place of eternal damnation. It's a pagan temple in Israel. Jesus chose to bring his disciples to Caesarea Philippi for one specific teaching point. A lesson quite different from what we see through an American lens.

I read the Bible differently now.

Context is everything. When we understand the geography, history, culture, and language of the Biblical passages, we see a depth of meaning and truth far beyond what we can glean from listening to sermons in church chairs. The Gates of Hell is a place where my life changed.

I pray that you have a similar experience.

Andy DeWitt

ABOUT THE AUTHOR

DR. ANDY DEWITT is an author, part-time missionary, and retired oral surgeon. His first book, the biography of a missionary, helped raise over a million dollars for the mission group. His other novels, memoirs, and nonfiction books are all aimed to stimulate spiritual discussions and challenge his readers to draw closer to Jesus.

Now retired from his surgical practice, Andy writes full time. He lives in the Midwest with his wife. His favorite activities are boating with family, taking long walks with his wife, and bragging about his three grown children.

WHAT DID YOU THINK?

If you could leave an online review, we'd love to hear your thoughts.

Go to Amazon.com and search for "Gates of Hell, DeWitt"

Thank you.

Made in the USA
Monee, IL
26 December 2022

19394474R00188